In the hot seat

The temperature of the mud bath continued to rise, and I realized it was reaching a dangerous point. My flesh was on fire, and my head pounded.

"Could you make the mud cooler?" I asked.

"That's not possible," she said. Her bitter, angry expression said she had no intention of doing that, and it occurred to me that she was the one who had turned up the temperature.

"I have to get out now," I said, attempting to sit up, but the mud blanket was too heavy. Mary Jane placed her hands—strong hands—through the mud on my shoulders, holding me down. "Let me up!" I snapped. "I've had enough."

"What do you know about Louis's death?" she hissed, continuing the pressure on my shoulders.

"Nothing, just that he was murdered." I now yelled, "Let me out, damn it!"

If she pushed down any more, I would drown in the boiling mud, and there wasn't a thing I could do about it. . . .

Other *Murder, She Wrote* mysteries

BLOOD ON THE VINE

A *Murder, She Wrote* Mystery

A Novel by Jessica Fletcher
and Donald Bain
based on the
Universal television series
created by Peter S. Fischer,
Richard Levinson & William Link

A SIGNET BOOK

SIGNET
Published by New American Library, a division of
Penguin Group (USA) Inc., 375 Hudson Street,
New York, New York 10014, USA
Penguin Group (Canada), 90 Eglinton Avenue East, Suite 700, Toronto,
Ontario M4P 2Y3, Canada (a division of Pearson Penguin Canada Inc.)
Penguin Books Ltd., 80 Strand, London WC2R 0RL, England
Penguin Ireland, 25 St. Stephen's Green, Dublin 2,
Ireland (a division of Penguin Books Ltd.)
Penguin Group (Australia), 250 Camberwell Road, Camberwell, Victoria 3124,
Australia (a division of Pearson Australia Group Pty. Ltd.)
Penguin Books India Pvt. Ltd., 11 Community Centre, Panchsheel Park,
New Delhi - 110 017, India
Penguin Group (NZ), 67 Apollo Drive, Rosedale, North Shore 0632,
New Zealand (a division of Pearson New Zealand Ltd.)
Penguin Books (South Africa) (Pty.) Ltd., 24 Sturdee Avenue,
Rosebank, Johannesburg 2196, South Africa

Penguin Books Ltd., Registered Offices:
80 Strand, London WC2R 0RL, England

First published by Signet, an imprint of New American Library,
a division of Penguin Group (USA) Inc.

First Printing, April 2001
20 19 18 17 16 15

Copyright © 2001 Universal City Studios Productions LLLP. *Murder, She Wrote*
is a trademark and copyright of Universal Studios. All Rights Reserved.

Ⓟ REGISTERED TRADEMARK—MARCA REGISTRADA

Printed in the United States of America

For David B. Agus, M.D.,
who gives medicine a good name.

Chapter One

"... and this Ladington Creek has always been one of my favorite cabernet sauvignons. I'm sure you'll agree that its sweet jammy nose, its big, rich, black-cherry aroma and lingering presence on the palate are extraordinary."

I glanced at Seth Hazlitt, who sat next to me in the single-session wine-appreciation course being taught by John St. Clair, a professor of business law at Cabot Cove Community College. John taught business to earn a living. His passion in life, however, was wine, and he'd been acknowledged for years as our town's most erudite connoisseur. A small man fond of tweed jackets and floppy bow ties, whose tortoise-rimmed glasses were round and oversized, he had an enthusiasm for the subject that was contagious. He'd started conducting the course ten years ago, and it was always fully subscribed, as it was this particular early October night.

"It is good," Seth said, savoring the wine's flavor.

John, who tended to be dramatic when discussing wine, threw up his hands. "*Good*?" he mimicked. "Seth, it is heavenly, a gift of the gods, a supreme affirmation of nature." He looked to me. "Don't you agree, Jessica?"

"Oh, yes," I said, suppressing a smile. "Definitely a gift of the gods. But will it help me get over this cold I've been fighting for weeks?"

"Absolutely," John said. "Better than any antibiotic."

"The Ladington of Ladington Creek vineyards," I said. "Is he still alive?"

"Very much so," said John. "Men like William Ladington never seem to die, and I hope he lives forever, as long as he turns out cabernets like this one."

The William Ladington we were discussing had been a larger than life character in years past. He'd made his fortune in Boston real estate, then gone to Hollywood where he bankrolled—which meant he produced—a succession of movies, the early ones receiving good reviews, later efforts pretty thoroughly trashed by the critics. Then he packed up and headed north, to California's vaunted wine country in the Napa Valley, where he bought a vineyard and started turning out Ladington Creek wines. Unlike his Hollywood experience, his early efforts weren't well received by those with the power to judge the relative worth of the product. But he continued refining his approach to turning grapes into wine and eventually produced vintages that met the approval of the leading critics, including Robert Parker, who never failed to praise Ladington Creek's output.

But it was Ladington's personal life that delighted the gossip columnists. He was known as a hard drinker and had been arrested for drunken driving on more than one occasion. He ran with Hollywood's macho crowd; he had his own "Rat Pack," it was said, all of them carousers and womanizers. Adding to his controversial image was an incident early in his career in which he was charged with the rape, and death, of a Hollywood starlet, a more contemporary replay of the Fatty Arbuckle case. Charges against Ladington were dropped for lack of evidence, but that dark shadow became a permanent part of his legacy.

Unlike some men on the Hollywood fast track, Ladington seemed to have a need to be married. The last thing I read, which was a few years ago, he'd taken his sixth bride, a failed Hollywood actress one-third his age.

"How old do you figure he is?" I asked.

"Got to be eighty," Seth said.

"Like fine wine, he improves with age," John added. He ended the evening by handing out a list of his current favorite wines, and urging us to upgrade our taste when purchasing. "A fine wine is priceless," he said as we filed from the room. Then he added a favorite quote of his from the Bible: " 'Like the best wine that goeth down sweetly, causing the lips of those who are asleep to speak.' "

Seth had driven me to the course, so he took me home.

"It's still early," I said. "Would you like a nightcap? Tea?"

"Ayuh," he said. "Cup of tea sounds fine.

"Glad you went tonight?" he asked after we'd settled in my living room to wait for the water to boil.

"Yes. One night won't make me a wine expert, but at least I have a heightened appreciation for the subject. I thought it made sense to attend John's course before I leave for California."

"Lot of damn nonsense."

"What is?"

"John's fancy descriptions of the way the wine tasted. 'Sweet jammy nose,' indeed. Tasted like any other wine to me."

I laughed. "Not according to John, and I must say he is inspirational. I never think much about the wine I buy, but I probably should. As he said, we should upgrade our taste."

"It's all a pretentious game, Jessica," my friend of many years proclaimed, "especially in restaurants. That silly ritual of sniffing the cork, smelling the wine, taking a tiny sip and holding it in your mouth, then sending the bottle back because it lacks bouquet or some other such thing."

Although I tended to agree with him—to an extent—I was glad the whistling kettle summoned me to the kitchen. When Seth becomes adamant about something, I've learned it's best to change the subject.

When I returned with our tea on a tray, he was perusing printed material we'd been given at the course. "When are you off for California?" he asked absently.

"Day after tomorrow."

"You'll be spendin' all your time at Margaret and Craig's bed-and-breakfast?"

"No. I'm staying at the Westin St. Francis in San Francisco for a few days, then going to Napa."

"Maybe you'll run into that old coot, Ladington, while you're there."

"Maybe I will," I said, refilling our cups.

Seth laughed. "John is probably partial to Ladington's wines because he wishes he was like him," Seth said. "You know, bigger than life, a woman's man."

"I doubt it," I said. "John St. Clair would never allow sentimentality to influence his selections. He's a purist when it comes to wine."

Seth looked at his watch. "Better be heading home," he said. "I've got a full house of patients tomorrow. Thanks for the tea. It had a sweet jammy nose, lingers nicely on the palate."

"Don't be so cynical," I said, walking him to the door.

"I was tempted to quote something else to John about wine," he said.

"Which was?"

"Disraeli. He said, 'I rather like bad wine . . . one gets so bored with good wine.' "

"I'm glad you didn't. Thanks for the ride. We'll talk before I leave."

I sat in bed and reread letters I'd received from former Cabot Covers, Craig and Margaret Snasdell. No matter where I travel, there always seems to be someone who's spent at least a portion of their lives here, and who enjoys touching base with current residents. Craig and Margaret were a popular, attractive couple in Cabot Cove. He was tall and solidly built, with a strong chin and reddish hair; there was a resemblance to the actor Robert Redford. Margaret, too, was tall and willowy, five feet nine inches, with an impressive mane of blond hair and a smile that melted snow in midwinter Maine. When they'd lived in Cabot Cove, Margaret was a nurse, Craig an independent insurance agent specializing in auto insurance.

They'd always talked of owning and operating a bed-and-breakfast, preferably in an area with less severe weather than we experience in Maine. They'd made their wishes known to real estate agents in northern California and waited patiently until the right property came on the market, a 10,000 square foot, 1892 manor house, Cedar Gables, designed by a British architect named Ernest Coxhead to reflect the Shakespearian era. They were thrilled when their bid was accepted, and we held an elaborate going-away party for them the night before they moved.

Their letters and occasional phone calls always ended with an invitation for me to be their guest at Cedar Gables Inn. The photographs they sent of the inn showed every aspect of it, inside and out, and the more I looked at them, and thought about it, the more I wanted to take them up on their offer. I was between writing books in October, and had been sneezing and coughing since the beginning of the month. This was a perfect time to get away for a week or two. There was an added incentive, however. I'd been toying with the idea of setting my next mystery novel in a winery, and this would give me a chance to do some research while enjoying myself.

"Lovely," I thought as I put the letters and pictures on my night table and turned off the light. A few days in one of my favorite cities, San Francisco, and then a relaxed, peaceful week in California's famed wine country.

Just what the doctor ordered.

Chapter Two

"That's it, Jess, trim the nose up a little and keep her flying straight and level."

I sat in the right-hand seat and did as Jed Richardson instructed, trimming up the nose of his Cessna 182 S single-engine airplane. I'd taken flying lessons from Jed a year ago and had received my private pilot's license. That didn't mean I was completely comfortable at the controls of an aircraft, although I'd passed my FAA test flight with flying colors, pardon the pun, and had aced the written exam, as the saying goes. My friends found it amusing that I'd learned to fly a plane but had never learned to drive a car. I suppose there is a certain irony in it, but that doesn't matter. I'd taken flying lessons as a challenge, much to Seth Hazlitt's chagrin, and was glad I had.

Jed was a former airline pilot who'd retired to start up his own small charter airline in Cabot Cove. This morning, he was flying me to Boston where I would catch a nonstop flight to San Francisco.

With the plane properly trimmed, we settled back and allowed the autopilot to take over.

"Sounds like a nice trip you're off on," he said.

"Yes, I'm really excited. It'll be wonderful seeing Craig and Margaret Snasdell again. From everything I hear about their bed-and-breakfast, it's lovely. And, of course, I'm looking forward to doing some wine tasting at all those vineyards."

"I suggest you have a designated driver with you," Jed said, laughing.

"I always have a designated driver, Jed. I don't drive."

"That's right—forgot about that."

"Seth and I were talking with John St. Clair last night about William Ladington."

"Is he still alive?"

"That's what we wondered. He hasn't been in the news for quite a while."

"Probably still kicking around. Damn fool with all those marriages. And that rape and murder of that actress."

"He was only charged, Jed," I said. "That doesn't mean he did it."

"I know, I know," he said, shaking his head. "Innocent till proved guilty and all that. Still, I wouldn't put it past him. You'd think he'd learn after two or three marriages didn't work. Of course, I give him credit for his successes. Everything he touches seems to turn to gold."

"Or wine in this case."

We passed the remainder of the flight making small talk. Then, as we entered the Boston air traffic control system, Jed disconnected the autopilot and navigated the intricate, busy Boston air space down to a smooth touchdown at Logan International. He taxied up to the private aviation area of the airport, took my bags from the rear of the plane, and walked me into the small terminal.

"You planning to stay in Boston awhile?" I asked after requesting ground transportation to the main terminal.

"Nope. Heading right back. Got an early-afternoon charter to Burlington. But I'll be here to meet you in ten days."

"And I'll be looking for you."

I watched him leave the terminal and stride to his plane. A few minutes later, an airport minibus took me to where the major airlines operated and I checked in for my San Francisco flight.

Although I travel a great deal, there's always a feeling of anticipation as I climb aboard a large jetliner and head for a favorite place. San Francisco certainly ranks as one of those, although there are plenty of other places I love to visit in this vast country of ours. San Francisco's physical beauty has always inspired me—the steep hills in the city that challenge even the strongest legs, the glittering bay beneath the Golden Gate Bridge, and the rugged mountains that form an exquisite scrim about the city. But it is the history of San Francisco that defines for me the spirit that permeates this magnificent jewel of a city. Even today, the rugged individuality of the Gold Rush and the dogged determination to survive after the 1906 earthquake say a lot about the character of the men and women living there. And the vast array of coin-operated newspaper boxes on many of the city's street corners are symbolic of the free and open attitude the residents of San Francisco seem to have toward one another.

Six hours later, as our captain banked left on our approach to San Francisco International Airport, I looked down from my window at the magnificent Golden Gate Bridge, shrouded in fog as happens virtually every late afternoon, its impressive span backlit by an enormous orange globe as the sun dipped toward the horizon.

My head cold seemed suddenly to disappear.

I felt wonderful.

Chapter Three

I checked into the Westin St. Francis Hotel, on Union Square, and had dinner in the Compass Rose Bar with Marsha Monro, an executive at the St. Francis with whom I'd become friendly during a book promotion tour a few years earlier. It was a relaxed, leisurely dinner; the conversation was easy, the laughs frequent.

"I think it's time for this lady to get to bed," I told Marsha after a superb rice pudding. "My circadian rhythms are acting up."

We stood in the opulent lobby waiting for an elevator.

"You know, you really didn't have to give me that wonderful suite," I said.

"I wouldn't have it any other way," Marsha said. "Looking forward to some serious wine tasting in Napa?"

"As long as it doesn't interfere with some serious relaxing. Actually, I'll be making notes about the wineries I visit. I might set my next novel in one. Other than that, I intend to sleep late, nap in the afternoon, and get to bed early."

An elevator arrived. "Well, Jess," Marsha said, "just don't get involved in the Ladington murder in Napa."

"Ladington, as in William Ladington?" I asked in surprise.

"Yes. Remember him?"

"I was talking about him with friends just a few days ago. Was he murdered?"

"No. A waiter who worked at a restaurant that Ladington owns was killed a few months ago. I guess the press was looking for a shorthand way to describe it. It's become *the* Ladington murder."

"Is he a suspect?" I asked.

"I don't know. I haven't been following it closely. You can read about it upstairs. All the newspapers are in your suite, along with some goodies to munch on. Pleasant dreams. Call if you need anything."

"I will, and thanks for your hospitality."

My suite was Number 1120—a spacious living room with couch, easy chairs, and desk, a large bedroom with a king-sized sleigh bed, two marble baths the size of my living room back home, and magnificent antique furniture everywhere. Two dozen red roses graced a coffee table in the living room, along with an overflowing platter of snacks, and a bottle of champagne, California vintage, of course. The hotel was built in 1904, badly damaged in the 1906 quake, and rebuilt to its present level of grandeur.

I spent more time than usual lingering in one of the luxurious baths, slipped a hotel terry cloth robe over my nightgown, and went to the desk. The drapes were open, revealing the city's lights. On the desk was a pile of newspapers and magazines, including the *Chronicle* and the *Examiner.* I picked up the *Examiner* and flipped through its pages. The Napa Valley murder was covered in an article on page three.

LADINGTON MURDER SOURS THE WINE

The recent murder in Napa Valley of Louis Hubler, a waiter, has residents on edge, and threatens the valley's lucrative tourist industry, according to Napa mayor, Warren Nielson. "As usual, the media blows an unfortunate event like this out of proportion," said

Nielson, "and some people planning to vacation here will be scared off. This unfortunate incident does not reflect a dangerous condition in Napa Valley, and I ask everyone to use common sense and not overreact."

The article went on to briefly describe the murder. The victim was a young waiter at Ladington's Steak House, in Yountville, a town noted for its excellent restaurants. He'd been stabbed to death, receiving a single fatal wound to his heart. The writer then gave a capsule background of William Ladington, rehashing highlights of his Hollywood career and his success as a vintner in northern California. A bed-and-breakfast owner in the area was quoted as having received a few cancellations because of the murder. That solitary comment certainly didn't represent a downward trend in tourism, although I know how such things can mushroom. But because murders are rare in places like California's wine country, I suppose even one tends to evoke a reaction from the public. In big cities, where murders are more common, there's less tendency to panic.

The final line said that Ladington had been questioned but was not considered a suspect at this time.

I was about to put down the paper and head for bed when a small boxed article at the bottom of the page caught my eye.

SHERLOCK COMES TO BAY AREA

George Sutherland, a top-ranking Scotland Yard detective, will address California law enforcement officials at the annual meeting of the Global Society of Crime Detection. Inspector Sutherland is a last-minute replacement for his supervisor at The Yard, Sir Malcolm Winston, who suffered a broken leg in a recent automobile accident in Oxford. The meeting will take place at the Stanford Court Hotel.

"I don't believe it!" I said aloud.

George Sutherland and I had met years ago when I traveled to England to address a mystery writers' conference. I'd been a guest during that trip at the manor house of Dame Marjorie Ainsworth, then the reigning queen of mystery writers. Marjorie had been in ill health and was quite frail that weekend, and I silently wondered how long she might have to live. But her life was cut even shorter when someone stabbed her to death in her bed.

Because of Dame Marjorie's esteemed position in British society, Scotland Yard was brought in to assist local police in solving the crime, and George Sutherland was assigned the case. He was a handsome widower, tall and distinguished with steel-gray eyes that failed to conceal a hint of mischief. I suppose it's safe to say that we developed an almost immediate attraction for each other, although because I was among the suspects—everyone staying at the house that weekend fell into that category—our personal feelings for each other didn't surface until we'd managed to solve the murder and I was about to leave London for Cabot Cove.

Since then, we'd stayed in touch by phone and through the mail, but time spent together had been limited by distance and our respective professional schedules. The most prolonged period of time we shared was when George hosted me and a dozen Cabot Cove friends at his small family castle in Wick, Scotland, situated on that magnificent country's most northern tip. He'd turned the castle into a hotel and we spent a wonderful week there, although the murder of one of his dining room staff tended to take the edge off any frivolity we might have been enjoying.

Neither of us had looked to advance our relationship—if

that's what you could call it—beyond that of close friends, although George had taken a few tries at moving it to another level. Were I interested in a romantic involvement, George Sutherland certainly represented everything I would look for in a man—bright, sensitive, caring, and with a subtle sense of humor which, once you tuned into it, could have you laughing until tears ran from your eyes. As it stood, we were content being friends.

I glanced at a small clock on the desk. It was ten in San Francisco, one in the morning in Maine, six a.m. in London. I was reluctant to call George at that hour, and made a mental note to get up early to call first thing in the morning. As I went to the bedroom and slipped off my robe, the phone rang.

"Hello?"

"Jess?"

"George? My goodness, I can't believe it's you. I was just reading that you're coming to San Francisco to address a group. I was going to call you except the sun's just coming up where you are."

"Yes, it is. I've been up working a case. This trip to San Francisco is very much a last-minute thing."

"So I read. A shame about Sir Malcolm breaking his leg."

"Nasty experience for him. He's getting on in age and probably shouldn't be driving. At any rate, I've been pressed into service and am leaving for San Francisco tomorrow."

"How did you know I was here?" I asked.

"When I was told to go to San Francisco, I decided I might be able to arrange my return trip to include your Cabot Cove. I reached your answering machine and heard your message that you would be out of town for ten days, so I took a chance and called your sheriff friend, Metzger. He told me you'd gone to San Francisco, of all places, and I wanted to make sure we could touch base, have a chance to see you if only for a short time."

"That would be lovely, George, except I'm only going to be here in the city for another day. I'm heading up to the wine country to stay with old friends from Cabot Cove who have a bed-and-breakfast there. I suppose I could stay in San Francisco a little longer, but I hate to change plans and disappoint them. Any chance of you joining me there after you've given your talk?"

"I don't know, Jess. Things have gotten terribly busy here. The murder rate is going up, or down, depending upon which politician is speaking. My personal observation is that it's definitely on the rise."

I laughed. "I suppose you can make statistics do whatever you want them to do, but you can't prove anything by me. The murder rate in the California wine country seems to be going up, too. I was just reading about a murder that took place there in the past few months. It's being treated by the press like a crime wave."

This time he laughed. "There you go again, Jess, always traveling to where murders are taking place. Or do they take place *because* you're coming?"

"I certainly hope not. Can you manage to stay a few extra days and join me in Napa? I would love to see you."

"I'll do my best. I'll give you a call at the hotel tomorrow when I arrive."

"I'll look forward to it."

Talking with George energized me and I sat up for another hour before finally feeling sleepy and succumbing to it. I climbed into bed and looked out the window at lights on a distant hill outside the city. All I hoped as I slipped into slumber was that there would be a chance to see this dear man, who, though we saw so little of each other, brought a spark to my life and enriched it, even from afar.

Chapter Four

"Margaret, it's Jessica."

"Hi, Jess. Are you calling from San Francisco?"

"Yes, I got in last night."

"I know, you're coming up a day early."

"No, that's not why I'm calling."

"It's okay if you do, Jess. Come early, that is."

"I'm really not calling about that. I'm still planning to arrive tomorrow. What I was wondering was whether you had an extra room."

"As a matter of fact we do. Are you bringing someone with you? An old friend from Cabot Cove?"

"Actually, a dear friend of mine from London, George Sutherland—he's a chief inspector with Scotland Yard—is coming to San Francisco to speak to a law enforcement group. I convinced him to join me for a few days in Napa."

There was silence on the line.

"Margaret, are you there?"

"Yes, I'm here, Jess. Tell me more about this Mr. George Sutherland."

"Not much to tell. As I said, he's a good friend I met in London years ago and—"

"Just how good a friend, Jess?"

"Oh, Margaret, it's nothing like that. I'm just happy he's going to be in the area the same time I am and I want to spend a couple of days with him."

Her laugh was slightly wicked. "Sure you'll be needing a second room?"

"Yes, I'm sure. Naturally, George will pay his way."

"How exciting, meeting a real live Scotland Yard detective. Of course we have a room for him, and we'll be delighted to have him as a guest. Is he driving up with you?"

"No. He'll be coming up a day or two later. Thanks, Margaret. I can't wait to see you and Craig."

"Same here. Enjoy your time in San Francisco."

The wonderful coincidence that George would be in California when I was had me walking with a light step all morning. He'd reached me on the cell phone provided to all guests by the hotel, a wonderful convenience—no need to miss incoming calls when away from your room, or to search for a pay phone to make outgoing calls. I was having breakfast in the dining room when his call came through. Although we had only a brief conversation, he'd said what I wanted to hear, that he had arranged to take a week's vacation while in California and would join me in the wine country.

I had a relatively free day ahead in San Francisco, my only real commitment a dinner date with an old friend from Cabot Cove, Neil Schwartz, a former New York City policeman who wrote poetry in his spare time. He'd moved to Cabot Cove after retiring from the force. Neil and I had developed a kinship shortly after his arrival in town because we both lost our spouses within six months of each other and found ourselves spending considerable time together, sharing many dinners at my house or at his, to the point that people began to gossip. There was never any romantic interest between us. It was simply a matter of two grieving people finding solace in each other's company.

Neil was never successful as a writer, at least not if defined by income. He and his wife, Sandy, lived on his police department pension and the occasional assignments he received from small magazines. Until she became ill, Sandy had worked as a nurse's aide. Neil eventually decided to move to Wisconsin, where his daughter and a grandchild lived. While there, he wrote a book called *Scarlet Sins*, a collection of true and startling murder cases. He sent me the manuscript hoping I would provide a quote for the cover, which I happily did. That put us back in touch.

Neil called me one day to announce he was moving to Sausalito, across the bay from San Francisco, where he had landed a job as adjunct professor at a local community college. Naturally, when making plans to travel to San Francisco, I let him know I was coming and we arranged to get together for dinner at Morton's steak house, directly across Union Square from my hotel.

I was surprised Neil chose to have dinner there. I'd been to Morton's in Georgetown and New York City and knew it was expensive. But Neil insisted, ending our conversation with a lighthearted "Things have turned around financially for me, Jess. I even have a mutual fund."

I was a few minutes early and waited for Neil in the small, cozy bar. My first impression as he came down the stairs from the street was that if dress reflects relative financial success, his nicely cut blue suit, sparkling white shirt, and muted burgundy tie certainly mirrored what he'd told me on the phone. I think the only time I'd ever seen Neil in a suit was at his wife's funeral in Cabot Cove. He was strictly a jeans and sweater type, with an occasional corduroy jacket with patches on the elbows thrown in when an occasion demanded more formal attire.

"Jess, how wonderful to see you," he said, wrapping his arms around me.

"It's been too long, Neil," I said. "You look dashing in that suit. Is it new?"

"As a matter of fact it is," he said, smiling broadly. He sported a beard, which he had occasionally done when living in Cabot Cove. His green eyes were very much alive,

with a twinkle that hadn't been there for a long time after
his wife's death.

"Feel like a drink at the bar before dinner?" he asked.

"Why don't we go right to our table? I'm famished."

We were shown to a corner table by the maitre d', and
our waitress, a perky young woman with a big smile, took
our drink order: a dry martini straight up for Neil, a glass of
Sterling Reserve pinot noir for me.

"Have a pleasant day?" he asked.

"I always do when I'm in San Francisco. I just walked—
my calf muscles are feeling those hills—and stopped in
shops, bought a few gifts for people back home. I ended up
having lunch at the Buena Vista."

"One of your favorite places."

The Buena Vista, on Fisherman's Wharf across from the
turntable for the Hyde Street cable car line, was where Irish
coffee was introduced in 1952 by the San Francisco columnist Stan Delaplane. The bartenders serve thousands of Irish
coffees each day, more than 20 million since Delaplane returned from Ireland with the recipe. What I especially love
are the communal tables where you always seem to end up
eating with interesting people. I'd sat at a table with cou-
ples from New York, Los Angeles, and Napa Valley. At one
point, the latter pair had brought up the murder of the
waiter at Ladington's restaurant.

"Just another drug hit," the young man said.

"How do you know drugs were involved?" I asked.

"Aren't they always?" his girlfriend replied.

I didn't challenge their assumption, for two reasons. First, I
was in too good a mood to get into a debate with anyone. Second, from all I'd read lately, drugs certainly were at the root
of myriad crimes. I contented myself with chatting about less
weighty matters and enjoying the convivial atmosphere at our
table and in the bustling bar and restaurant itself.

Now, I tasted the wine and declared it satisfactory, although I knew I would never send back wine unless it was blatantly bad. I thought of Seth and his jaded view of the ritual of wine sniffing and tasting, and had to smile.

"What's new with my favorite poet?" I asked Neil.

"Let's see," he said, raising his glass and clicking it against the rim of mine. "What's new with me? Well, I'm no longer teaching."

"That certainly is news. How long ago did you leave?"

"It's been about a month."

"What brought it about?" I asked, hoping he hadn't been asked to leave.

"A magazine assignment. Remember *Scarlet Sins*?"

"Of course I do. I gave you a quote for the cover."

"Yes, you did, and I'll always be grateful. Anyway, a top editor at *Vanity Fair* got interested in the murder of a waiter in Yountville because of William Ladington's connection to it. He owns the restaurant where the victim worked."

"So I've heard."

"They offered me a big advance, no haggling, and wired me the first half. Of course, it might not be big by your standards, but it's the biggest payday I've ever seen. Poetry doesn't pay much, you know."

Nor do magazines, I thought, although I hadn't tested those waters for years.

"This is really exciting news, Neil. I read a short piece in the paper last night about the murder."

"I've been spending a lot of time up there recently," said Neil. "It's not easy getting information from people in Napa Valley. They tend to be an insular bunch, pretty much stick together and don't like talking to what they consider outsiders. Being there as a journalist labels me as one of those."

I laughed. "I know what you mean. We have a few insular types in Cabot Cove, too, I'm sure you remember. But I know you'll keep digging. Have you made any headway? Who do people up there think did the killing?"

"Not one of their own—that's for sure. Had to be some nut passing through. I don't argue with them because I'm trying to get them to open up, but some of them are downright nasty, like Ladington himself. He's a crusty SOB if I've ever met one. Maybe you remember him from all the press he used to get."

I laughed.

"What's funny?"

"Ever since I decided to spend a week in Napa, his name has been coming up with regularity. I suppose it's akin to deciding to buy something, say a certain new car model, and all you see on the streets are that same car. We were wondering back home whether he was still alive. Obviously, he is. Are the police considering him a prime suspect?"

"Not officially. He was at the restaurant the night of the murder but claims he knew nothing about it, says he'd left for home before it happened. He lives in a castle at his vineyard. At any rate, I stopped by to ask him a few questions."

"And?"

"And Ladington told me in no uncertain terms to get lost. The shotgun he carried helped make the point."

"I don't blame you for getting out of there. I'll be doing some research for my next novel while in Napa, although I'm not committed to setting it in a winery. Any suggestions where I might go?"

"Sure. Stop by Ladington's place. He doesn't shoot women, just marries them."

Although I try to be prudent in what I eat these days, opting for red meat only now and then, I dug into the huge, tender porterhouse that was big enough for two. If I was home and had a dog, I would have requested a doggie bag. As it turned out, Neil did have a dog, and the waitress packaged up what we both had left over for what would undoubtedly be a very happy canine.

We parted on the street.

"If I can be of any help while you're here, Jess, just yell. Where are you staying in Napa?"

"A bed-and-breakfast owned by Margaret and Craig Snasdell. Remember them?"

"Vaguely. They moved out here?"

"They bought a beautiful place, Cedar Gables Inn. You can reach me there." I almost mentioned that George Sutherland would be joining me but decided not to. People tend to assign romantic motives to such situations, which I wanted to avoid.

"I'm really pleased for you, Neil," I said. "*Vanity Fair* is such a good magazine."

And a generous one, I thought, again wondering how much magazines paid these days for lead articles.

I walked back to the hotel and went to my suite where the little red light on the phone flashed to indicate someone had left a message. It was Seth Hazlitt. I would have returned the call were it not for the time difference.

I settled on the couch and resumed reading a book I'd started on the plane. It was called *Sunlight into Wine,* by an Australian viticulturist, Dr. Richard Smart. I wanted to learn all I could about growing grapes and making wine, but I bogged down in early technical material and found my eyes closing. When that happens, I seldom fight it.

I climbed into bed and thought of the dinner conversation with Neil Schwartz. What a coincidence that Bill Ladington had surfaced and had some connection to a murder, as innocent as the connection might be. But I decided to put any such thoughts out of my mind. Murder was of interest to me only in the books I wrote.

The real thing was none of my business.

Chapter Five

"We have two choices how to go to Napa, Mrs. Fletcher. We can go over the Golden Gate Bridge and head up 101, or we can take the bridge to Oakland and use Route 80."

"I'll leave that up to you. You're the professional."

"Six of one, half a dozen of another," he said. His name was Harry, a pleasant, middle-aged man who wore a gray uniform, black tie, and black chauffeur's cap. I'd hired him through a car service in San Francisco. Margaret and Craig Snasdell had offered to come down to the city to pick me up, but I didn't want to impose any more than necessary. As it was, they were being gracious enough to put me up for a week.

"On second thought," I said, "let's take the Golden Gate. I remember going over the bridge to Oakland a few years ago. It was terribly congested. Besides, I love the view from the Golden Gate."

"I was hoping you'd say that," he said, smiling and opening the rear door of a Lincoln Town Car. He got behind the wheel and we pulled away from the hotel. Fifteen minutes later, he joined sparse traffic on the famous bridge that links the city of San Francisco with Marin County to the north. The bridge was the symbol of home for thousands of GIs returning from the Pacific Theater during World War II. I looked back through the window over the bay and city. It was a sparkling clear day, the sun shining brightly, visibility unlimited. People who live in places with such stunning beauty are indeed fortunate, I thought, as we reached the end of the bridge. Down to our right was the picturesque waterfront village of Sausalito where Neil Schwartz lived. What a joy it must be to wake up every morning and sip your coffee while taking in the unique vista that is the Bay Area. If I ever decided to move from Cabot Cove, it could easily be to this part of the country. Then again, London has always appealed, too. But thoughts of leaving the town I love so much have always been just that, pleasant, fanciful thoughts, moments of idle daydreaming, what-if exercises.

An hour later we had passed from the congestion of lower Marin County into the beautiful and unique farmland that is California's famed wine country. I looked out over tree-topped mountains and luxurious valleys, with thousands of acres of tilled fields creating what looked like giant quilts. We followed Route 101 to a town called Petaluma, then headed east on Route 116, which took us across the southern end of the Sonoma Valley, one of Northern California's five primary wine districts, or appellations. Each appellation has a different topography, climate, and soil, which gives the grapes grown in those areas their own special properties. The Sonoma Valley dates back earlier than Napa, but the wines produced in Napa Valley have become more popular over the years, perhaps because of the more favorable conditions, but more likely due to aggressive marketing.

"It's such an unusual landscape," I said to Harry. We'd been chatting throughout the trip, and he demonstrated knowledge not only of the wine country, but also of the wine-making process.

"Yes, it is," he said over his shoulder. "All the trellising gives it a different look. I've always found it interesting, Mrs. Fletcher, how the early settlers came here and realized conditions were perfect for making wine. And it hasn't been that long, you know. Thirty-five years ago there were only something like twenty-five wineries in all of Napa Valley. Last count, I think, there were about a hundred and sixty-five, and the state of California must have more than seven hundred by now."

"Funny," I said, "but I tend to think of wineries as being small businesses. Obviously, it's big business in California."

"It certainly is," said Harry. "Ranks right up there with making movies."

"Those early settlers who established the first vineyards must have been rugged individualists," I said. "You have to have a lot of faith to take a patch of land and plant grapes on it, then hope Mother Nature will be good to you before it's time to harvest them and turn them into a wine that people will like and buy."

"I suppose so," he said. "Lots of faith—and lots of money."

We both laughed.

"Do you know anything about Ladington Creek wine?" I asked.

"They produce very good wines," Harry said. "My wife and I enjoy a bottle of Ladington Creek cabernet on special occasions."

"I understand there's been some excitement in Napa the past month."

"You mean the murder."

"Yes. What have you heard about it?"

"Just what I've read in the papers, and that isn't much. I suppose you're interested in it because you're a mystery writer."

"No, not at all. But since I'll be spending a week here it caught my attention."

Eventually, we ended up on Route 12, and not long after that we entered the city of Napa. I handed Harry a map the

Snasdells had sent me, and after one false turn we pulled up in front of 486 Coombs Street, the bed-and-breakfast my friends from Cabot Cove had traveled three thousand miles to buy. The impressive house was set back from the road with a brick pathway leading to a front door covered by a portico supported by six white columns. To the left was a flagstone circle containing curved stone benches and a bird-bath. Parking for four cars was located to the right of the house.

"Nice place to spend a week," Harry said.

"It's charming, isn't it?" I said. "Picture perfect."

Harry got out and took my luggage from the trunk. I stepped from the car and stretched against a knot in my back. The sun warmed my face—the temperature was in the seventies—and a slight breeze ruffled my hair. "I'll bring these right inside for you," Harry said, picking up my two heavy bags as though they were empty and leading the way to the front door. He stepped aside and I prepared to knock when the door opened and Margaret Snasdell was facing me, a wide, familiar smile on her pretty face.

"I made it," I said, grinning.

"So I see. My goodness, you haven't changed a bit, Jess."

"You have," I said. "California must agree with you. You've gotten younger."

"And you're as diplomatic as ever. And don't kid a kid-der. These silver streaks among the gold tell the tale."

"This is Harry," I said. "He drove me from San Francisco."

"Thank you for bringing this dear friend to us safely. Come in, please."

Harry carried the luggage through the open door to a large foyer with gleaming black and white tile. He put the bags down and said, "It was a pleasure meeting and driving you, Mrs. Fletcher. I wonder if I could ask a favor?"

"Of course."

He pulled a paperback edition of one of my books from his jacket pocket and held it out for me. "My wife loves to read, and when I told her I'd be driving you, she gave me this to see if you'd be kind enough to sign it for her."

"I'd be delighted. What's her name?"

"Marie."

I inscribed the book and handed it back to him.

"Stay for tea, Harry?" Margaret asked.

"That's kind of you, but I'd better get back to the city. There'll be another assignment, I'm sure." He thanked me again and left.

"This is such a lovely place," I said, taking in what I could see from my vantage point in the foyer, which included what Margaret termed the main parlor, a large room with dark paneling and dense, wall-to-wall raspberry carpeting. A small red couch and a window bench were in front of leaded windows overlooking Coombs Street. In the center of the room stood a table containing a vase of fresh-cut flowers and a guest registry. A chandelier hung gracefully above it. At the far end of the room was a fireplace flanked by high-backed chairs. Between them was a silver tray on a stand holding etched red cordial glasses and a pitcher. The overall impression was of a warm and inviting place from a bygone era.

"Want to see your room?" Margaret asked. "Freshen up after your trip?"

"Sounds like a good idea."

A woman appeared from the dining room.

"This is Barbara," Margaret said. "She manages the inn when Craig and I are away. Couldn't survive without her."

We shook hands.

"I've been looking forward to your arrival," Barbara said. "I've enjoyed your books."

"That's very kind."

"I was just about to take Jess to her room," Margaret said. They each grabbed a piece of my luggage and led me up a wide staircase to the second floor.

"We decided to put you in the Churchill Chamber, Jess," Margaret said as we went down a short corridor lined with antique photographs to a room at the end. "We have two very special and, I must say, popular rooms—the Churchill, named after Alice Ames Churchill—this house was built for her—and Count Bonzi's Room."

"Count Bonzi? Who was he?"

"He lived here at Cedar Gables back in the twenties. I thought your Scotland Yard friend would enjoy that room. Some guests leave believing it's haunted. It even has a secret back stairway. When is he arriving?"

"Tomorrow."

"I'm sure he'll enjoy sleeping where the count slept. Here we are."

She opened the door and I stepped into the Churchill Chamber, my home for the next week.

The room was large and furnished with heavy, ornate furniture including a queen-size feather bed set between a thick, dark wood head and footboard. A gas-fired fireplace occupied one end of the room. At the other end was the door to the bath, in which there was a whirlpool tub large enough for two, framed with dark, aged wood, and a shower.

"Did you and Craig create all this?" I asked.

"Pretty much. We remodeled a room at a time. Like it?"

"Love it. I may never leave."

"And miss all those good wine tastings? Why don't you relax, Jess, unpack, and grab a quick nap. We serve wine and cheese in the den at five. You can meet our other guests then, and Craig should be back. We've made dinner reservations at seven. The Napa Valley Grille. The chef, Bob

Hurley, is a good friend. His herb-crusted sea bass melts in your mouth."

"I have a feeling my diet is about to go out the window," I said lightly.

"No dieting allowed, Jess. This may be health-crazed California, but the rules have to be broken now and then. Relax. If you need anything, just yell for me or Barbara."

I explored the room more closely, then unpacked, hanging my things in an oversized armoire and placing folded items in the drawers of a chest. I went to the window and looked out on a large house next door that appeared to be empty. The sun was now behind clouds that had rolled in since my arrival. I felt a chill and examined the gas fireplace, figured out how to start it, and stood in front of it for a minute to allow its heat to wash over me. The feather bed looked inviting so I kicked off my shoes, pulled down the comforter, slid beneath it, and was asleep in seconds.

According to my watch, I'd slept almost an hour. I freshened up, changed clothes, and wandered downstairs where Margaret, Barbara, and two young women who worked part-time at the inn were busy laying out the wine and cheese to be served at five, a half hour away.

"Caught twenty winks?" Barbara asked.

"Yes," I said. "It felt good."

Cedar Gable's den was an eclectic mix of high-tech and antique furniture. A large projection TV dominated one corner, and there was a shelf containing videos of dozens of movies for guests to watch. Comfortable chairs and couches were scattered throughout the great room. There was a fireplace and a grand piano, and three imposing black Triumph motorcycles, buffed to a mirror finish, stood amid the furnishings like in a motorcycle showroom.

"Craig's?" I asked, pointing to the cycles.

"Yes," Margaret said, laughing. "You know him, always has to have a project going. There was a Harley before these, and an Austin Mini he rebuilt. We don't have a garage so they end up in here. They serve a purpose, though. They're a great conversation topic. When men check in and see them, they sigh with relief that they haven't been dragged by their wives to some frilly B-and-B."

I wandered around the rest of the downstairs, pausing to admire individual pieces of furniture, taking in the dining room with its long table exquisitely set, and a hutch on which books on wine and the region, colorful neckties and T-shirts, and CDs of local jazz musicians were for sale. The CDs were played throughout the house through small speakers in every public room, creative, relaxing music that added to the overall feeling of well-being. A male singer in the Sinatra vein was singing *Fly Me to the Moon.*

"Who's he?" I asked.

"His name is Bob Dalpe. He did a few weekends recently here in Napa. He usually works the Compass Rose Bar at the St. Francis in San Francisco."

"I'll make a point of hearing him next time I'm there. My kind of music."

Magazines and newspapers were laid out on a table in the main parlor. I scanned them until the front page of a local weekly paper that had been delivered that day stopped me cold. Staring up at me was *me*—my photograph. A headline beneath it read: J.B. FLETCHER, NOTED MYSTERY WRITER, VACATIONING IN NAPA.

I took the paper into the den and showed it to Margaret.

"That devil," she said.

"Who?"

"Winston." She pointed to the byline on the article— Winston Wallace. "I bumped into him at the post office and told him you were spending a week with us. I never dreamed he'd turn it into a story. Hope you're not upset to be losing your anonymity."

"No, of course not."

Truth was, I would have preferred that my week in the Napa Valley go unnoticed, but it really didn't matter. I returned to the main parlor, sat in one of the chairs next to the fireplace, and read the article. It consisted of nothing more than information the reporter had taken from the jacket of my latest novel, mentioning a few things about me and listing other books I'd written. The piece ended with a line that I'd be spending my week at Cedar Gables, owned by old friends from Maine.

I returned the newspaper to the table and rejoined Margaret in the den.

"Wine?" she asked, indicating the tabletop that offered a variety of cheeses and crackers, raw vegetables and dip, and bottles of red and white wine. Some of the bottles were labeled Cedar Gables.

"Your own vineyard?" I asked.

"No. Wineries custom-label wines for private use. This chardonnay is a favorite of mine."

It was a lovely wine, with a buttery taste that lingered on the tongue and . . .

I thought back to my evening with Seth Hazlitt at John St. Clair's wine-appreciation seminar. Despite Seth's cynicism about those who took wine tasting seriously, I was committed to using this week to sharpen my palate and heighten my appreciation of wine.

I held up my glass: "Cheers!"

Chapter Six

The Napa Valley Grille was everything Margaret had said it would be. We were greeted warmly by a handsome maitre d' named Joel who obviously knew Craig and Margaret well. "He's the best dancer in the valley," Margaret said as the tall, lithe man led us to a table in a prime area of the restaurant. Craig ordered a bottle of sauvignon blanc, and we settled in for a leisurely dinner.

"It is so wonderful having you here," Craig said. He was tanned and fit, and wore a brown suede jacket, chinos, and a yellow shirt. "Brings back all those memories of Cabot Cove—"

"And Maine winters," Margaret added with a chuckle.

"All in the mind," I said.

"The mind?" Craig said. "I felt those winters in my bones."

They recommended a special appetizer, breast of duck in a cabernet sauce, and we caught up on our respective lives, including mutual friends from back home. It was over endive and frisée salads that the topic of murder was raised.

"Been reading about our murder?" Craig asked me.

"Yes," I replied. "Have you had any cancellations because of it? I understand your mayor is concerned about the impact on tourism."

"Our mayor," Craig said, not attempting to disguise the displeasure in his voice. "No, no cancellations—yet. Our mayor is a good man with good intentions, but the notion that someone might be murdered on his watch is anathema. I suppose his concerns about what it might do to tourism are justified, but there is such a thing as reality."

"I understand William Ladington owns the restaurant where the victim worked," I said.

Craig and Margaret looked at each other, raised their eyebrows, and shook their heads. "Bill Ladington," Craig said. "The original angry man."

"I thought he was a lover," I said, "not an angry man."

"Bigger than life," Margaret said. "And powerful. We've only run into him a few times. A big, gruff older man with a perpetual scowl and not a kind word in his vocabulary."

"Is he married?" I asked.

"I don't know," Craig said.

"Yes, he is," Margaret said, "to a woman in her late twenties, early thirties at best. He must be close to seventy-five, eighty."

"What number wife is that?" I asked myself aloud. "Number seven?"

"An honorable man," Craig quipped. "Believes in the sacred act of marriage. No one-night stands for Mr. Ladington. I will say this. Ladington Creek wines are among the best coming out of Napa Valley. He's got a wall in his tasting room filled with awards. Planning to visit him while you're here, Jess?"

"No, but if his wine is as good as everyone says, maybe I ought to do a little tasting."

"He's got quite a place out near Halton Mountain," Margaret said. "A castle that's been here since the Spanish."

"Halton Mountain?" I said. "I think I read something about that."

"The finest grape-growing land in all of California," said Craig, "and the most hotly contested."

"Why?"

"Perfect conditions for a vineyard," Craig said. "Some vintners would kill to own a piece of it." He must have realized his comment was provocative because he added, "Figuratively speaking, of course."

"Of course."

"I don't know the specifics," said Margaret, "but people have been talking for years about Halton Mountain as though it possesses some sort of magical grape-growing powers."

"Hillsides are always prime land for vineyards," Craig offered. "Halton Mountain evidently is better than most."

"Who owns the mountain?" I asked.

"That's what's being contested," Margaret replied. "As I understand it, Ladington and other vintners are claiming rights to a prime area of it. According to rumors, the dispute has turned ugly. So, Jess, tell us more about your Scotland Yard friend."

"George? That's exactly what we are, friends, nothing more." I recounted how we'd met in London but had found so little time to nurture a relationship. "I'm sure he'll love the room the count slept in. Bonzi?"

"Yes. Your timing was perfect. I'm sure you noticed that we're short on guests this week. Only three of the six rooms are occupied, including yours. It runs in cycles. Some weeks we're fully booked, with dozens of callers being turned down. Then we have a week like this. Plenty of room at the inn."

"Not good for the bottom line," Craig said with a laugh. "But that's the nature of the business."

"I've tried to clear the slate for the week so we can bounce around together," Margaret said. "Still don't drive?"

"No, but I fly," I said, which led to some good-natured kidding as I told them about having become a licensed private pilot. "And don't feel a need to chauffeur me. George is renting a car in San Francisco."

We feasted on the crusted sea bass and topped off dinner with raspberry tarts and coffee, then sat up until midnight back at the inn, chatting away, joined briefly by the only other guest, a Mrs. Marshall, whose husband had died within the past year and who was taking a long, leisurely car trip to help lessen her grief.

"Time for bed," I said.

"Breakfast is between nine and nine-thirty," Margaret said. "My special almond French toast in honor of our special guest and friend."

I changed for bed in the Churchill Chamber and picked up the paperback of *Playing with Cobras,* a novel written a few years back by a close friend, Craig Thomas, whose work I admire. Craig and his wife, Jill, live outside London, and I'd been their houseguest on a few occasions.

But as I reclined in bed and was about to start reading, my eyes strayed to a heavy chest of drawers across the room. I got up, went to it and picked up a leather-bound, oversized book I'd noticed earlier but hadn't opened. It was a diary of sorts written by previous occupants of the room, mostly honeymooners. Their entries waxed poetic about their stay at Cedar Gables, and some included rather intimate details of their first nights together in the two-person whirlpool tub. I took the book back to bed with me and spent the next half hour chuckling at some of the entries, tearing up at others. It always amazes me— and often touches me—that people are willing to bare their personal lives to strangers. Many of the entries went back a long time, long before Margaret and Craig had bought Cedar Gables and renovated it. Some people inserted their photographs along with their entries. There were crushed flowers, labels from the bottles of wine they had enjoyed on their stay, poems (Neil Schwartz would have cringed at most of them), and reviews of local restaurants.

My eyes closing, I placed the diary on the nightstand next to Craig's book, silently apologized to my friend for being distracted from starting his novel, turned out the light, and snuggled in for the first of what I anticipated would be many peaceful nights in Napa Valley.

Chapter Seven

I answered a knock on my door the next morning.

"Someone here to see you," Barbara said.

"Thank you. I'll be right down."

I hadn't expected George to arrive so soon, although I knew he was an inveterate early riser. I checked my watch. Not that early after all. Eight o'clock. I'd been up for an hour, and after showering and dressing had been sitting by the window reading Craig Thomas's book. Now, I stood in front of the mirror and fluffed my hair and scrutinized my makeup and outfit—heather tweed skirt, coffee-and-cream blouse, pale green cardigan sweater, and sensible walking shoes.

I left the room, walked down the hall, and descended the stairs, stopping once to say good morning to a life-sized suit of armor guarding the first landing. I continued and reached the foyer, expecting to see George. Instead, another man stood in the main parlor. He was short, no taller than five feet, five inches, but he was solidly built with a short neck, and a chest that pushed against the front of his shirt and jacket. He wore a black suit, white shirt, and brightly colored tie and held a hat in his hands.

My first instinct was to return upstairs. Obviously, he was not there to see me. I'd never seen him before.

But he turned, spotted me standing on the staircase, and approached.

"Mrs. Fletcher?"

"Yes."

"My name is Raoul Sebastian."

"Yes?"

"Mr. Ladington sent me."

"Mr. Ladington? *William* Ladington?"

"Yes, ma'am."

"Why—why did Mr. Ladington send you to me?"

"He wants you to be his guest at lunch today."

I wasn't sure how to respond. After a pause that seemed endless, I said, "Why does Mr. Ladington want *me* at lunch?"

"I don't know, ma'am, but he instructed me to bring you to the winery."

"What if I don't wish to go to lunch at his winery? Did it ever occur to Mr. Ladington to call and issue a proper invitation?"

"I can't address that, ma'am. All I know is that he's expecting you for lunch. I'll be happy to wait until it's time to go. You're due there at noon. We should leave here at eleven-thirty."

"I don't wish to be rude, Mr. Sebastian, but I find Mr. Ladington's approach to be out of line, even offensive. I have no intention of joining him for lunch at his winery today, or any other day for that matter. I happen to be waiting for someone to join me, and my schedule does not include lunch with Mr. Ladington."

Barbara had been standing in the dining room doorway, listening to our conversation. Sebastian turned to her: "May I please make a phone call?" he asked.

"Local?" Barbara asked.

"Yes, ma'am. To Ladington Creek."

"The phone is over there," she said, pointing to the single phone in the inn for guest use. As he went to it, Barbara and

I looked at each other, raised our eyebrows in unison, and moved a little closer to hear what he was saying.

"Mr. Ladington, it's Raoul. I'm at Cedar Gables Inn. Mrs. Fletcher refuses to come for lunch."

He held the ꞁhone away from his ear, and Ladington's shouting could be heard across the room. Sebastian turned to me and held out the receiver. The look on his face was one of pleading. I crossed the main parlor and took the receiver from him.

"Hello?" I said.

"Jessica Fletcher?"

"Yes."

"Bill Ladington here. Glad you can make it."

"Make it? No, I'm sorry. I'm not free for lunch."

"Nonsense! I'd like to meet you, get to know you, get your advice about something."

"I'm sorry, buꞇ I won't be at lunch," I said. "I have other plans."

"I won't take no for an answer, Jessica."

I considered suggesting that since we didn't know each other, his informality was annoying. But he didn't give me the chance. "Tell you what, Jessica. Nice name. I like that name. What do they call you, Jess? You come on out here with Raoul, enjoy a fine meal, see how a *real* winery operates, and lend me an ear. What have you got to lose? You've got a date with somebody else? Bring him along. No need to dress up. We're informal out here, laid back."

"How did you know I was here?" I asked.

"Saw your picture in the paper. You must be a real star. Didn't think writers got that much attention."

"I'm nothing of the sort."

"Like you to see my place. A real castle, built back when the Spanish ran things in Napa Valley. Got a chef who puts all those fancy French chefs to shame."

"I—"

Margaret came from her office. "Jess," she said with a smile, "a call for you. Heavy British accent."

"Oh?" I said to Ladington, "I'm afraid I have another call. It was nice speaking with you."

"Go ahead and take it," he said. "I'll hold on till you're through."

Exasperated, I placed the receiver on the table and went to the office, where Margaret handed me the phone.

"George?" I said.

"Yes. Glad I caught you. I'll be delayed a bit."

"I'm sorry to hear that. How long?"

"I've been roped into a panel discussion later today. I should be able to pick up the rental car by three. What is it, two hours to Napa?"

"Approximately."

"Look for me about five, in time for a quiet drink and dinner. Sorry, love, but it can't be helped."

"Of course. I understand. I'll do some things on my own for the day and be here when you arrive."

"Splendid. Can't wait to see you. Cheerio."

"He's not coming?" Margaret said.

"Later. About five."

"Who are you on the phone with out there?" she asked, pointing to the main parlor.

"William Ladington."

"What does *he* want?"

"Wants me to have lunch with him at his winery. He sent an emissary to bring me."

"Oooh, sounds intriguing. You're going, right?"

"No, I'm not. He's arrogant."

"But now you're free until five when your Scotland Yard friend arrives. Go to lunch. See what's up. You can bring back all the gossip, tell me what's going on with Ladington."

I left the office and went to where the phone still rested on the table. Raoul stood in the parlor with Barbara.

"Hello?" I said.

"Got rid 'a that other call, huh? Good girl."

I started to say that I wasn't a "girl." Instead, I said, "I've decided to accept your luncheon invitation."

"That's what I wanted to hear. You tell Raoul to stay around until it's time to head over here, take you anywhere you want to go, give you anything you need."

"I have to be back early this afternoon," I said.

"Whatever you say. Got a new book out? Bring it along, sign it for me and the wife. We don't read much but like to have signed books on the shelves, especially hardcovers. They look a lot better. Make it to Bill and Tennessee."

"Tennessee?"

"That's her name. Ever hear anything so dumb? But she's a real stunner, a real beauty."

We ended the conversation and I hung up. Margaret and Barbara stood looking at me, smiling.

"Satisfied?" I asked.

"As long as you tell us everything that happens," said Margaret.

"I'm only doing it for research," I said, sounding defensive, like an alcoholic who claims to drink only for medicinal purposes. "I may set my next book in a winery. What better way to learn than to be hosted by the owner of one of the better wineries?"

"Of course," Margaret said.

"If George arrives early, tell him I'll be back as soon as possible."

"Don't worry," Margaret said. "And if you don't come back, you'll have Scotland Yard on your case."

Her comment caused me to remember what Neil Schwartz had told me: that William Ladington owned the restaurant where the waiter had worked before being knifed to death, and that he had a vile temper.

"Yes," I said, "that will be comforting in case I don't come back."

I said to Raoul, "I'll be ready to leave at eleven-thirty."

"Yes, ma'am."

"What are you going to do between now and then, Jess?" Margaret asked.

"Go upstairs, get out my book on growing grapes and making wine, and bone up on those subjects before meeting Mr. Ladington. I'd hate to look stupid."

"Breakfast at nine," Barbara called as I headed up the staircase.

"My special almond French toast," Margaret added.

"Wouldn't miss it," I said over my shoulder without missing a step.

Chapter Eight

The vehicle driven by Raoul was a red four-wheel drive Jeep Grand Cherokee. I don't pay much attention to cars, but this sort of Jeep is familiar to me because we get so much snow in Cabot Cove. Four-wheel drives, with their ability to handle slippery conditions, are the most popular vehicles in town—perhaps in all of Maine, for that matter.

Raoul held open a rear door for me, but I opted for the front passenger seat, from which I'd have a better view and could more easily converse with him.

We left Napa City on Route 121, but quickly turned onto what Raoul said was the Silverado Trail. "Mr. Ladington told me to bring you this way, Mrs. Fletcher," he explained. "It takes longer but the views are prettier."

"I'm glad he did," I said. "Pretty views are always appreciated."

The Silverado Trail wound along the eastern edge of Napa Valley, running parallel to the more congested and commercial Route 29, the main artery from the valley's southern boundary to Calistoga at the northern end. Raoul had handed me a map shortly after leaving town. On it were listed all the major wineries in the valley. Ladington Creek was almost at the end of the Silverado Trail, near the town of St. Helena. Two mountains were noted on the map: Howell Mountain, and the one that Craig and Margaret had mentioned at dinner, Halton Mountain. Ladington Creek was located at the base of the latter.

Bill Ladington had been right. The views along the Silverado Trail were spectacular. I looked down over the valley and its thousands of symmetrical rows of grape trellises that followed the contour of the land as far as the eye could see. Some vineyards were relatively flat; others twisted up hillsides and disappeared over their crests. All were brightened by lovely yellow wildflowers called mustard flowers, which inspire a number of festivals throughout California's wine country. Besides the trellises, the other distinguishing feature across the sprawling landscape were windmills, hundreds of them spaced throughout the vineyards.

"Do those windmills generate power?" I asked.

"No, ma'am," Raoul replied. "The vineyards turn them on when the temperature gets cold enough at night. The air above the ground is warmer than the air at the ground. The breeze created by the windmills circulates the warmer air over the vines."

"Seems like a sensible, low-tech solution to a problem," I said.

"Yes, ma'am."

Some of the wineries we passed looked like European estates, with huge iron gates, and access roads lined with poplar trees reaching far into the vineyards' inner recesses. Others, more recently built—at least the main buildings looked more contemporary—were closer to the road, and large signs invited visitors to come sample the product.

When we reached Halton Mountain, Raoul turned off onto a very narrow, winding macadam road edged with tall, thick bramble bushes. Then, suddenly, he made a sharp left turn and we were on a dirt road wide enough for only a single car. I looked up and was surprised to see tall, swaying palm trees along the sides of the road; had we left northern California and driven to sunny Los Angeles?

I looked ahead. Looming large on a rise of land was a castle, obviously the one inhabited by William Ladington that, according to him, had been built by the Spanish. I don't know enough about architecture to question any castle's origins, but I knew one thing for certain about this one: It was huge. And as we got closer, I realized we were about to cross a drawbridge over a moat.

"A moat?" I said.

"Yes, ma'am. Mr. Ladington had it dug years ago."

"For security purposes?"

"I wouldn't know, ma'am. I don't question what Mr. Ladington does. Ever!"

I glanced at Raoul, whose face was set in what appeared to be anger, although he was such a serious, unsmiling young man that it was hard to gauge. I looked down and saw that the moat, which I judged to be twelve feet wide, was half filled with brackish, green water; huge boulders lined the bottom.

I didn't have time to ponder it because we were over the bridge and on a circular gravel drive in front of the castle. Massive black wooden doors opened and the lord of the manor stepped through them and stood at the top of the steps. There was no doubt it was William Ladington; I'd seen his picture in enough tabloids to recognize him immediately—six feet, four inches tall, broad shoulders, square, tanned, and deeply lined face, and a full head of steel-gray hair. He wore tight jeans, a little too tight considering the overhang of his stomach, a white gauze shirt open halfway down his chest, and highly polished cowboy boots. He stood with his hands on his hips and a smile on his craggy face.

I opened my door before Raoul had a chance to come around to do it for me, and stepped out of the Jeep. Ladington didn't bother to come down to greet me. He simply motioned for me to join him on the steps, which I did.

"Well, well, well," he said in a loud, hoarse voice, "the famous Jessica Fletcher. You bring that book for me and Tennessee?"

"No. I didn't have one with me."

Ladington turned to Raoul. "Hey, get yourself over to town and buy up some of the lady's books. Go on. Get going. Fletcher. Jessica Fletcher. Get the ones with hard covers on them."

Raoul, who had been standing next to the Jeep, got back in it and drove off.

"Come on in, sweetheart," Ladington said.

I didn't move.

"You planning on standing out here all day?"

"Mr. Ladington, if we're going to get along, I prefer that you not call me sweetheart or any other term of endearment."

He laughed. "One of those fem libbers, huh?"

"No, just someone who believes in and demands respect between people."

His face screwed up into exaggerated shock at what I'd said. Then he broke into a wide grin again. "Fair enough. What would you like to be called? Mrs. Fletcher? Jessica? Jess?"

"Jessica will be fine," I said, extending my hand.

"And I'm Bill. Plain ol' Bill," he said, shaking my hand and guiding us through the huge doors.

He led me into a foyer the size of my home in Cabot Cove. Here, the Spanish influence was more evident to my untrained eye. Huge, colorful oil paintings, heavy tapestries, and sizable wall ornaments made of steel or wrought iron lined the walls. We made our way down a lengthy hallway to the rear of the castle. He opened glass doors and we stepped out onto a broad brick patio that overlooked an Olympic-sized pool, and an expanse of vineyard that stretched to the base of a barren hill. Separating us from the vineyard was the moat, narrower at the back than in front. A wooden footbridge that could be raised and lowered by hand spanned it. It was down. An armed security guard sat in a yellow director's chair next to it.

"Is that Halton Mountain?" I asked.

"Yes, ma'am, Jessica, that's exactly what it is. How do you know about Halton?"

"Friends told me about it last night at dinner."

"They tell you it's the finest piece of land in the whole damn valley?"

"They said it was a good place to grow grapes."

"Your friends are fond of understatements." He pointed to his right, to another mountain on which grape trellises were strung up to its crest. "That's Howell Mountain. It's almost as good as Halton."

"Why aren't there vineyards on Halton Mountain?" I asked, returning my attention to the bare hillside.

"There will be, Jessica," he said sternly. "There will be."

I pointed in the direction of another vineyard that seemed to butt up to the southern edge of Ladington Creek. The trellises were different from those on the Ladington property. "Is that your land, too?" I asked.

"No. It belongs to a rotten SOB named Jenkins."

"I take it you and Mr. Jenkins aren't friends."

"I'd like to see him dead. That's how friendly we are. Talking about Robert Jenkins just sets my blood pressure off, and it's high enough as it is. Come on inside and meet some of my people."

Some of my people. This was an arrogant man used to being in control of his world, including its human inhabitants.

The dining room easily accommodated a table with thirty chairs, as well as massive pieces of furniture along the walls. I noticed that seven places had been set for lunch, all at one end of the table. There were three chairs on each side of the table, and one at the end that was more of a throne, obviously Ladington's place of honor.

There were two people in the dining room when we entered, a short, chubby man whom I judged to be in his late forties and a woman a foot taller than he. Her brunette hair hung loosely over her cheeks and neck. She wore a loose-fitting, ankle-length, multicolored dress that would have looked very much at home on a Caribbean beach. Although they stood together at the far end of the room, their body language said all was not well between them. The woman kept her back to us.

"Hi, Dad," the man said, smiling and quickly circumventing the table.

"Hello, Bruce," Ladington said.

Bruce extended his hand to me without any introduction from his father.

"I'm Jessica Fletcher," I said, shaking a pudgy, soft, sweaty hand.

"The mystery writer?"

"Yes."

"Jessica is joining us for lunch," Bill said.

"That's great," said Bruce.

"You take care of that business this morning?" the elder Ladington asked.

"No," his son replied. "I thought I'd—"

"I suggest you stop thinking and start doing. Go on, take care of it now!"

"Sure, Dad." Bruce turned to where the woman continued to stand with her back to us. "Come on, Laura."

She responded by giving us a wide berth and leaving the room. Bruce smiled weakly at me, mumbled something about being back in time for lunch, and left.

"Is he your only son?" I asked Ladington when we were alone.

"Unfortunately, yes."

I didn't comment on the callousness of the statement, and if I hoped he wouldn't have more to say about his son, I was disappointed.

"Got his mother's genes—that's for sure. Weak-willed, half a backbone, no spunk."

"What ah . . . which of your wives is his mother?" I asked, knowing I shouldn't but having decided that what would be considered inconsiderate to most other people probably didn't apply to Ladington.

"Second, I think. Wasn't the first—I'm sure of that."

"How many . . ."

"How many women have been Mrs. Ladington?" he said with a laugh. "Tennessee's number eight. I finally got lucky and found somebody who wasn't crazy or drugged or drunk, and who wasn't after my money."

Quite a testimonial to seven previous women, I thought.

"He married that pitiful excuse for a woman," Ladington added, referring to the woman who'd just left. "Ever see anything so pathetic? Got the personality of a dead clam."

I was spared having to respond when an older woman of Latino origin entered the dining room from a door at the far end. She carried a tray on which a selection of breads was displayed, placed it on the table, and left without saying a word.

"That's Consuela. She and her husband, Fidel—like Castro—they help around the house, do some gardening, help out in the kitchen. They were here back before I bought the place. Didn't think it would be right to can 'em, although I was tempted. They don't do a hell of a lot."

It was the first expression of compassion from him since I'd arrived.

We had just stepped outside again when a man almost as tall and wide as Ladington, and wearing gray coveralls and knee-high green rubber boots, came up onto the patio from a set of steps on the pool side.

"What's up, Wade?" Ladington asked.

"I need you down at the press, Bill."

Ladington said to me, "You'll have to excuse me, Jessica. This is Wade Grosso, my vineyard manager."

"Ma'am," Wade said.

Ladington went to the open door and bellowed, "Hey, Tennessee, come on out here and keep Jessica Fletcher company."

"No, that's all right," I said. "It's lovely out here. You go ahead and . . ."

A woman appeared in the doorway. She was tall, almost six feet, and had a mane of blond hair that exploded from the top of her head and cascaded down over her shoulders. She was heavily made up, her lips enlarged by an overuse of crimson lipstick. She wore a leopard-skin blouse with the top four buttons unfastened, and tight black slacks. Open sandals exposed rather large feet with polish the same shade as her lips. A cigarette dangled from long, talon-like fingers with inch-long red nails.

"Say hello to Jessica Fletcher," Ladington said. "Got to tend to some business."

He walked off with Wade Grosso, leaving his wife and me facing each other.

"Hello," I said.

"Hello," she said, dropping the smoldering cigarette to the brick patio and extinguishing it with the heel of her sandal. "His majesty said you were coming for lunch."

" 'His majesty?' "

"The great man, William Ladington." She laughed. "He likes to be called that. Come on inside. I'll give you a house tour."

"A castle tour would be more apt," I said under my breath, following her inside.

Twenty minutes later, after I'd been shown the bedrooms, baths, library, and a few other spaces, Tennessee

Ladington led me to a series of rooms segregated from the main house. "The offices for the winery," she said, lighting another cigarette and plopping down behind a desk in a high-back red leather office chair. "Sit down," she said. "This is where his majesty rules his domain."

Her constant snide remarks about her husband, delivered with apparent humor but pointed nonetheless, made me uncomfortable, and I silently wished he would return. I tried to make small talk: "Must be challenging to run a winery like Ladington Creek," I said.

She responded by puffing on her cigarette and adding it to an already overflowing ashtray.

"You've garnered so many awards for your wine," I said. "I took a wine-appreciation course before coming to California. The instructor is quite a fan of your wines, especially the cabernet."

Tennessee Ladington was spared having to join the conversation when a man entered the office. "Hello, Tennessee," he said.

"Hello, Roger."

Roger, who wore a greenish suit that was slightly too big for his slender frame, started for a door leading to another office, stopped, turned, and said to me, "Aren't you that writer, Jessica Frazier?"

"It's Fletcher, Roger," Tennessee said. "Jessica Fletcher. Bill invited her for lunch."

"Honored to have you," he said, coming to where I sat and extending his hand. "Welcome to Ladington Creek."

"Thank you," I said. "I'm pleased to be here."

"See you later," he said, disappearing through the door and closing it behind him.

"Roger Stockdale," Tennessee said. "He's our business manager. Bill thinks he steals."

"Oh, I . . . I, ah . . ."

She smiled, her first since I'd met her. "Bill thinks everybody's stealing from him, including me. He carries paranoia to new heights. I assume you noticed the moat when you arrived."

"Yes, I did. I'd never seen a real moat before."

"Stupidest thing I've ever seen. Cost a fortune to have it dug. Made us the laughingstock of the valley."

I started to say that I'd been told Ladington Creek had an impressive tasting room—I had a sudden urge for a glass of wine, alone—when loud voices in the hall caused me to turn in that direction. The dominant voice belonged to Bill Ladington, who yelled, "I'll be damned if that mealy-mouthed low life is going to intimidate me. You go back and tell him I'll break his damn neck if he tries it again."

Ladington's large frame filled the open doorway. He said to his wife in the same bellowing voice, "Jenkins is out there telling Wade he's going to bring in some new French rootstock and plant it alone, no grafting to American stock. Damn fool will kill every vine in the valley if he does that." He looked at me: "Tennessee take care of you?"

"Oh, yes. I had a tour of the house—the castle—and—"

"You hungry? I sure as hell am. Tennessee, tell the cook to get things moving. We've got a hungry guest here. Can't have a hungry murder-mystery writer, can we? Where the hell is Raoul with those books? Bruce back yet?"

Ladington continued to bark questions and orders as he led me back to the dining room where his son, Bruce, and daughter-in-law, Laura, stood where they had when I first encountered them.

"Hey, Mercedes, let's get some food out here," Ladington shouted through an open door to an unseen person.

Roger Stockdale, the vineyard's business manager, joined us along with Wade Grosso, who'd removed his rubber boots and replaced them with carpet slippers. As expected, Ladington took his place at the head of the table and we occupied chairs on either side. Tennessee sat to my left, the seat furthest from her husband.

A woman who I assumed was Mercedes appeared from the kitchen followed closely by Consuela. Both carried platters of food that they placed before us. One platter over-flowed with meaty ribs and chicken glazed with barbecue sauce; the other contained steaming vegetables, a large bowl of mashed potatoes, and a silver gravy boat with extra barbecue sauce. I looked across the table at Laura, who looked as though she might become ill at any moment.

"Come on, dig in," Ladington said, attacking one of the salads that had been put on the table earlier.

"Do you always eat this big a meal at lunch?" I asked, laughing.

"Always," Stockdale said.

"Do you serve American food at your restaurant?" I asked.

"Of course," Ladington replied through a mouthful of food. "It's a steak house. Steak and lobster and chicken.

"The chef is Greek," Tennessee said.

"But no Greek food," Ladington said. "Not at *my* steak house. His name's Nick. Never can tell what he'll come up with for lunch. Ladington's Steak House is the best damned restaurant in the valley. When Nick's cooking for me, he keeps it simple, like ribs and chicken. He whips up lunch for us here at the castle, then heads over to the restaurant to make dinner. I'll take you over there myself tonight, Jessica, let you see for yourself."

"That's kind of you," I said, "but I have dinner plans."

"With who?"

"Maybe Mrs. Fletcher doesn't want to—"

Ladington interrupted his son with, "Don't be telling me what to ask anybody, Bruce."

"Sure, Dad, I—"

"Where the hell is Raoul with those books?" Ladington growled as he filled his plate with ribs and chicken.

It didn't take me long to adapt to the conversational flow at the table, which was virtually nonexistent. Ladington pontificated while we listened. I asked a few questions early in the meal but soon stopped and ate in silence along with the others. Laura Ladington nibbled on a small piece of roll before excusing herself. "I'm not feeling well," she said, which prompted Ladington to say when she was gone, "Of course she doesn't feel good. How the hell can you feel good if you don't eat? Just eats vegetables and all that organic garbage. One of those health Nazis we've got all over California."

If Bruce had a defense of his wife, he kept it to himself.

Over dessert, talk turned to vineyard business. I would have preferred to absent myself and yearned to be taken back to Cedar Gables, but there didn't seem to be an appropriate moment to make that request. As I sat there and heard Ladington lodge a series of complaints directed at everyone, I wondered what had possessed me to accept his invitation. He'd said on the phone he wanted to discuss something with me, but that was probably a ruse to get me to agree to come for lunch. Could it be, I wondered, that William Ladington was starstruck and simply wanted a well-known writer to be his luncheon guest? If so, was it to impress his wife, or some of the others? I decided that might be a good possibility, considering how much he wanted autographed books for his shelves.

Raoul arrived as we were about to vacate the table. He'd purchased two of my novels in hardcover, prompting Ladington to berate him for not buying more.

"The others were in paperback," Raoul said. "You said to only get the ones with hard covers."

Raoul departed with the others, leaving Ladington and

me alone in the dining room. He placed the books before me and I signed them to him and his wife.

"You just sold a couple of your books, Jessica," he said. "You made a few bucks coming out here today."

"Yes, I suppose I did. Could Raoul take me back to the inn now?"

"Nonsense! You haven't been here long enough to get to see the place. Come on, I'll give you a tour of the vineyards, show you how good wine is made."

I was tempted to insist upon leaving, but remembered that I'd intended to learn about wine making as a possible backdrop for a novel. Besides, I still had time to kill before George would arrive.

"All right," I said. "Show me how good wine is made."

Chapter Nine

". . . and that's what makes a truly fine cabernet, Jessica."

We'd been walking through one of his vineyards for almost an hour. During that time he'd pointed out with pride certain aspects of the Ladington Creek approach to growing grapes and turning them into award-winning wine. He showed me how to use a refractometer, a handheld instrument that allows light to pass through a drop of grape juice. "See?" he said as I read a graduated scale on the refractometer. "It reads in Brix units, the percent of sugar concentration in the juice. The sugar molecules bend the light and give the reading. It's up to sixteen now."

"What does that mean?" I asked.

"It means it's time to keep a close eye on the grapes. Close to time to harvest them now. Maybe another week, ten days. That's when the picking crew will come in. I don't use machines to do the picking. No, sir. All by hand, and at night, too, when it's cool."

His demeanor had changed from what it had been during lunch and the hour leading up to it. Then, he'd demonstrated brusqueness and arrogance bordering on outright meanness. Now, as the sun slipped lower into the western sky, casting long shadows over the land, he became increasingly reflective, almost gentle in his comments.

"You see," he said as we stood at the far end of the vineyard devoted to grapes for his award-winning cabernet sauvignons, "the key is to *care* about the wine you produce, treat it like the precious thing it is, not be satisfied with taking shortcuts to produce more of it to rake in bigger bucks. Hell, I could modernize this place so you'd think it was DuPont or some other big chemical factory. But that would rob my cabernet of its uniqueness. I turn out only about three thousand cases of cab every year. That's a spit in the barrel compared to the big boys in the valley."

"You're obviously very proud of what you've accomplished here," I said.

"You bet I am, but I'll be even prouder once I get hold of a piece of that mountain over there and plant some of my new rootstock on it," he said, pointing to the gray and gold slope of Halton Mountain. "See, Jessica, grapes love rock, especially shattered rock. You've got to use dynamite to shatter that rock, give it lots of crevices where the roots can grab hold. There's soil a couple of hundred feet deep on that mountain, and down below there's a gravel swath a couple of hundred feet wide. Used to be a riverbed. Most perfect spot on this earth to grow grapes. When you grow grapes under stressful conditions, you improve the taste. The grapes are smaller but sweeter, packed with flavor."

"I understand you're not the only vintner who wants Halton Mountain," I said.

"You've picked up a lot in a short time."

"Well, actually I'm hoping to learn more, a little first-hand research I might use in my next mystery."

"I can help you there. I'm fighting people who won't know what to do with that mountain if they ever get hold of it. There's the conservationists raising hell, too. If it's up to them, no more land in the valley can be used for growing grapes. They claim planting on hillsides like Halton Mountain causes soil erosion and the like. Not true, not if you know what you're doing."

"And I don't doubt you do, Bill. Know what you're doing, that is."

"I appreciate the compliment, Jessica. Now I suppose you'll be wanting to get back to your friends."

A glance at my watch told me he was right. It was almost four.

"You didn't ask about the murder at my restaurant," he said flatly.

"I didn't think it was any of my business."

"It's everybody's business. Everybody ought to care about all these damn drugs our young people get involved with."

"Drugs were involved?"

"That's the way I see it. Used to be that the junkies and dealers stayed down in San Francisco and fried their brains, what they had of 'em. But they've been running drugs up here into Napa Valley the last couple 'a years, always looking for new users, new markets."

"Was the waiter involved with drugs?" I asked.

"That's what some folks are saying. Can't prove it by me. He was a nice enough kid. Didn't seem like the sort who'd get involved with that junk, but I suppose you never can tell about young people these days. I know one thing. I'd like to find the bastard who killed him and have him alone for a few minutes. The State wouldn't have to worry about a trial or anything. I'd take care of him myself."

Not wanting to feed into the topic of vigilante justice, I said instead, "Before I go, I'd like to know what it was you said you wanted to talk to me about. Obviously, it's not how to make wine."

He rubbed a large hand over the stubble on his chin and nodded. "When I read you were going to be in Napa Valley for a week, I decided you might be the perfect person to help me write my autobiography."

"Me? No, that wouldn't be possible. I write fiction,

murder-mystery fiction. I don't write nonfiction or collaborate or—"

"The way I figure it, a good writer can write anything."

"And you figured wrong," I said, laughing to take the
edge off the comment. "No, Bill, I'm afraid I'm the wrong
person. I'm sure you have a fascinating story to tell. You've
been in the press for many years and—"

"That's the whole point, Jessica," he said, a sad expression occupying his broad face. "All that press was when I
was acting like a damn fool, running around Hollywood
with a bunch of madmen, all the women, that sort of thing.
No, I want to tell a different story about Bill Ladington."

"Which is?"

"That I accomplished something worthwhile here at Ladington Creek. That I gave the world the best cabernet sauvignon it's ever tasted."

I turned from him and looked out over the expanse of
vineyard. He'd explained that he was about to begin "the
pick," the picking of grapes to be used to create the cabernet. "I bring in a crew only at night," he'd told me. "Once a
grape is off the vine, even a little sun can start the fermenta-
tion before they get to the crusher. The vineyard's full of
natural yeast. Costs me more to do the pick at night but
that's all right. Like I said, if you're going to make a great
wine, you have to care about how you do it more than your
pocketbook."

He walked me back to the castle where Roger Stockdale,
his business manager, stood next to a black BMW in the
gravel driveway. "Roger will drive you back," Ladington
said. "Raoul's off picking up somebody at the airport."

"Thank you for a lovely day," I said, not entirely meaning it. His interaction with his family and business associ-
ates had been unpleasant, but I was grateful for the hour
spent with him away from them.

"Tell you what," he said in a voice low enough so that

Roger wouldn't hear, "you come spend the rest of your time out here at the castle. I'll give you all the secrets about wine making for your book. Be my houseguest. There's a whole wing with four nice guest bedrooms. You spend some time here, bring your friends, and see what I'm talking about. Then, if you decide you don't want to write the story of Bill Ladington, wine maker, you can just head off and write your murder mysteries."

"Bill," I said, offering my hand, "it's been a pleasure meeting you. And I appreciate your confidence in me as a writer. But no, I couldn't possibly write your book. As for staying here as your guest, it's tempting, but my friends would be extremely disappointed if I left their B-and-B."

"Maybe you'd change your mind if you knew who Raoul is picking up at the airport later," he said.

"Oh?"

"Edith Saison."

My blank look said I didn't know who she was.

"My new business partner. Saison Winery? In Bordeaux? Never heard of it?"

"No. I'm not terribly wine-literate, although I'm determined to correct that while in Napa."

"She's bringing new cabernet varietals she and her beau have developed at their vincyard. Once they're grafted to my rootstock—and planted on Halton Mountain—the world will get what I want to give them, the finest cabernet sauvignon ever produced, California, France, anywhere! It's going to be a great story, Jessica. It'll turn the wine world on its ear."

"I'm sure it will. Thanks again for inviting me."

I got in the front seat of the BMW with Stockdale and we pulled away. I looked back at Ladington, whose posture was less self-assured than when I'd arrived.

"An interesting man," I said after we'd crossed the moat and were headed back to Napa City.

"Everyone who meets him for the first time says that, Mrs. Fletcher. It's after you get to know him that you start coming up with other words to describe him."

I said nothing.

"Bill's a lot happier when his wife and son aren't around," Stockdale added. "A different person when they're traveling, or down in Curaçao. Bill has a house there, in Daai Booi Bay."

"I've been to Curaçao," I said. "It's a lovely island, not as commercial as other islands in the area."

"Yeah, I like it, too. I get to spend a week there every year. One of the perks of working for Ladington Winery."

We didn't discuss Bill Ladington for the rest of the trip, although I thought of virtually nothing else. Strange, how even the most abrasive, seemingly callous person can demonstrate a softer side, given the right situation. I can't say I'd grown to like Ladington during our hour together in his vineyards, but he had mitigated, to some extent, my initial reaction to him.

Oh well, I thought, it had been a fascinating exposure to a vineyard and its owner, and the odd assortment of people surrounding him. And I'd made a good beginning, learning something about wine making. Chalk it up as just another of life's interesting moments.

As we approached the Napa city limits, thoughts of Ladington became past tense, replaced by the pleasant contemplation of seeing the most interesting person in my life these days, George Sutherland.

Chapter Ten

I'd no sooner said good-bye to Roger Stockdale, entered Cedar Gables, and gone to my room to freshen up when one of the young college girls who worked part-time at the inn came to tell me I had a visitor. I took a look at myself in the mirror and bounded down the stairs. Sure enough, there he was, George Sutherland. I crossed the main parlor, stopped a few feet from him, and we both beamed.

"As they say," he said, "you are a bonny sight for sore eyes."

After a welcoming hug, I stepped back and took him in. He never seemed to change, even after long periods of not having seen each other. He wore his usual tweed sports jacket with leather patches at the elbows, a blue button-down shirt, muted green paisley tie, gray slacks that looked as though they had just come through a press, and ankle-high brown boots polished to a mirror finish.

"I'm so pleased you're here," I said. "Easy drive—on the wrong side of the road?"

"No problems. Piece of cake, as the saying goes. How was your day?"

"Ah—interesting. I'll fill you in over dinner. Come, let me show you the inn."

Margaret emerged from her office and I introduced them.

"I don't think I've ever met a real, live Scotland Yard inspector before," she said.

"That's only when I'm in England," George said pleasantly. "For this week in California, I'm simply George, Jessica's friend and enthusiastic tourist."

"Fair enough," said Margaret.

"I was about to give him the tour," I said.

"I'll do it," Margaret said. "Bring your suitcase, George, and we'll stop by your room first."

After we'd shown George the house and returned to the main parlor, Margaret suggested a restaurant for that evening, Chanterelle. "Very romantic," she said slyly. "The owner, Karl, is a friend. I'll call and make a reservation."

Two hours later George and I sat at one of the restaurant's quiet corner tables and touched the rims of our wineglasses.

"Here's to a wonderful week together," he said.

"Yes. That's worth toasting."

Over appetizers—Dungeness crab for me, portobello mushrooms for him—he said, "Tell me about what you did today. You said it was interesting."

"It may not seem as interesting to you as it was for me. Ever hear of William Ladington?"

He frowned, then said, "The film director?"

"Producer. He left Hollywood many years ago and bought a winery here in Napa Valley."

"An interesting switch in careers. Was he successful?"

"Yes, and still is. He's very much alive, although he's nearing eighty. I had lunch with him today at his castle."

"Castle? A real one?"

"Yes, from when the Spanish occupied the valley."

"Is it as large as my family castle in Wick?"

"Bigger. He has a moat."

George burst out laughing. "A moat? With crocodiles?"

I laughed, too. "No, but I wouldn't have been surprised if Ladington had included a few crocs."

"Was Mr. Ladington a pleasant host?"

"Not at first. He treats people who work there, and his

family, like a Prussian general. Very off-putting. But he gave me a tour of his vineyards after lunch and I saw a different man, a very proud man, passionate about his work. I grew almost to like him. He invited me—us—to be his guests at the castle for the week."

"That's intriguing? Are we going to stay there?"

"Oh, no. We're staying at Cedar Gables. Margaret is such a delight. You'll meet Craig, her husband, when we go back."

The owner, Karl, personally took our order. He recommended the venison, but I opted instead for hazelnut-crusted rack of lamb; George chose baked Chilean sea bass. We settled in for a leisurely dinner, catching each other up on what had been going on in our respective lives since we last spoke, recalling times spent together in London, especially the first time we'd met, during the investigation of Dame Marjorie Ainsworth's murder, and the trip I'd taken with Cabot Cove friends to his family castle in northern Scotland. Unfortunately, a murder had taken place there, too.

"I think we should make a pledge to each other, Jessica," George said after the waiter had removed our empty wine bottle and poured coffee.

"What are we pledging?" I asked.

"To not allow murder to intrude ever again on our time together."

"I hereby pledge," I said.

"And so do I."

Craig and Margaret were sitting on a small patio off the kitchen when we arrived. The black sky was filled with stars; classical music played softly from a portable radio on a table. After George was introduced to Craig, we joined them on the patio where the only illumination came from two flickering candles. As I sat next to George I felt like a schoolgirl out on a date, sitting quietly next to someone special in my life and with old friends, no one speaking, content after a wonderful meal, at peace with myself and with the world.

Until a news bulletin broke into the musical program:

> We've just learned that former Hollywood film producer, and more recently owner of Ladington Creek Winery, William Ladington, has died at his home in Napa Valley. Details are sketchy at this moment. We'll report more on his death as we receive further information.

"You were just there!" Margaret said after an initial gasp.

"I know."

"Did he appear to be ill to you?" Craig asked.

"No. I mean, he was quite old, but he seemed vibrant, walked with a spring in his step, talked of his determination to produce the world's finest cabernet. He did mention he had high blood pressure, but—"

"What an unfortunate coincidence that you were with him today," George said. "It must be upsetting."

"It certainly is shocking," I said, taking a few deep breaths.

"I wonder . . ." Margaret said.

"Wonder what?" Craig asked.

"I wonder whether foul play might have been involved."

George and I looked at each other.

"You're wondering the same thing?" Margaret asked.

"No," I said. "George and I made a pledge at dinner tonight. No murders to intrude on our time together."

"Why are you talking about murder?" Craig asked his wife. "The man was eighty years old. He undoubtedly died of old age, pure and simple."

"Of course," I said.

George nodded his agreement.

"Who else did you meet there this afternoon, Jess?" Margaret asked.

"Oh, his wife, son, daughter-in-law, business manager—
he drove me back here, name's Stockdale—household staff,
vineyard manager."

"A cast of suspects," Margaret said.

"Margaret!" Craig said.

"How can I not think about it maybe being murder?" she
asked. "We're sitting here with one of America's most famous murder-mystery writers and a detective from Scotland Yard."

"Both of whom are decidedly off duty," George said with
a chuckle.

"Amen," I added. "And this off-duty mystery writer's
eyes are getting heavy."

"Not too upset to sleep?" Craig asked. "Would you like a
drink?"

"No, no, I'm fine," I said. "I didn't know the man, but
spent what turned out to be a pleasant few hours with him,
at least at the end of my visit. He wanted me to collaborate
on his autobiography."

"He did?" Margaret said.

"Yes. I told him no, of course, but I'm sure someone will
do his biography now that he's gone. Should be interesting.
You will excuse me. Time for bed."

"Sure you don't want a nightcap?" Craig asked.

"Positive."

George took Craig up on his offer. I bid everyone good
night and went to the Churchill Chamber where I assumed
I'd fall quickly asleep. But the news of Ladington's death
proved to be more upsetting than I'd thought, and I spent an
hour in bed reading more entries from the guest diary.
Eventually, the long day caught up with me and I turned off
the light and lay there in the darkness, hearing the wind
outside my window, and processing everything that had occurred that day. I didn't get very far; my eyes closed and I
slipped into welcome slumber.

Chapter Eleven

George and I sat at a small table in the dining room the next morning.

"Sleep well?" I asked.

"Oh, yes. I wondered whether Count Bonzi would make an appearance in the middle of the night, but no such luck."

The door to Margaret and Craig's office was open and we heard her answer the ringing phone.

"Cedar Gables Inn," she said smartly. "Hello, Mrs. Kaplan. Yes, of course I remember you. What? Today? This week? Oh, I'm sorry, but both the Churchill Chamber and Count Bonzi's room are taken for the week. Yes, I understand. Last-minute vacations are always the best. I wish we could accommodate you but—"

I heard the front door open. A few seconds later two men stood in the dining room entrance.

"Hello," I said. George's confusion was written on his face. "George, this is William Ladington's driver, Raoul, and Ladington's son, Bruce." I said to Bruce, "I was so sorry to hear about your father. It must have been a terrible shock for all of you."

Margaret said into the phone, "Hold on, Mrs. Kaplan, please. We have other rooms and—" She poked her head out of the office to see who'd arrived.

"Could I speak with you, Mrs. Fletcher?" Bruce asked. He was perspiring, and had a frantic expression on his face.

"Yes, of course," I said. "Excuse me, George?" As I followed Bruce to the main parlor, I said to Margaret, "They're from Ladington Creek. Bill Ladington's son and the driver."

Margaret's expression asked why they were here. I shrugged in response.

"I'm sorry to bother you like this, Mrs. Fletcher," Bruce said hurriedly, "but I didn't know whether to call or to just come here and see you in person."

"It doesn't matter," I said. "Why *are* you here?"

"My father's death."

"I heard it on the news last night," I said. "I was sorry to hear it, but—"

"Mrs. Fletcher, they say he committed suicide."

"Oh, my. Did he?"

"No. He was murdered."

I sensed that George was standing in the doorway listening to our conversation and looked at him, then turned back to Bruce. "Are you sure?" I asked. "How do you know that? He only died last night. Surely, an autopsy will have to be done to determine the cause of death."

"I don't care about any autopsy, Mrs. Fletcher. I know my father didn't kill himself. You met him. Did he seem to you like a man planning his own death?"

"No, he certainly didn't, but that doesn't prove anything. Look, Bruce, I know you're upset. If what you say is true and someone murdered your father, the authorities will do their best to determine the killer's identity. In the meantime—"

"Mrs. Fletcher, I want you to help prove my father was murdered."

I wasn't sure what to say.

"I know you're out here in Napa on vacation," Bruce went on, "and that solving murders isn't what you do for a living, but my father really took a liking to you. He told me he invited you to come stay at the winery and help him write his autobiography."

"Yes, he did, but—"

"Will you come stay with us and help me prove that my father did not take his own life?"

"I'm sorry. I can't do that."

Bruce turned to George, who now stood next to Margaret. "Won't someone help me?" he asked, extending his hands palm-up in a gesture of helplessness. "You must have known my dad. Everyone in the valley knew him."

"I met him a few times," Margaret said.

"Sorry," said George, "but I'm a stranger here. I only knew of your father through what I read in the newspapers."

"The gossip sheets, you mean," Bruce said. "The tabloids. He was better than that." He returned his attention to me. "Please, Mrs. Fletcher, at least come to the castle for the day and see what you think after you've talked to me and the others. You may be a writer, but I know you've actually solved some murders. Please!"

"I think it's obvious the lady doesn't wish to go with you," George said in his Scottish brogue, modified a bit from having lived and worked for years in London.

"This is Chief Inspector Sutherland of Scotland Yard," I said.

"Scotland Yard?"

"Yes," said George.

"Then you and Mrs. Fletcher could come together and help."

"Are your local authorities investigating?" George asked.

"Sure, but what do they know? They don't know how to solve a murder. All they do is give out traffic tickets and arrest an occasional drunk. They've already said it looks like a suicide."

"Why have they reached that conclusion so quickly?" I asked.

"An empty bottle of pills and a note found in his study."

George and I looked at each other and knew we were thinking the same thing: an empty bottle of pills and a farewell note weren't bad reasons for authorities to suspect suicide at the outset of their investigation.

I said, "Bruce, I hope that if your father was murdered, his killer is found. But I'm not the one to help in that effort."

"Oops, I almost forgot I left someone hanging on the phone," Margaret said, heading for her office.

"Margaret," I said, following her into the office, "we overheard your conversation with someone wanting the rooms George and I are occupying."

"Doesn't matter," she said. "They're regular guests, always show up with enough people to fill the place. Mr. and Mrs. Kaplan always take Count Bonzi's room, and her mother—she's very old—likes Churchill Chamber."

"I feel terrible depriving you of paying guests," I said.

"Don't be silly," she said. "Craig and I are thrilled to have you and your friend staying with us for a week."

I lowered my voice. "You heard what Ladington's son wants us to do, go back out to the castle."

"Yes. How exciting."

"I'm not sure it's that, but it seems to me that by our going out there, you could free up our rooms for your paying guests."

"Please, Jess, don't make a decision based on that. If your natural bent as a sleuth makes you want to dig into his death, by all means go. Do you think George will want to go too?"

"I'll ask him."

She smiled. "Can't resist, can you?"

"Oh, I could resist, Margaret, but I suppose I don't want to."

She picked up the receiver from her desk and said, "Sorry to keep you waiting, Mrs. Kaplan. Good news. The guests who were occupying the rooms you want have had a sudden change in plans and are leaving. Happy to have you."

I returned to the main parlor and motioned for George to join me in the dining room. I started to say something, but he put his index finger to my lips and said with a grin, "I have a feeling we're about to cross a moat and spend a few nights in a Spanish castle."

"You don't mind?"

"I would if it meant seeing less of you. But since we'll be together—and since you have this insatiable need to get to the bottom of things—I wouldn't think of protesting. Besides, we haven't worked as a team in a long time, not since that week at my family's home. It might regenerate a whole new career for us, the Scotland Yard detective and the beautiful murder-mystery writer."

"You are wonderful," I said.

"And so are you, Jessica Fletcher. I'll go pack."

Chapter Twelve

Bruce wanted us to go to Ladington Creek in the Jeep driven by Raoul, but we insisted on taking George's rental car. Although I'd decided to make the trip, I wanted the ability to leave whenever we wished, and at a moment's notice. We followed the Jeep; this time we took the more congested, but shorter Route 29, which took us through Yountville, Oakville, and Rutherford until we reached St. Helena. The Jeep passed over the drawbridge that spanned the moat, but we stopped before crossing it.

"Aha," George said, "the famous moat."

"Yes," I said.

"Do they ever raise the bridge?" he asked.

"I don't know. It was down the last time I was here. I suppose they do. Why bother having a drawbridge if you don't raise it now and then?"

"I was just wondering if it was up or down last night, when he died."

"We'll ask."

Raoul beeped his horn and motioned for us to cross. George did, and we parked next to the Jeep in front of the castle where Raoul and Bruce had exited their vehicle. Once we'd crossed the moat, Bruce went to a wooden box near the front door and activated a switch that caused the drawbridge to slowly, noisily creak to a vertical position, cutting off access to the castle.

"Was the bridge raised last night?" I asked.

"Yes," Bruce said. "Dad always raised it at night."

"Which would mean no one had access to the castle except those already in it," I said.

Bruce pursed his lips and frowned. "I suppose so," he said, as if he wasn't sure he liked the idea. "We might as well go inside."

George lagged behind as we approached the massive front doors. I turned to him. "Coming?" I asked.

"There isn't any sign of the police having been here," he said, hands in his pockets, eyes taking in everything.

"Because they say it was a suicide," Bruce replied. "They were in and out of here in less than an hour. Great police work, huh?"

George ignored his comment and continued to pace in front of the castle. Finally, he shrugged and joined us as we entered the expansive foyer with all the symbols of its Spanish heritage.

"These are most impressive," George said, admiring the wall hangings. "Very nineteenth century, Francisco de Goya influenced."

Tennessee Ladington appeared through a doorway. She was dressed less casually and provocatively this time in black slacks and a black blouse, closed black shoes, and less jewelry and makeup.

"Hello, Mrs. Ladington," I said. "I'm terribly sorry about your husband."

"Thank you," she said.

I searched her face for signs of grief. There were none. "This is George Sutherland," I said. "He's a friend of mine from England."

"Mrs. Ladington," George said, extending his hand, which she took and quickly released.

"George is a chief inspector with Scotland Yard," I added.

"Scotland Yard." The respect in her voice was mock. "I don't think it would be out of line to ask why you're here, Mrs. Fletcher, you and your British friend."

"They're here because I asked them to be," Bruce said.

His stepmother's expression was as menacing as a loaded gun.

Roger Stockdale joined us. "Hello again, Mrs. Fletcher," he said. "I didn't know you were coming back."

"Nor did I," Tennessee said. "You'll have to excuse me if I seem distracted. Bill's death has been a terrible shock for me."

"I'm sure they understand," said Stockdale. "One minute he's here, big as life and running things, the next minute he's dead." He shook his head. "What a tragedy."

"I asked her to come," Bruce told Stockdale, referring to me. "This is her friend, Detective . . ."

"Sutherland," George said. "George Sutherland."

"British, huh?"

"Close enough, I suppose," George said with a smile. "Scottish."

"Scotland Yard," I said.

"Why would Scotland Yard be interested in Bill's death?" Stockdale asked.

I spared George having to reply. "Mr. Ladington had invited me to stay here as his guest," I said. "Inspector Sutherland is an old friend who joined me here in Napa for a holiday. Bruce came to where we were staying and reissued the invitation."

"Impressive, Bruce," said Stockdale, "taking action. Now that your father's dead, maybe you'll find that missing backbone."

I expected Bruce to respond angrily. He didn't. His face reddened and he focused his gaze on the tile floor.

"Please excuse me," Tennessee said. "I have a lot of things to take care of."

"I'll go with you," Stockdale said, touching her arm. To me he added, "I'm glad you've come back. We can use some clear thinking."

"Any chance of a cup of tea?" I asked Bruce after they'd left.

That snapped Bruce out of his funk. "Oh, sure," he said. "Come in the kitchen."

George and I followed him to where Nick, the dinner chef from Ladington's Steak House, was preparing lunch. The main housekeeper, Mercedes, was helping.

"Could we get some tea, Mercedes?" Bruce asked.

"Tea? What do you think this is, a restaurant?" she said without turning.

"It's for guests," he said hurriedly. "Jessica Fletcher, the mystery writer, and a Scotland Yard inspector."

Mercedes slowly turned, wiping her hands on her apron as she did. She was a stout woman with gray hair pulled into a tight bun and a ruddy, round face.

"You came back, huh?" she said to me.

"I don't really need tea," I told Bruce.

"I'll make it for you," the housekeeper said, heading for a huge six-burner stainless-steel stove.

"We'll be in Dad's study," Bruce said.

"Are you sure we should be there?" I asked as we went down a hallway. "He was found there, wasn't he?"

"Oh, no, Mrs. Fletcher. He was found in the moat."

George and I looked at each other.

"You said there was an empty bottle of pills on his desk," George said as Bruce opened the door to the study.

"There was, but he was found in the moat. That's strange, isn't it?"

"Not necessarily," George answered.

"A bigger concern is whether the police will want to come back and do a crime scene investigation in this room," I said.

"They won't," said Bruce, closing the door behind us. "To them it's a suicide. Remember?"

Bill Ladington's study was decorated and furnished as I would have expected it to be, a reflection of a dominating character. But unlike his office, this room was more personal, a quiet refuge where he could retire and indulge in more reflective thought, read a book, think about things other than the day-to-day running of the winery. One wall was dominated by huge blowups of posters for the movies he'd produced, with dozens of photographs of him with recognizable movie stars interspersed between them. The walls were southwestern tan stucco, the carpet purple, thick and plush, the color of royalty. The cherry wood desk was easily twelve feet long, the large swivel chair behind it in tan leather. The wall displayed stuffed animal heads—elk, tiger, leopard, and a few deer. Floor-to-ceiling bookcases, an elaborate bar, and a tan leather couch and armchairs completed the room.

George went to the bookcases and perused what they held while I sat in one of the armchairs. The desk was immaculately clear of papers and other signs that a busy person had been using it. The only items on it were a fancy telephone with a dozen buttons, and a single black leather portfolio.

"This is where the empty bottle of pills was found?" I asked Bruce.

"Yes."

"Was it a prescription drug?"

"No. It didn't have any label on it. One of those amber-colored bottles."

"So there was no way for the police to know what had been in it?" I said.

"I guess not. They took it."

"The police lab will determine what was in that bottle—if anything," I said.

George took a chair next to me. "Your father had quite a collection of technical books on wine making," he said to Bruce.

"Dad was serious about making wine," his son replied. "Lots of people didn't think he was serious, that Ladington Creek Vineyard was just a hobby of his. But he was determined to create the world's finest cabernet sauvignon."

"So he told me," I said.

"The moat," George said absently.

"What?"

"I've been thinking about the moat where Mr. Ladington was found," George said. "It seems unlikely he would take an overdose of some sort of pills for the purpose of killing himself, then get up from behind his desk, leave this room, and go to the moat to die."

"Exactly!" Bruce exclaimed, coming to his feet for emphasis.

As he did, Mercedes arrived with our tea. She placed the tray on the desk without a word and left. I served.

"Who was here last night when he died?" George asked.

Bruce screwed up his face in an exaggerated attempt to remember. "Let's see," he said, rubbing his round chin, "there was Tennessee, Roger, Raoul, my wife Laura, Wade Grosso, Mercedes, Consuela and Fidel, some of the vineyard workers who met with Dad, the security staff, and . . . oh, right, Madame Saison."

"The French vintner," I said. "Your father told me she was coming. They were involved in some sort of joint venture, I believe."

"Yeah, something like that," Bruce said, not attempting to disguise his displeasure.

"And security staff?"

"Three of them. They live in their own quarters at the back end of the main vineyard."

"Which would be on the other side of the moat," George said.

"Right, although one of them was here at the house last night. They take turns at the night shift."

"The suicide note," I said. "I assume the police took that."

"Yes, they did," Bruce replied.

"What did it say?" George asked.

"I didn't see it," Bruce said, picking up his cup and saucer but quickly replacing it on the tray because his hand shook visibly. "They just took it."

"Then how do you know it was a suicide note?" I asked.

"Because that's what they told me. Dad had a small, battery-powered Canon typewriter in here. They took that, too." He laughed. "Dad had no use for computers. Even using an electric typewriter was a big deal for him."

"They'll test it to see whether the note was written on it," George said.

Our conversation was interrupted by a knock at the door. It opened and Mercedes announced, "Sheriff Davis is here." She stepped aside to allow him to enter. He was a big man, almost as imposing as Bill Ladington. He wore jeans, a pale green V-neck sweater over a white button-down shirt, and white sneakers. Obviously, law enforcement in Napa Valley was a casual undertaking.

"Sorry to barge in on you like this," he told Bruce, "but I was passing and thought I'd stop by."

"Is the drawbridge down?" Bruce asked.

Davis laughed. "It wasn't, but I rang the bell and announced who I was on the intercom." He looked directly at me and George.

"This is Jessica Fletcher," Bruce said. "And her friend, George Sutherland. He's a Scotland Yard detective."

"That so?" Davis said, crossing the room and extending

his hand to George. "Pretty much out of your jurisdiction, I'd say."

"Just a tourist," George said, smiling and shaking his hand.

Davis also extended his hand to me, which I took.

"Jessica Fletcher," he said. "Sounds familiar."

"Mrs. Fletcher is a famous mystery writer," Bruce said.

"Yes, that's probably where I heard it. I'm not much of a reader so no offense if I haven't read any of your books."

"Of course not," I said.

"Your name came up this morning," the sheriff said.

"Oh? Why?"

"A writer from San Francisco was in my office. He said he was a good friend of yours."

"Neil Schwartz?"

"Yeah, that's him. You are his friend?"

"Yes."

"He's a pesty guy."

I laughed. "Sometimes to get a story you have to be a bit of a pest."

Davis turned to Bruce. "Appreciate a word with you, alone," he said pleasantly.

Bruce looked nervously at George and me as he followed Davis from the room and closed the door behind them.

"Maybe the police have more interest in Mr. Ladington's death than his son thinks," George said.

"I wonder what he wants," I said, going to the bar and examining the dozens of bottles displayed on the back bar. "I doubt very much if he was just passing by and dropped in for a social visit."

George laughed and joined me at the bar. We didn't turn immediately at the sound of the door opening because we assumed it was Bruce. But when we did turn, we were face-to-face with a woman.

"Mrs. Fletcher?" she asked in a heavy French accent.

"Yes," I said. "You must be Edith Saison."

She smiled, came to us, and shook our hands. She was of medium height. A pin spot in the ceiling shone down on ink-black hair cut short, causing it to glisten. Her features were sharp and well defined, cheekbones high, chin and nose prominent. Her large, oval eyes were as black as her hair. She wore a black pants suit subtly trimmed in gold and cut to accent her good figure. I judged her to be in her late forties, although she could have been in her early fifties. Hard to tell.

"It must have been a blow having Mr. Ladington meet such a sudden, unexpected end," I said.

"Yes, it was," she said. "I still can not believe it."

"You arrived last evening," I said.

"*Oui.*"

"Had you spent much time here at the vineyard, and in Napa Valley?"

"Oh, no. This is my first trip. Bill and I did all our negotiations in France or Curaçao. We both have homes there. Bill told me you were going to help him write his autobiography."

"That isn't exactly true," I said. "We did discuss it, but I told him it was out of the question."

"But he did talk to you."

"About making wine."

"About me and our plans?"

"Just in passing. He said you were bringing varietals to graft to his vines."

"That's right," she said. "It's such an exciting project. The combination of the varietals we've developed in France, and the excellent growing conditions here, promise to create a truly superior cabernet."

I was about to ask whether Ladington's death changed those plans, but she walked from the room. Bruce and Sheriff Davis returned. Bruce looked as though he'd been given bad news by the large, affable sheriff, but the lawman's expression was unreadable.

"I understand you'll be staying here for a week or so, Mrs. Fletcher," Davis said.

"That's right, Sheriff."

"A shame Bill Ladington won't be around to play host," Davis said. "Well, I'll be going now."

"Are you still considering Mr. Ladington's death a suicide?" George asked the sheriff.

"I'm not at liberty to discuss an ongoing investigation."

"Investigation?" I said. "Bruce told me it was definitely ruled a suicide."

"Well, now, Mrs. Fletcher, even though everything points to Bill Ladington's taking his own life, until we've got the autopsy results, it's still considered under investigation. But that shouldn't concern you or Detective Sutherland. You wouldn't be here to conduct your own investigation, would you?"

Bruce answered for us. "No, Sheriff, they're just houseguests. When I learned Dad had invited Mrs. Fletcher, I thought it was only right to honor what he wanted."

Davis's expression said he didn't necessarily believe it, but he didn't press. He bade us a good night and Bruce escorted him from the study, leaving George and me alone.

"What do you think?" I asked.

"About what?"

"About staying. We don't have to."

"You've already given up our rooms at your friends' inn."

"I'm sure we can find something else."

He went behind the desk, placed his hands on it, and leaned forward, a chairman of a board about to break news to stockholders. "I rather think I'd like to stay, Jessica," he said, grinning broadly. "Interesting group of characters, perplexing situation, many questions but few answers, and so much to learn about turning grapes into fine wine."

I smiled and shook my head. "So much for our pledge last night at dinner to avoid murder at all costs."

George laughed. "Simply a matter of life intruding on otherwise well-laid plans. We should get our luggage from the car."

Raoul, Ladington's driver, was in front when we exited the castle and he helped us inside with our bags. Tennessee Ladington awaited us in the foyer, arms folded across her chest.

"Your room is—" she said.

"Rooms," I corrected. "We'll need two separate rooms, if that isn't too much trouble."

We were shown to a wing in which four empty guest rooms were located. Mine was on the west side, affording a view over the main vineyard where Bill Ladington and I had our conversation the previous afternoon. George's accommodations were on the east side, separated from me by a short hallway.

"Dinner is at eight," Tennessee said. "Informal. Cocktails at seven in the drawing room."

We watched her walk away. When she was out of earshot, I said to George, "This is absolutely bizarre. Cocktails? Dinner at eight? It's as if no one has died, no talk of funeral plans, no grieving, except for Bruce."

"Undoubtedly they're in shock," George said. "You can never judge people by their reactions to a sudden death. Some fall apart, others forge ahead."

"Maybe it's denial," I said.

"Or they're all glad to see him gone."

"What a sad thought," I said. "I wonder—"

"Yes?"

"I wonder whether the murder of the young waiter at the

restaurant Ladington owned is in any way linked with his death."

"One of many things to find out while we're here," he said. "See you downstairs for cocktails?"

"Yes. George, are you sure we should stay? I mean, instead of a leisurely week visiting vineyards, we're smack-dab in the middle of a possible murder."

"Not an unusual situation for either of us, Jessica."

"I just don't want to spoil our week."

"To the contrary. No better way to forge a close relationship than to investigate a murder together." He kissed my cheek, stepped into his room, and closed the door. I went back to my room, unpacked, and took a shower. When I was dressed for dinner, I paused at the window overlooking the vineyard. Edith Saison stood alone on the terrace peering out over the vineyard. Bill Ladington had said she'd developed the varietal with her "beau" in France. Would he be arriving? I wondered.

I answered a knock on my door. It was George, dressed in a handsome blue suit, white shirt, and burgundy tie. "Ready?" he asked.

"Ready as I'll ever be."

"You're bonny, as usual."

"Thank you," I said in response to his calling me beautiful. "What's the Scottish word for handsome?"

"*Braw. Weill-faured.*"

"Well, you're both of those things."

He held out his arm, which I took, and we descended the wide staircase together. I glanced over and saw the trace of a smile on his lips, which made me smile too. He was enjoying this in a pixieish way, a side of him I'd seen before and found appealing, among so many other sides.

Chapter Thirteen

Although we walked into the drawing room at precisely seven, we were the last ones to arrive. It was as though everyone else couldn't wait to get a drink. Raoul served as bartender behind a rolling cart on which a variety of liquors and Ladington Creek wines were displayed. Frank Sinatra singing *I've Got You Under My Skin* crooned incongruously through hidden speakers. Bruce immediately came to greet us. His wife, Laura, stood alone in a far corner. In another corner of the large room, Tennessee Ladington spoke with Roger Stockdale and Wade Grosso. The vineyard manager had exchanged his rubber boots and coveralls for gray slacks, green blazer, and white shirt. All three held drinks in their hands.

Bruce led us to the bar where I asked Raoul for a glass of sparkling water while George selected a single-malt Scotch, on the rocks. Consuela passed through with a tray of canapés.

"I'm so happy you're here," Bruce told me.

"I feel a little awkward," I said, "being here the day after your father's death. And I wasn't expecting a cocktail party."

"That's Tennessee for you. I'm surprised she didn't book a band to celebrate Dad's passing."

George changed the subject by asking, "What did your sheriff have to say this afternoon?" He sipped his Scotch and sighed in appreciation.

"That clown? He didn't like it that you and Mrs. Fletcher were staying here."

"Why, for heaven's sake?" I asked.

"He said he doesn't want anybody making more out of Dad's death than it was. 'Just a suicide,' was what he said."

"I trust you informed him of your feelings on the subject," George said.

"Of course I did, but he's not interested in hearing them."

I looked around the room and was struck with the reality that if Bruce Ladington was right, and his father was murdered, that murderer was likely enjoying cocktails in that very room. Unless, of course, the killer had managed to vault the moat, come in from the outside, and leave the same way.

Roger Stockdale broke away from his group and joined us next to the bar. "Good evening," he said.

"Good evening," I replied.

"I hope all the ringing phones haven't disturbed you," he said.

"Ringing phones? I wasn't aware of any."

"Good. The damn media vultures have been calling nonstop about Bill's death. Oh, by the way, Mrs. Fletcher, there was a call for you." He fished in his shirt pocket and handed me a slip of paper. Written on it was Neil Schwartz's name and phone number.

"Your pesty friend?" George asked, reading the paper over my shoulder.

I laughed. "Yes. From Cabot Cove. He's the writer and poet I told you about. I had dinner with him in San Francisco before coming to Napa. He has a contract to write an article for *Vanity Fair* about the murder of that young waiter at Bill Ladington's restaurant."

"I suppose Mr. Ladington's death makes the story even more compelling," George said.

"Or kills interest in it if he committed suicide," I countered. I asked Stockdale if there was a phone I could use.

"Of course."

I followed him from the drawing room to a small office down the hall. "You can use this one," he said.

He closed the door. I settled behind the desk and dialed Neil's number. He answered on the first ring.

"Neil, it's Jessica."

"You got my message. I was afraid they wouldn't give it to you."

"Why?"

"Because I'm obviously part of the dreaded media. I called Cedar Gables Inn. Your friend Margaret told me you'd moved to Ladington's castle. You're *staying* there?"

"It's a long story, Neil, but yes, I'm staying here along with my friend from London, George Sutherland."

"The Scotland Yard inspector."

"Right."

"You're there because Ladington died?"

"Right again. I'd been here as his guest for lunch yesterday and he invited me to stay. I declined the invitation, but Margaret at Cedar Gables had a last-minute request for rooms and Ladington's son, Bruce, arrived and asked me to come and—as I said, it's a long story."

"Did he really commit suicide?" Neil asked.

"Ladington? I don't know. That's the official word so far."

"But you suspect he didn't."

"I'm told he did." I debated telling Neil that Ladington's son thought otherwise, but held my counsel.

"All the press reports say it was suicide. I spoke with my editor at *Vanity Fair*. She says that if Ladington did commit suicide, it waters down the murder story about the waiter. But if Ladington was murdered, that's an even bigger story."

"I have to get back to a cocktail party, Neil."

"Cocktail party? The guy just died."

"I know. Unusual, isn't it? These are unusual people."

"Jess, any chance of getting me in there?"

"Here? At the castle?"

"Yeah."

"I don't know, Neil. There hasn't been any press as far as I can determine—yet. I don't think you'd be especially welcomed."

"Will you try?"

"Let me play it by ear. I really should get back. I'll stay in touch."

"Great. I can't believe you're actually there. I'd sell my soul to be in your shoes right now. Go back to the party. Party! Jesus! What a weird crowd."

Weird crowd stayed with me as I rejoined the assembled in the drawing room.

"Is there a problem?" George asked when I rejoined him.

"No. Neil wants me to see if I can arrange for him to visit the castle."

"For his article?"

"Yes."

Edith Saison, who'd been huddled with Roger Stockdale, interrupted us. She looked stunning in a floor-length, low-cut white dress. It was hardly attire for grieving, but then again, no one seemed to be in an especially somber mood. *Weird crowd* indeed!

"Mrs. Fletcher, I wonder if we could find some quiet room where we can talk."

"All right."

George raised his eyebrows, turned, and asked for a refill. Edith escorted me from the drawing room to the same office from which I'd called Neil. She took the chair behind the desk; I sat in the room's only other chair, upholstered in gray.

"We only have a few minutes before dinner," she said in her charming French accent, "so I'll be direct. What did you and Bill talk about yesterday?"

My initial reaction was to be offended. It was no business of hers what Bill Ladington and I discussed. But since our conversation was certainly innocuous enough, I saw no reason not to repeat it. No state secrets were exchanged, no confidences passed on with an admonition to keep them secret.

"We talked about growing grapes and making wine mostly," I said. "He said he wanted to create the world's best cabernet, and that you were coming to help him do just that. Were you to be partners?"

She closed her eyes, drew a deep breath, opened them, and said wistfully, "Yes. We signed the papers not long ago."

"I'm sorry you've lost your partner," I said. "Does this affect ownership of Ladington Creek Winery?"

"Of course. I suppose it will be a tangled legal mess, lawyers fighting with each other, Bill's estate claiming outright ownership. His wife, that dreadful woman, is already staking her claim by virtue of having married him."

"A wife does have rights," I said, not wishing to engage in a debate on the subject but compelled to state the obvious.

"Rights! Pooh!" Edith said, fairly snarling. "She's been nothing to Bill but a garish blonde thing on his arm. She may have rights, Mrs. Fletcher, but she deserves nothing. They were about to divorce, you know."

"No, I didn't know."

"He didn't mention it to you during your talks?"

"Talk. Singular." I glanced at my watch, stood, and said, "I'd better get back to George, Ms. Saison. Once again, I'm sorry for the loss of your partner, and I'm sure, your friend."

I felt her eyes on me as I left the office and returned to the drawing room where George was talking with Wade Grosso.

"Have plans been made for Mr. Ladington's funeral?" I asked the vineyard manager.

"Probably not," he replied. "There's the autopsy and all that. I suppose Tennessee will get around to it when she has to. I see you and Edith Saison had yourselves a little talk."

"Just a chat, getting to know each other. I understand she and Mr. Ladington were partners in developing a new cabernet."

"Over my objections."

"Why did you object to it?" I asked, feeling comfortable enough to probe.

"You wouldn't understand," he said. "Making wine is a complicated process. Edith and her French partner think they know it all and sold Bill on it. Frankly, I think they're a couple of frauds. I tried to get Bill to see it, but he could be the most stubborn man ever born. Excuse me. I want to get another drink before dinner."

"Interesting," George said. "I assume you've come up with your own thoughts about Ms. Saison's character."

"Not yet," I said. "She seems pleasant enough. Mr. Grosso is right. I'd have to know a lot more about growing grapes and making wine to make that sort of judgment. I—"

Mercedes entered the room and announced in a distinctly unwelcoming voice, "Dinner is served!"

Chapter Fourteen

We were spread out at the dining room table, which left plenty of space between us. George was to my right, Wade Grosso to my left. Directly across was Laura Ladington, whose uncommunicative solemnity hadn't changed. Her husband, Bruce, tried to engage her in small talk but she managed only an occasional grunt and nod of the head. I felt sorry for both of them. She was a pretty young woman, but much of her natural attractiveness was lost in what seemed to be a pervasive depression. Her light blue eyes were lifeless and dull. She seemed to be a dreadfully unhappy person, which must be difficult for her husband to cope with.

Tennessee sat at the head of the table where her husband had been the previous day. Conversation during the early portion of dinner, which we were told had been cooked by Mercedes and was being served by Consuela and Fidel—a tomato and onion salad, pot roast, glazed carrots, thin home fries, and raspberry pie for dessert—was directed by Tennessee, who spent most of it complaining about how much work would be involved in settling her husband's estate. "He wasn't very organized, you know. He never changed his will after his fourth divorce, although Lord knows I urged him to hundreds of times. It isn't fair to those who have to wade through everything when a disorganized person dies."

It seemed to me from my observation of Bill Ladington that he was an extremely organized man. I mentioned that.

Tennessee answered me in a tone usually reserved for a teacher correcting a slow student. "Bill could show many sides to many different people, Mrs. Fletcher. He certainly was organized when it came to his business. When it involved his personal life, he was—"

"Go ahead and say it," Stockdale said. "When it came to his personal life, William H. Ladington was a mess." He looked to me and quickly added, "I speak from experience, Mrs. Fletcher. Supposedly, I handle the vineyard's business and finances. But Bill brought me into his personal affairs on a regular basis. I told him as recently as a few days ago that he should update his will. His answer was to wave his hand and say he'd get to it. He never did."

"If I'm out of line asking about his will, please say so," I said. "Who benefits from the existing, out-of-date will?"

"His fourth wife," Tennessee responded. "Isn't that wonderful? My attorney says I have every right to fight it. Obviously, Bill didn't intend for anything to go to her." Was she about to cry? She didn't, saying in a voice tinged with exaggerated sweetness, "Of course, Bruce here is in that will, aren't you Bruce, dear?"

"Dad left me a little."

"The lawyers will sort this out," Stockdale said.

"And take their huge fees," Tennessee said.

Edith Saison, who'd sat silently during this conversation, suddenly spoke up. "His intentions were very clear," Edith said. "He wanted our partnership to survive, wanted this winery to continue under his name—and under my leadership."

"Rubbish!" Tennessee said.

"Any word on when the autopsy will be completed?" Stockdale asked, more to head off further confrontation between the two women than because he cared.

"No, but it can't be soon enough," Tennessee answered. "Bill always said he wanted immediate cremation, and that's what he'll have."

"No service?" Bruce asked.

"If you want one, dear Bruce, have one. Your father told me that—"

"Stop it!" Laura said, springing from her chair, slamming her hands on the table, which caused her plate to jump, and violently shaking her head. "You people are all sick. He just died and all you care about is money and your own selfish needs. God, I hate you all." She ran from the room, her crying resonating from out in the hall.

"Go tend to her, Bruce," said Tennessee.

Bruce stood.

"Why don't you stay here, Bruce, and let her get over her hysterics?" advised Wade Grosso, who didn't sound as though he was trying to be helpful.

"I'll go," Stockdale said, standing.

Bruce jumped to his feet. "No, I will," he said. "She's right. All anyone here cares about is money."

As Bruce left, Raoul appeared: "You have a call, Ms. Saison."

Edith quickly left the room. George said quietly and casually, "If Mr. Ladington was murdered, there won't be any cremation, at least not until the authorities are satisfied with their findings."

"I'm impressed," said Tennessee. "Spoken by a member of Scotland Yard. Does that make it official?"

"Simply standard police procedure, Mrs. Ladington," George said, not sounding at all piqued at her tone, as I was.

"I don't believe we need the British version of standard police procedures," Tennessee said. "We have all the competent authorities we need right here."

My anger had now risen to the point where I was prompted to speak. "Mrs. Ladington," I said, "if you'd like us to leave, please say so. Your husband invited me to stay here as a guest for the week, and your stepson renewed that invitation. But I assure you it would not be a hardship for us to pack up and spend the week in more welcoming surroundings."

"Mrs. Fletcher is right," Stockdale said. "We aren't treating our guests the way Bill would have wanted us to. We're on edge, Mrs. Fletcher, as I'm sure you can understand. Bill's passing shocked us all. Please forgive us—and don't think of leaving."

Edith Saison returned to the room to announce, "That was Yves. He's coming to stay here."

"When?" Tennessee asked.

"He called from Curaçao. He's getting on a plane within the hour."

Stockdale answered the question written on my face. "Yves LeGrand. Edith's partner in their French vineyard."

"Oh."

Wade Grosso, who stood to my left, snorted but didn't comment.

I looked to Tennessee, who didn't seem pleased with the news.

Bruce reappeared and took his seat. "Laura's not feeling well," he said. "A bad headache." To me he said, "She gets migraines."

"Poor thing," Tennessee said, standing. "Excuse me. I don't eat dessert."

After dinner, Bruce suggested we retire to his father's study for a nightcap, but George and I declined.

"I have to talk to you," Bruce said. "About Dad's death."

"I think it had better wait until morning," I said. "I'm very tired."

"Sure, I understand," he said. "We'll spend the day going over it."

"Do you feel like some air?" George suggested when we stood alone at the foot of the stairs leading to the second level and our rooms.

"Oh, yes," I said.

We stepped outside into a chilly, damp night. The clouds were low and fast-moving, and a dense fog had enveloped the winery. The air was filled with a hum.

"Giant fans in the vineyards," I said. "It must be cold enough for them to go on. They circulate the warmer air above the vines to keep the lower portions from freezing."

"You already sound like an expert," he said, pulling a pipe from his jacket, tamping tobacco from a pouch into it and lighting it. It smelled good.

"What do you think of our friends inside?" I asked lightly.

"I've been in the company of some strange people following a death," he said, "especially when murder is a possibility, but these characters elevate dysfunctional to new heights."

We fell silent and breathed in the damp night air. But we stiffened at a sound from behind. We turned. A man emerged from the shadows holding a rifle. It was pointed directly at us. "Identify yourselves," he said.

"We're guests here," I said. "Who are *you*?"

"Security. Guests? Nobody told me about any guests."

"I don't care what anyone told you," George said. "Put down that ridiculous gun before you hurt someone."

He seemed unsure of what to do, which made him especially dangerous. I glanced beyond him to a window next to the front door and saw Roger Stockdale's face. He realized I'd seen him, opened the door, and said, "It's all right, Willy. They're houseguests."

Willy lowered the rifle. "Just doing my job," he told Stockdale.

"Of course," Stockdale said. "It's all right."

"That's better," said George. "I have a particular aversion to having strange men point a loaded weapon at me."

"Can't blame you," Stockdale said. "It won't happen again."

George's anger was palpable. He took my arm and said, "Let's go inside, Jessica, before we end up dead like our host."

Chapter Fifteen

Rain pounding against the window woke me early the next morning. I pulled open the heavy drapes and looked out at a windswept torrent of water cascading from an almost black sky.

The weather was disappointing. George and I had decided before retiring to our rooms that we'd find some time to get away from the castle and explore the surrounding countryside. Although we'd made a commitment of sorts to Bruce to investigate his father's death, I was also determined to relax and take in the valley's sights.

Before falling asleep, I'd perused my Napa Valley guidebook and had noted a few places to visit, including Sterling Vineyards, where you have to ride an aerial tram to get to the chateau and tasting room. I was also intrigued with the notion of taking a hot air balloon ride, and wrote down the number of Napa Valley Balloons, which offered daily trips. In the past, the thought of going up in a balloon and hanging from it in a wicker basket while flames were shot up inside the balloon to give it lift, had never appealed. Now that I'd learned to fly, however, I was eager for the experience.

But those excursions would have to wait for a sunny day.

I joined George for breakfast in the dining room where, we'd been told, we could have breakfast any time up until noon. Consuela served us eggs and toast and fresh-squeezed orange juice. We were either early or late; we were the only ones there.

Bruce Ladington joined us as we were finishing.

"I thought we could have that talk now," he said.

"Looks like a perfect day for talking," George said. "This weather isn't good for much else. Very much like home in Scotland."

"Before we have that talk," I said, "I'd like to see the tasting room. I understand your awards are displayed there."

"Yeah. Dad was really proud of them. Nobody knew that side of him. He never bragged about all the money he made in real estate in Boston, or movies in the Hollywood days. But this was different. It was as if wine became a transfusion, a new supply of blood for him."

"Was the partnership with Ms. Saison as important as he thought it would be?" I asked.

Bruce lowered his voice to a conspiratorial level. "That's what he believed, but as far as I'm concerned she's a fraud. And now this lover of hers—what's his name? Yves LeGrand? I don't know what kind of deal Dad cut with them, but Roger told me once that they really took Dad to the cleaners."

"How so?" I asked.

"Dad never shared his business with me. Kept it to himself. Probably figured I was too dumb or something."

Hearing him say that saddened me. This young man was so unlike his father in every way, physically and emotionally, and had desperately wanted and needed his father's approval, which, I suspected, he'd never received.

"How's your wife feeling this morning?" George asked, sensing the discomfort I was experiencing and changing the subject.

"Better. When she gets those migraines, the only thing she can do is go to bed."

"I've heard how painful they are," I offered.

"Pretty bad," Bruce said. "It's always worse when we're here at the castle. She never has them when we're at the Curaçao house."

"Do you spend much time in Curaçao?" I asked.

"As much as we can. Come on. I'll show you the tasting room."

I'd assumed we'd be going to another part of the castle. But we had to leave it in order to get to a separate building that was considerably newer than the castle. We took large, striped golf umbrellas from a stand and held them above us as we crossed a level grassy area to the newer building, which was one-story and designed to look like an oversized log cabin.

"It isn't open to the public until ten," Bruce said once we were inside.

The tasting room took up almost the entire building, with the exception of three small offices at one end. While the building's exterior was rough-hewn, the inside was decidedly modern. A long stainless-steel counter ran the length of the room. Behind it were display racks for the different wines produced by Ladington Creek. Two large trays of small glasses occupied one end of the counter.

"This is where people come to taste," Bruce said. "It used to be free, but the other wineries started charging and we did, too. It got to be too expensive handing out free wine."

"I can imagine," George said, going behind the counter and examining some of the bottles and their labels. I strayed to the wall opposite, on which dozens of framed awards were displayed. They came from all over the world. Most had been given for the winery's cabernets, although there were also citations for a Ladington Creek merlot. It was evident that white wine was not the winery's strong suit.

Bruce joined me.

"Your father told me," I said, "that the varietals Ms. Saison was bringing to graft to his vines would create a truly superior cabernet one day."

"I guess he believed that, Mrs. Fletcher. I wish he hadn't. If you ask me, Edith Saison should be a prime suspect in his murder."

George had come up behind us. "*If* it was murder," he reminded the younger Ladington.

"Can there be any doubt?" Bruce said. "You saw the way everybody acted at dinner last night. They're all glad he's dead."

"Why?" I asked.

"For control, Mrs. Fletcher. For the money. Edith claims Ladington Creek becomes her property because of her partnership with Dad. Boy, did she sell him a bill of goods. He met her and her boyfriend, Yves, in Curaçao. They have a house there, too, over on Knip Bay. Dad was like any big tough guy. They're the easiest to con, if you know what I mean, like salesmen being the easiest people to sell."

"What about your stepmother?" George asked.

"Her? Oh, she wants the money, too. It isn't fair that she can lay claim to it just because she got him to marry her."

"Got him to marry her?" I repeated.

"That's right. Dad was a big, tough guy, but he was a pussycat when it came to women. You know he'd been married many times. Tennessee told him what a great man he was and he fell for it, like he usually did. She even said he should run for President. They were married a month after they were introduced."

"Is there anyone else you suspect?" George asked.

"Bob Jenkins."

"Who is he?" George asked.

"He owns the vineyard next to Ladington Creek. Shelton Reserve. Ever hear of it?"

"I believe I have," I said. "I attended a wine-appreciation course before leaving Maine. Our instructor had a number of wines for us to taste, and I seem to remember one was Shelton Reserve."

"Jenkins has been trying to run my father out of business since Dad bought Ladington Creek. It was called Opel Vineyard then, until he changed the name."

"Your father mentioned Mr. Jenkins to me," I said. "Said something harsh about him."

Bruce smiled. "I don't wonder. He hated him. Jenkins's vineyard is on higher ground than ours. That means any problems Jenkins has with disease, especially phylloxera, can run down onto our vines in a heavy rain."

"Phylloxera?" George asked.

"A plant louse that pretty much wiped out vineyards in Europe and California last century," I said. "It's made a comeback in California recently."

"I am impressed by your explanation, Jessica," George said.

"I read it in the book I brought with me on wine making."

"It's a really bad disease," Bruce said.

"I'll take your word for it," said George.

"Would you like to taste some of the wines?" Bruce asked. "Before the tourists arrive? I sometimes work the tasting room. It was the only thing Dad let me do around here."

"I doubt you'll see many tourists on a nasty day like this," I said.

"A little early for a taste of the grape for me," George said. I agreed.

"Want to go back to Dad's study?" Bruce asked.

We nodded and went to the door. The rain had stopped; a lovely rainbow spanned the horizon where the sun attempted to displace the grayness. We returned to the castle and were on our way to Bill Ladington's study when voices from an adjacent room caused Bruce to stop.

"Sounds like the *shirra*," George said.

"The what?" Bruce said.

"Sorry," George said. "I slipped into my Scottish mode. *Shirra*. Scottish for sheriff."

"Oh."

Sheriff Davis appeared in the hallway. "Been showing your houseguests the property?" he asked Bruce.

"We were in the tasting room," Bruce replied.

"Enjoying an early-morning eye-opener, Mrs. Fletcher?"

"We didn't have any wine," I said.

"Did you come to see me?" Bruce asked.

"Matter of fact, no," the sheriff said. "I came to see your stepmom."

We waited for a further explanation. None was forthcoming. Instead, he said, "I got back a preliminary autopsy report this morning, just before I headed here."

We stood silently.

"Looks like it wasn't as clear-cut as we first thought."

"Dad didn't commit suicide?" Bruce said excitedly.

"I didn't say that," said the sheriff, "but the investigation's going to remain open until we have the answer."

"Could you be more specific?" George asked.

The sheriff turned and smiled at George. "Sounds to me like you're not so much of a casual tourist as you said you were."

"Just curious," George said.

"Professional curiosity?"

George didn't respond.

"Tell you what. How would you like to spend some time with me, see how we catch the bad guys in Napa Valley? You know, hands across the sea and all that."

George looked at me before saying, "I assume that invitation extends to Mrs. Fletcher, too."

"Give you some research for your next book, Mrs. Fletcher?"

"Perhaps."

"Sure. How about tomorrow morning? Nine?"

"That sounds good to me," George said. "I always enjoy seeing how other law enforcement agencies function."

Davis gave us directions to his headquarters and left.

"I can't believe that," Bruce said.

"Generous offer of him," George commented.

"Maybe you'll find out things about how Dad died. This is great."

"We'll see," George said. "Now, let's go to your father's study and have that talk you've been anxious to have."

Chapter Sixteen

Our conversation with Bruce was short and nonproductive. He had nothing to offer in the way of evidence that William Ladington had been murdered, just kept repeating his belief that someone had killed his father. I was grateful when Mercedes entered the room and announced that Laura needed him. He excused himself, leaving George and me alone in the study where an unexpected shaft of sunlight slashed through a gap in the drapes and across the purple carpeting.

George stood, went behind the desk, and took the chair once occupied by Ladington. He narrowed his eyes as he took in the room.

"You're thinking?" I asked.

"I'm thinking that your friend Mr. Ladington did not take his own life."

"Based upon?"

"Common sense, and the sheriff's comment. Pretend I'm Ladington. Pretend I've decided to end my life by ingesting some sort of pills. What time was his body found, Jessica?"

"I don't think anyone said."

"We must ask. In the meantime, I sit here at my desk staring at the pill bottle. Yes, I tell myself, it's time to leave this world. I swallow the pills. What do I wash them down with?"

"Water, I suppose."

"Was there a glass found on this desk along with the empty pill bottle?"

"Something else to ask about."

"Yes."

He got up and came around the desk.

"I've taken the pills. Now what do I do? Leave this room in which I'm supremely comfortable, surrounded by meaningful momentos of my life? Why would I? Death by pills is a quiet, tidy way to die. If I were William Ladington, I would simply remain in my comfortable chair and spend my last minutes on earth reflecting on what I'd accomplished."

"Go on," I said. "You make sense so far."

"Thank you. No, I don't do the logical thing. I get up, go to the door, and leave this room."

I followed him to the door and into the hallway.

"If I did—leave the room, that is—I'd certainly be aware that my final moment might come at any time, here in the hallway, in the presence of others. But I ignore that and leave the castle."

We stepped into welcome sunshine.

"It's night. I've taken enough pills to kill me. I'm outside now, where there are security guards who might come upon me. But that does not deter me. I decide to walk to the edge of the moat to die, perhaps fall into it. Not an especially neat and considerate way for a proud man like Ladington to be found. Totally against the type I understand him to be. Do we know precisely where in the moat his body was found?"

"Another question to be answered. We could ask here at the castle, but I'd rather get it from the sheriff. The *shirra*." I laughed. "I'm not sure we'd get a straight answer from anyone here."

We went to the edge of the moat and looked down into its brackish water.

"How deep is the water?" George asked.

"I have no idea, although it looks deeper than the last time I looked. Those rocks are covered now. They weren't before. I suppose it depends to some extent on how much rain falls."

"It can't depend solely on nature," George said. "There must be a man-made means of flooding it."

We followed the natural curve of the moat to the rear of the castle.

"You're right," I said, pointing to a large pipe with a cut-off valve. I went to where it jutted out over the moat and looked down. "Yes, it definitely is deeper than the first time I saw it, the day I had lunch with Ladington."

George didn't respond.

"I assume that if it can be filled by this pipe, it can also be drained," I said.

George nodded, took out his pipe, and went through the ritual of filling and lighting it. I turned and looked into the distance.

"That's Halton Mountain," I said.

George looked to what I was seeing. "Is that part of this vineyard?" he asked.

"No, but I just realized it could have some meaning in Ladington's death."

"How so?"

"There's evidently a dispute over ownership of land on the mountain. Ladington explained to me that vines thrive in rocky, pitched hillsides. Margaret and Craig Snasdell also talked of how Halton Mountain is perfect for grape growing."

"Does Ladington own part of it?"

"I don't believe he did, but he wanted to."

"Who else wants it?"

"I suppose his neighbors, the other vintners."

"Like Mr. Jenkins?"

"I'd like to find out," I said.

"Another question on our growing list." He looked up into a mixed sky, patches of blue interrupted by residual fast-moving clouds. "Why don't we take that ride we talked about? No telling when it will rain again." He chuckled as we started back toward the front of the castle. "The weather here is like Scotland," he said, exaggerating his Scottish brogue. "V-e-r-y changeable."

Like my life, I thought.

Chapter Seventeen

The drawbridge was down when we left, eliminating the need to ask that it be lowered. Nor did we bother telling anyone we were leaving. But our departure was observed. As I stood next to George's rented silver Ford Taurus waiting for him to unlock the doors, I looked back at the castle, specifically to windows on the upper level. Laura Ladington, Bruce's brooding wife, stood at one of them, her attention focused on us.

After we'd crossed the drawbridge and were on our way down the narrow lane leading from the vineyard, I let out a loud sigh that caused George to turn.

"Is that a statement of contentment or distress?" he asked.

"Relief," I said. "I hadn't realized how tense I've been until we crossed that bridge."

"They are an anxiety-producing group, aren't they?"

"To say the least. I feel guilty plopping you smack-dab in the middle of a dysfunctional family."

He laughed. "'Dysfunctional' hardly does them justice, Jessica. Daft is what they are."

I laughed too, and it felt good.

We didn't have any specific destination in mind as we drove south on Route 29. Traffic was heavy, which gave us a chance to take in the passing scene at a leisurely pace. Both sides of the road were lined with wineries, their signs inviting those passing by to stop in and taste the fruit of their efforts. George asked a few times whether I wanted to stop, but I declined. "Not in the mood," I said each time. "Maybe after we've had some lunch."

We didn't have much to say to each other, which, I've always believed, is the test of a true friendship. It was obvious that George's mind was active, as was mine, but we left each other space and time to process our thoughts. I found myself doing what I've done before, trying to divide my mind into separate compartments in which to segregate conflicting ideas. In this instance, I assigned a compartment to each of the people in the castle. They'd been a blur until now; a group of people without individual definition. But once they were placed in my imaginary stalls, I was able to focus on them with greater clarity. Of course, they were of interest to me only if William Ladington had been murdered. In that case, they were suspects. But if he had, in fact, taken his own life, they were nothing more than odd characters engaged in a fight over the spoils of the deceased's life.

Tennessee Ladington loomed large in my thinking. It was easy to paint her stereotypically—sexy blonde who displays her feminine charms to a bigger-than-life wealthy older man, whose penchant for marrying was well known. According to Bruce, they'd married after knowing each other for only a month. That probably said more about Bill Ladington's impetuousness than her designing ways. It wouldn't be fair, I knew, to hypothesize about whether she was glad to see her husband dead, although her demeanor didn't suggest to me a grieving widow devastated by such a tragic event. If that were true, money would be her motivation. But it seemed that the legal question of who would inherit his wealth, including Ladington Creek, was up in the air. Bruce had told us that Edith Saison was laying claim to the winery by virtue of her partnership with the deceased Ladington. If that were true, she, too, would have motive for seeing her partner dead.

There was soon to be another face at the castle, Edith's French partner and alleged lover, Yves LeGrand. Was he flying to California to comfort Edith and to join in mourning William Ladington? Or was it strictly business, his presence there lending weight to what might become a battle over Ladington Creek?

I placed Bruce and Laura Ladington together in my series of mental boxes. Theirs was hardly a marriage made in heaven, although I wondered to what extent Bruce's father's overt disdain for his son's choice of a wife exacerbated the couple's problems. Not having parents' approval of a mate places a strain on any relationship. Was Laura's apparent depression a result of such a strain, or had it preceded the marriage? One thing was certain: Laura's outburst at the dinner table the night before represented her true feelings about the family into which she'd married.

My brief encounters with Roger Stockdale and Raoul had been characterized by somewhat hostile comments about William Ladington. Raoul's facial expression was one of constant anger. When asked whether his boss had had the moat dug for security purposes, he'd responded, "I wouldn't know, ma'am. I don't question what Mr. Ladington does. Ever!"

And when Stockdale drove me to Cedar Gables Inn after my lunch at the castle and I'd labeled Ladington "an interesting man," Stockdale had replied, "Everyone who meets him for the first time says that, Mrs. Fletcher. It's after you get to know him that you start coming up with other words to describe him."

It's not unusual for employees to have negative views of their employers from time to time. But to express such feelings so openly to a stranger said to me that their anger ran deep, and that they needed an outlet for it. Was that outlet the murdering of Bill Ladington?

The vineyard manager, Wade Grosso, bothered me, although if pressed I wouldn't be able to come up with a tangible reason. And there was Robert Jenkins, the competitive neighbor and fellow vintner, who wanted a piece of Halton Mountain as badly as Ladington did. And, of course, household staff, including the husband and wife team of Consuela and Fidel, the head housekeeper, Mercedes, and members of the security squad, might also have harbored ill feelings toward their employer.

But this was purely supposition on my part. As far as the police were concerned, Ladington's death was still being considered a suicide, although Sheriff Davis's comment that morning indicated that that finding wasn't set in stone.

"Hungry?" George asked as we approached the town of Yountville.

"As a matter of fact, I am."

"Looks like plenty of choices," he said, nodding left and right at restaurants lining Washington Street.

"How about you?" I asked. "Any preferences?"

"I'd be happy with some good pub fare, bangers and mash," he said, smiling, "bangers" being British for sausage, and "mash" for mashed potatoes.

"I don't see any British pubs," I said. I pointed ahead of us. "There's Bill Ladington's place."

A parking space was open directly in front of Ladington's Steak House, and George deftly backed into it.

"Game?" he asked.

"Always."

We stepped through the entrance into a large, brightly lit room, with multiple skylights providing additional natural illumination. The restaurant was arranged on two levels, with the raised portion at the back of the room. A small bar was to our right. Everything—walls, columns, bar, and tables—was made of light wood with a golden patina. Huge, colorful flower arrangements provided attractive separation among groups of tables. In one corner was a sushi bar with a hand-lettered sign indicating it was closed.

"Sushi in a steak restaurant," George commented. "That seems an odd combination."

We were early; there were only a handful of diners when we arrived.

A pretty young redhead wearing a white tux shirt open at the neck and black slacks greeted us at the reservation podium. "Two for lunch?" she asked pertly.

"Yes, please," said George.

We were seated on the raised platform, which gave us an unrestricted view of the entire room. Our waitress, wearing the same uniform as our greeter, brought us menus and asked if we wanted a cocktail. We both declined, opting instead for a bottle of sparkling water and some lemon wedges.

The menu gave credence to the restaurant's name. Most of the items were of the meat variety, although there was salmon, grouper, and snapper for those preferring fish. A separate sushi menu had a note clipped to it: *"Our sushi bar will be closed until further notice."* The day's luncheon specials were sliced sirloin steak on a garlic wedge, or homemade chicken salad. Soup of the day was onion.

"A respectable menu," George said.

"Yes, and it reminds me of something. There's another person to consider."

"Another person? To consider for what?"

"To consider as a suspect if Ladington was murdered. The chef cooks lunch each day at the castle, then comes here to handle the evening meal. I'd forgotten about him. His name is Nick."

"Was he at the castle the night Ladington died?"

"I presume he wasn't, based upon the schedule I was told he kept. But schedules can always be changed."

"The young man who was murdered," George said, "he worked here as a waiter?"

"Yes. He was stabbed to death."

"Was Ladington considered a suspect?"

"He was questioned, from what I read. But whether he was a suspect is conjecture. He claimed to have been at the castle when it happened, although he had been here at the restaurant earlier in the evening."

"Probably nothing more than coincidence. The chicken salad appeals."

"Two chicken salads," I told the waitress, "and iced tea."

"What was the young man's name?" George asked.

"Louis something. I forget the last name."

"Miss," George said to the waitress as she passed our table, "we understand that someone who worked here, a waiter, was recently murdered."

I wasn't sure whether she'd respond, but she did. "That's right. Louis Hubler."

"Yes, Louis Hubler," I said. "Did you work with him?"

She nodded. "I sure did. Not always the same shift, but we were friends."

"A dreadful way to die," George said.

"Are you from Scotland Yard or something?" she asked.

George laughed. "As a matter of fact, I am."

"I figured, with the accent and all. Are you investigating Louis's murder?"

"Unofficially," I answered. "We're—we're friends of Mr. Ladington."

Her expression, which had been noncommittal, soured. "He's dead," she said.

"Yes, we know," I said. "He committed suicide."

"You believe that?"

"Is there a reason why we shouldn't?"

"I don't know. It's just that he didn't seem like the sort of man who'd do that."

"I agree," I said. "Had your friend, Louis, and Mr. Ladington had any problems between them?"

Her small laugh was rueful. "I'd say so."

"What sort of problems?" George asked.

"Ask Mary Jane."

"Who is she?" I asked.

"A waitress who used to work here. She left the night Louis was killed. I have to get going. I'll see if your chicken salads are ready."

"Where can we find Mary Jane?" I asked.

"Calistoga, I guess. She's working at one of the spas."

"And her last name?"

"Proll. Mary Jane Proll."

She returned with our dishes and quickly left the table. The only further conversation we had with her was when she served us a piece of apple crumb pie to share.

Afterward, I told George, "Bill Ladington said the day I had lunch with him that drugs might have been involved in the waiter's murder."

His eyebrows went up. "Doesn't look like a place where drugs would be sold," he said. "But you can't assume that about any place on the planet these days."

"Ladington didn't say that this Louis Hubler was a drug user or seller. He based his comment on rumors. Feel like a ride to Calistoga?"

"A strange name for a place," he said, removing a credit card from his wallet and placing it on the bill our waitress had delivered with the pie.

"Named after the famous spa in Saratoga, New York," I said. "Or so I read. 'Cali' for California. It's famous for mud baths."

"Mud is for pigs to bathe in, Jessica. Not people."

"But this is California, George. Things—and people—are different here."

"So I've noticed."

Chapter Eighteen

We retraced our steps back up Route 29, passing the turnoff to Ladington Creek Vineyards in St. Helena and continuing north until we reached Calistoga. For some reason, I expected a town out of the old west, with saloons, wooden sidewalks, and tall cowboys in large Stetsons sitting around in front of a jailhouse. The name Calistoga had that ring to it.

Instead, we drove down Lincoln Avenue, the busy main street lined with art galleries, upscale clothing stores, attractive restaurants, and an assortment of small shops that might have been found on any prosperous main street.

"Where to?" George asked.

"To the spa where Mary Jane Proll works."

"And where might that be?"

"I haven't the slightest idea, but a good start would be the first spa we come to."

Which was only a hundred yards in front of us. George parked, and we stood on the sidewalk beneath a large red sign promising the ultimate in mud baths, steam rooms, and massage. George laced his fingers together, stretched his arms in front of him, pivoted left and right, and grimaced.

"Stiff?" I asked.

"Yes. The back acts up now and again. Are we going in?"

"I will if you'd prefer to stay out here."

"You go ahead," he said. "I'll try and walk off this kink in my back."

The spa's reception area was spartan but welcoming. The walls were painted stark white, broken only by two large, colorful Kandinsky posters. A woman wearing a white lab coat sat behind a gleaming black, free-form Plexiglas desk.

"Hello," she said pleasantly.

"Hello," I replied.

"Can I help you?"

"If you mean am I looking for a mud bath and massage, the answer is no. I'm touring the wine country with a friend. I'm from Maine—Cabot Cove, Maine. A dear friend back home asked me to look up a family member while I was in Calistoga. I thought you might know her."

"What's her name?"

"Proll. Mary Jane Proll. Her mother told me she was working here in a spa."

"I don't know anyone by that name. Did her mother say which spa she works at?"

"Unfortunately, no."

"Sorry, but I can't help. Try the Hampton Spa. It's over near Sterling Vineyard."

"Really? That's on my list of places to visit. It has an aerial tram."

"Right. Once you get up to the chateau you have a great view of the valley."

"That's where I'll go then. The Hampton Spa. Thank you."

"Hope you find your friend."

"Oh, I'm sure I will. Thanks again."

George was standing in front of an art gallery smoking his pipe when I came out of the spa.

"Feeling better?" I asked.

"Yes, much. Any luck?"

"No, but a lead."

We got back in the car and I consulted a map of Calistoga on which many of the spas were noted. "We're going here," I said. "Hampton Spa. And then maybe we'll take that ride I mentioned, on an aerial tram."

He laughed. "Sounds as though you're shifting from murder investigator to tourist."

"A little of both wouldn't hurt. That's why we're here, isn't it, to take in the sights?"

"That was the original plan."

"Murder tends to change plans, doesn't it?"

"It certainly does. All right, to the Hampton Spa we go."

Unlike the spa I'd visited downtown, Hampton Spa was set back from a narrow road on the outskirts of Calistoga. It looked more like a ranch than a spa. A breeze that had picked up sent dry, red dirt surrounding the building into the air, giving some credence to my initial perception of what Calistoga would be.

We parked directly in front of the entrance in a space a car had just vacated. Judging from the number of vehicles, Hampton Spa was doing a brisk business.

"Coming in with me this time?" I asked.

"Absolutely. This might be my one and only chance to see what a spa, California style, looks like from the inside."

Although the building's exterior was rough-hewn, a quintessential western look, the reception area was opulent, the sort of room one might associate with a European anteroom. The floor was covered with thick Persian area rugs; the furniture was period reproductions. The sound of soft classical music and the aroma of bath oils and soaps were soothing.

"Hi," said a young woman in white slacks and blue turtleneck as she entered the room from an area behind it. "Are you being helped?"

"No," I said.

"Be right back."

She disappeared through the door, to be replaced by an older woman wearing an oversized white terrycloth robe and disposable white slippers, who smiled at us as she crossed the room and left through another door. Then, a middle-aged man, also wearing a robe and slippers, appeared, followed by the woman in white slacks and turtleneck. "The massage rooms are through that door," she told the male client. "Someone will be with you in a minute."

When the man was gone, she smiled at us and asked, "Do you have an appointment?"

"No," I said. "Actually, we were—"

"We have an opening," she said as she sat behind a desk and consulted an appointment book. "Mary Jane had a last-minute cancellation. Would you like the full treatment—mud bath, whirlpool, steam, and massage?"

"Mary Jane has an opening?" I said, more to delay answering her question than seeking clarification.

"Yes, she' s—"

Another young woman came through a door. She wore a white lab coat over jeans and a pale blue button-down shirt. She was tall and solidly built, and had short red hair and a pretty face that skirted being masculine. The large nametag pinned to her white coat said: MARY JANE PROLL.

"This is Mary Jane," her colleague said.

"Hi," Mary Jane said.

"Hello," I said. "I'm Jessica. This is my friend, George."

"Here for a treatment?" she asked.

"Well, maybe. I understand you have an opening. What does a treatment entail?"

She ran through the list as her colleague had done, but added, "You'll feel like a million dollars after it, relaxed and at peace with the world."

I smiled at her enthusiasm.

"What does it cost?" George asked.

"The complete session is a hundred and twenty-five dollars," Mary Jane said. "We take all major credit cards. Or you can just have a mud bath or massage. Your choice."

"Actually," George said, "we really came in to—"

"I'll have the works," I announced, causing George to frown at me.

"You, too, sir?" Mary Jane asked George.

"I, ah—"

"You don't mind, do you?" I asked him. "Calistoga looks like a pleasant place to browse. Being at peace with the world is very appealing."

"Sure you want to, Jessica?" he asked, his tone suggesting that I should reconsider.

"Yes," I said. I asked Mary Jane how long it would take.

"An hour and a half," she replied.

"All right," George said. "I'll mosey about the town, as you Yanks like to say, and be back to collect you in ninety minutes."

"I'll get your robe and slippers," Mary Jane said, following the other woman from the room and leaving George and me alone.

"I can't think of a more perfect chance to have a long talk with her," I whispered.

"Have you ever had a mud bath before?" he asked.

"No, but I'd never flown a plane either. Even if this doesn't result in useful information, I'll have had a new experience."

"Sounds daft to me, but you know best."

He kissed me on the cheek, shook his head, and left as Mary Jane reappeared with my robe and slippers. She led me to a room with two square tile tubs sunk into the floor. Each contained a grayish substance I assumed was the mud. One thing was certain: the temperature in the room was considerably hotter than the reception area.

She pointed to a set of curtains. "You can change in there," she said, and handed me a white sheet. "Wrap yourself in this sheet when you've finished undressing."

I hesitated. Deciding to have the spa treatment in order to

spend time with her had been easy. Now, I thought of George's comment that only pigs bathe in mud, and I wasn't quite sure I wanted to go through with it. Mary Jane's expression said she was waiting for me. I took the sheet and stepped through the curtains. The small dressing room was concrete, too, including a narrow bench on which to sit. Plastic hangers hung from two hooks in the wall. I removed my clothing and hung it on the hangers. Naked, I wrapped the sheet around me, drew a breath, and stepped back through the curtains.

"All set?" Mary Jane asked.

"I suppose so," I replied.

"Hand me the sheet and I'll hold it up while you get in the tub."

"Which one?" I asked, trying to forestall the inevitable.

"This one," she said, indicating the closest one. "Just get in and let yourself sink."

She took the sheet from me and I sat on the rim of the tub and lowered my bottom into the mud, which had the consistency of wet peat moss. Slowly, tentatively, I swung my legs over and stretched out, the buoyant mud supporting my body. My head rested on a slim, hard pillow at one end. Mary Jane methodically folded the sheet, placed it on a chair, slipped on a pair of plastic gloves, got down on her knees, and began to slather more mud over me, using a small wooden paddle.

"Comfortable?" she asked.

"It's very warm," I said. "Hot" would have been more accurate. It was becoming uncomfortable, and I sensed that my blood pressure was rising. I wasn't sure how much longer I wanted to stay submerged in hot mud, and decided to get to the real reason I was there.

"I must admit," I said, "that I came here today for something other than a mud bath."

"Really?" she replied, continuing to smear more hot mud over me.

"Yes. My friend and I—he's a chief inspector with Scotland Yard in London—we've been looking into the death of William Ladington."

I looked up into a face that reflected surprise, and concern.

"We had lunch at Ladington's Steak House and got talking with a waitress there. She's the one who told us about you, that you worked there until the young waiter, Louis Hubler, was murdered."

"What business is it of yours?" she asked as she continued to mold the mud around me. Her movements seemed to become slower and more deliberate, more forceful. I started to answer, but she cut me off. "What do I have to do with it?" she asked brusquely.

"Probably nothing," I said, forcing a smile and moving in the mud. My discomfort was increasing and I decided to end this as quickly as possible and leave. "The other waitress at the steak house said there might have been trouble between Mr. Ladington and Mr. Hubler, and said you'd know about it."

"I thought you said you were investigating Ladington's death. What does Louis have to do with it?"

"I don't know," I said. "I was hoping you could tell me. I think I've had enough. I'd like to get out now."

She ignored my request and continued moving the mud over me with the paddle.

"Do you know what problems existed between the waiter and Mr. Ladington?" I asked.

"I used to work there," she said flatly.

"I know," I said. "Were you friendly with Louis?"

"Who are you?"

"Jessica Fletcher. I write crime novels. I'm—"

"I don't have to talk to you."

"Of course you don't," I said. "All I wanted to ask you was—"

"I don't know anything. Excuse me."

She stood and left the room. I decided to try to extricate myself from the tub in her absence, but she was back before I could even start.

"What do you *really* want?" she asked, again on her knees and moving mud over me.

"Look," I said, "I didn't mean to upset you. I don't have any official reason for asking questions. Mr. Ladington's son asked me to help prove that his father was murdered."

"He killed himself. I read about it."

"Yes, he might have. I won't ask any more questions. Just help me out and I'll be on my way."

The mud was now up under my chin, and movement was difficult. The mud also seemed to have gotten hotter, and my discomfort level was rising with it. She made a sudden, forceful move with the paddle, causing some of the hot mud to splash on my cheek and lip. The temperature of the mud continued to rise, and I realized it was reaching a dangerous point. My flesh was on fire, and my head pounded.

"Could you make the mud cooler?" I asked.

"That's not possible," she said. Her bitter, angry expression said she had no intention of doing that even if she could, and it occurred to me that when she'd left the room, it might have been to raise the temperature.

"I have to get out now," I said, attempting to sit up, but the mud blanket was too heavy. Mary Jane placed her hands—strong hands—through the mud on my shoulders which, combined with the weight of the mud, rendered me incapable of moving. "Let me up!" I snapped. "I've had enough."

"What do you know about Louis?" she asked, continuing the pressure on my shoulders.

"Nothing, just that he was murdered." I now yelled: "*Let me out, damn it!*"

For a moment I thought she was about to push me under, submerge my face in the mud—drown me in it. If so, I was helpless to prevent it. Sweat poured down my forehead into my eyes. The heat was unbearable.

"Please," I said. "Don't do this to me."

I actually believed I was going to die in that tub filled with mud. But then she released her grip on me, knelt, and began scraping the mud from my body into the side of the tub. "Come on. Get out before you boil," she said.

She held up a clean sheet as I struggled to pull myself free of the mud's sucking grip. She extended a hand, and I managed to first sit up, then pull my legs over the side of the tub and finally stand. She wrapped the sheet around me. "The shower is in that room," she said, pointing to a door.

I was furious as I stood there, shaking with anger and fear. I glared at her; she locked eyes with me and never wavered. I drew a series of deep breaths before being able to say, "Coming here was foolish. Trying to ask you questions under false pretenses was even more foolish. But what you just did to me is inexcusable."

She said nothing. I entered the shower room and washed the hot mud from me. My skin, every inch of it, was fire-engine red; I felt as though thousands of tiny needles had been injected into me. My robe and slippers were there. I put them on and returned to the mudroom where Mary Jane sat in the chair, leaning forward, elbows on her knees, face cradled in her hands, hair in disarray. I intended to say nothing else, simply ask for my clothes and leave.

But she said, "I don't know you or why you're interested in Louis's murder, and I don't care. Who sent you?"

"No one sent me. My friend, George, and I are staying at the Ladington winery. We're interested in determining whether Bill Ladington was a suicide or a murder victim.

The murder of your friend was probably just a coincidence."

"Ladington hated Louis."

"Hated him? An employee? Why did he hire him?"

"He didn't hate him when he hired him. It was after."

"What caused it?" I asked, pleased that she'd begun to open up.

"Ask the bitch."

"Pardon?"

"That old hag, Ladington's wife."

It was true that Tennessee Ladington was older than the young woman in the room with me, but she was hardly an "old hag." I suppose it was all a matter of perspective.

"What about Mrs. Ladington?" I asked.

"She was after Louis."

"I see."

"She seduced him. That's what always happens, I guess, when a woman marries an old guy with megabucks but has to get her sex somewhere else, like from a young waiter at her husband's restaurant."

"Are you certain they were having an affair?" I asked.

"Of course I am. Louis told me all about it."

"He bragged about it to you?"

"He wasn't bragging. He said he was breaking it off, wasn't going to see her anymore. He promised me."

She averted her eyes. She had obviously been involved with Louis Hubler too.

"That's right," she said, reading my thoughts, "Louis and I were going out. It got pretty serious. At least I thought it was, until I found out about Ladington's wife. God, guys can be so stupid, falling for some bleached-blonde bimbo because she wears clothes cut down to here and lots of lipstick. What a jerk he was. Look what it got him." She lifted a trembling hand and smoothed her hair.

"Yes," I said sadly. "Why did *you* leave the restaurant?"

"To get away. If Ladington knew that I knew about his wife and Louis, he'd come after me, too."

"After you too? Are you saying Ladington murdered Hubler?"

"It's obvious, isn't it? He killed Louis because he was climbing under the covers with his wife. Doesn't take a rocket scientist to figure that out."

If Louis had, indeed, broken off the affair with Tennessee, I thought, she too might have had reason to kill him, either because her heart was broken—unlikely—or because he'd threatened to tell her husband about her sexual dalliance.

"You can't be afraid of Bill Ladington anymore," I said. "He's dead."

"Not him personally," she replied. "He's dead, and I couldn't care less about that. But there're the others."

"Who?"

"Everybody, including that bitch Tennessee, his stupid son, that thug Raoul who drove him everywhere. Don't think I'm paranoid. But I am smart enough to know that knowing too much about Bill Ladington can get you killed. I used to work in the spas up here in Calistoga, and got back as fast as I could after Louis was killed. Satisfied? Do you want the rest of the treatment? Massage?"

"No."

She retrieved my clothes and handed them to me.

"Know what I'm going to do?" she said.

"What?"

"Calistoga isn't far enough away. I'm getting out of here, maybe Hawaii, Russia, someplace at the opposite end of the earth."

"Did Louis use drugs?" I asked.

"Why don't you just get out of here," she said. "And don't bother coming back. I won't be here."

Chapter Nineteen

I stepped into the fresh air and said a little prayer of thanks for being out of that infernal cauldron called a mud bath. Maybe it would have been therapeutic if a slightly deranged young woman hadn't decided to turn me into a french fry. But for me, it would be one of those first-time experiences never to be repeated.

I looked down the road toward the center of town, which wasn't more than a quarter of a mile away. The silver Taurus was gone, as I expected it would be. I looked at my watch. I'd been in the spa for an hour, thirty minutes less than I'd told George. Nothing to do, I decided, but to walk into town and look for him.

I checked cars parked along the curb and eventually spotted ours in front of an art gallery. I entered. No George. I eventually found him in another gallery specializing in local contemporary artists. He was admiring a particular painting, head cocked, eyes half narrowed, when I walked up to him.

"Nice," I said.

He turned and his eyes widened. "Good Lord, Jessica, what happened to you?"

"Do I look that bad?"

"Like a lobster just out of boiling water."

"I had a mud bath."

"I know that, but you didn't say the purpose was to sauté you."

"Frankly, I thought it was going to end up even worse."

"Does it hurt? Like a sunburn?"

"A little. Unless you're seriously considering buying that painting, I suggest we leave."

The gallery owner, a stout woman wearing a floor-length black dress and multiple gold chains around her neck, intercepted us. "If you'd like to buy that painting today, I can give you a substantial discount. The artist is ill and needs the money."

"Thank you, no," George said, ushering me out of the gallery. When we were on the sidewalk, he said, "I heard her give that line to another browser about a different painting. The going-out-of-business approach."

We got in the car. George started the engine, turned and asked, "Care to tell me what happened at the spa?"

"Every minute detail of it. Oh, look, there's Neil Schwartz coming out of that restaurant." He was heading on foot in our direction.

"Your writer friend?"

"Yes."

When Neil was almost abreast of the car, I lowered my window and called his name. He stopped, leaned forward to see who it was, broke into a grin, and came to me. "Jessica," he said enthusiastically. "What are you doing here?"

"I took a mud bath."

"Really? Where?"

"Hampton Spa. Neil, this is George Sutherland."

"Heard lots about you," he said to George. "Jessica, I need to talk to you. Hey, you look funny."

"Thank you."

"No, I mean, sort of—sort of red. Is that from the mud bath?"

"Yes. Very unpleasant. The young woman at the spa raised the temperature to almost the boiling point."

"Deliberately?" George exclaimed.

"Yes, deliberately. George, maybe we'd better skip the tram ride and find a quiet place where we can talk."

"Follow me," Neil said, taking off in the direction of his car, a champagne-colored Lexus.

"I'd say your friend does quite well," George said as we fell in behind the Lexus.

"I'm so pleased for him. He's always struggled. He was a New York City police officer, you know. Retired from the force and moved to Cabot Cove. His financial picture seems to have improved dramatically, although I can't imagine one magazine piece doing it. But I'm out of touch with magazines and what they pay."

"I didn't realize magazines paid that well, either. Chaps I know who write for magazines for a living are always complaining about low rates."

Fifteen minutes later we'd pulled into a parking lot for a restaurant and bar on the outskirts of St. Helena. It was three o'clock; the parking lot was empty. Inside, the cleanup from lunch was underway, and tables were being set for the dinner crowd. A rosy-cheeked young man stood behind the bar washing glasses and squeezing lemons.

"Are you serving?" Neil asked.

"Yes," the bartender replied.

We took a table in a far corner of the bar area and were served frosty mugs of draft beer.

"Seems like sacrilege ordering beer in wine country," George said, raising his mug. "Cheers!"

After George and Neil exchanged getting-to-know-you pleasantries, Neil and I looked at each other. "You first," he said.

"I haven't gotten very far," I said. "George and I went to Ladington's restaurant. A waitress told us about another waitress who used to work there, Mary Jane Proll."

"You found her?" Neil asked.

"Yes. At Hampton Spa. Do you know who she is?"

"I heard something about her."

"Didn't people at the restaurant mention her to you?" I asked. "I assume you've interviewed everyone there for your article."

"Her name did come up, just in passing. Go on. What did she tell you?"

"Well, I signed up for a mud bath, figuring if I had her one-on-one, I could get her to open up. But when I started asking questions—I was in the mud bath at the time, captive in it is more apt—she became upset and raised the temperature on me."

"You might have died," George said.

"That crossed my mind."

"What did she tell you?" Neil repeated.

"Not very much. She's afraid of Bill Ladington. Or was. She thinks he killed the waiter, Louis Hubler."

"What does she base it on?" Neil asked.

"Supposition. Nothing more than that. She'd dated Hubler."

"She said that?"

"Yes."

I sat back and pretended to be enjoying my beer. What I was really doing was taking a break from the conversation to decide how much to share with Neil. On the one hand, I wanted to be helpful to him for his article. On the other hand, George and I had been drawn into the situation at the behest of Bill Ladington's son, and it was obvious that neither he nor any other member of the household wanted to cooperate with the press.

"What's going on inside the castle?" Neil asked. "I called this morning and asked for an interview. My ear still hurts from the hang up."

"They're not interested in talking to reporters," I said,

"Fine," said Neil, "but you're on the inside. What's going on there? I've been talking with people, regular folks, in St. Helena. They laugh about the story that Ladington killed himself. Got to be murder, is what they tell me. What does his family say?"

George sensed my discomfort and answered for me. "Obviously, Jessica is in an awkward position. We're houseguests at the castle and—"

Neil regarded me with disappointed eyes. "Look, Jessica, if you don't want to help me, that's okay. I mean, I just thought that because we go back a long way as friends, and are both writers, that you'd, well, that you'd be happy to share things with me."

"You're right, Neil, absolutely right. It's just that—"

"Maybe I'd better be going," Neil said, motioning to the bartender that he wanted the check.

I made up my mind to help him. There really wasn't any ethical or moral reason not to.

"We're at the castle because Ladington's son, Bruce, came to Cedar Gables the morning after his father died and asked me to come. He's adamant that his father didn't commit suicide, although he doesn't have anything to prove it. I tend to agree with him only because my brief time spent with Bill Ladington said to me that this was not a man who would take his own life. George doesn't buy the suicide scenario either, based upon Ladington's actions the night he died."

George explained to Neil the incongruity of Ladington swallowing a bottle of pills at his desk and then going outside to die.

"Doesn't make sense to me, either," Neil said. "Who's the most likely suspect?"

I shrugged. "They're all unusual people, and one gets the distinct feeling that few of them liked William Ladington. But whether their dislike went deep enough to prompt killing him remains to be seen."

"What about this Mary Jane character?" he asked. "Is she linked in some way to Ladington's death?"

"I can't imagine how," I said. I told him about Mary Jane Proll's accusation that the murdered waiter, Louis Hubler, had been having an affair with Tennessee Ladington.

Neil made a note in his reporter's spiral-bound notebook. "That would give Ladington a motive for killing the kid. His wife, too, if Hubler was breaking off the relationship."

"Exactly," George said.

"Let's not forget Ms. Proll," I said. "She was evidently in love with Hubler, and he'd been cheating on her. A woman scorned. And, I might add, she's a very strong young woman with a streak of cruelty in her."

Neil nodded and sat back in his chair. He said, more to himself than to us, "Damn, I wish I could get inside that castle with you." He came forward again. "Any chance of my arriving with you as an old friend, Johnny Jones or Willy Smith?"

"I'd be uncomfortable perpetrating a falsehood," I said. "I think the best you can expect is to benefit from what we observe. Sorry."

"Nothing to be sorry about, Jess," Neil said. "I understand. I really do. Getting the inside scoop from you will be enough help." To George he said, "Not much of a holiday for you, huh, trying to figure out a murder?"

George smiled as he took his pipe from his pocket and lit it.

"Sorry, no smoking," the bartender announced from behind the bar.

"Not even in a bar?" George asked.

"California law," the bartender said. "No smoking in any restaurant or bar."

"An uncivilized practice," George muttered, tamping the tobacco to extinguish it.

"I did manage to get a hold of the sheriff who's handling Ladington's death and the Hubler murder," Neil said.

"Sheriff Davis," George said.

"Right. Nice enough guy, only he wouldn't tell me much. Said he wasn't able to discuss an ongoing investigation. It's what they all say. Have you met him?"

"As a matter of fact, we have," replied George. "He didn't seem especially keen on my being at the castle."

"Professional jealousy?" Neil said.

"I wouldn't know," George said.

"We should be heading back," I said. "We'll take the aerial tram ride another time. What are you up to for the rest of the day, Neil?"

"I thought I'd swing by one of the local newspapers, see if I can pick up any scuttlebutt from reporters who've been following things."

"Try Winston Wallace," I said.

"Who's he?"

"A local reporter. He did a piece about my coming to Napa and staying with Craig and Margaret at Cedar Gables. I'm surprised I remember his name."

"What paper?" Neil asked.

"That I don't remember," I said. "I can call Margaret and find out."

"Great." Neil handed me his cell phone.

Margaret or Craig wasn't there, but Barbara answered my question.

"The *Napa News*," I told Neil, handing him back his phone. "Should have been easy to remember. It's a weekly. Margaret Snasdell is a friend of the reporter."

"I'll look him up," Neil said. "What else have you learned about the waiter's murder?"

"Nothing, except that drugs might have been involved."

Neil frowned, and paused before saying, "I've heard that, too. What are they saying? About drugs, I mean."

"Actually, Bill Ladington was the one who brought it up."

"Ladington himself, huh? What did *he* say?"

"Just that there were rumors. I don't think he knew anything for certain. Are you staying in the area, or going back to Sausalito?"

"Staying here. A motel in Napa. Nothing fancy but it's all I need." He handed me a business card from the motel.

"I'll call," I said. "Better that you not try to reach us at the castle."

"Fair enough."

We parted in the parking lot and drove off in separate directions.

"Think I'm making a mistake in confiding in him, George?" I asked.

"Not at all. He seems like a trustworthy chap. Besides, he's liable to dredge up something around the valley that we'll miss by being at the castle. What's our next step?"

"See if we can get answers to that growing list of questions. I think it's time we got to know our hosts a little better."

Chapter Twenty

The drawbridge was up when we arrived and we had to call on the intercom to have it lowered. Standing on the castle side was Wade Grosso. He wore his usual high rubber boots, coveralls, and a broad-brimmed straw hat. He watched us get out of the car, and was about to turn and walk away when I called to him.

"Yes?" he said.

"I was wondering whether we could steal a few minutes of your time, Mr. Grosso."

I couldn't tell from his expression whether my request annoyed him, or if he didn't care one way or the other.

"What do you need?" he asked.

"We were wondering exactly where Mr. Ladington's body was found in the moat the night he died," I said.

"Why?"

"Pardon?"

"Why would you want to know that?"

"Just curious," I said.

"Bull! You and your limey friend here want to make it look as though Ladington was murdered instead of taking his own life. Isn't that right?"

"No, it isn't right. Bruce Ladington has asked us to learn the truth. We want to know what really happened that night. If he committed suicide, fine. Don't you want to know what happened to him, what *really* happened?"

"All I want to know, Mrs. Fletcher, is that he's dead. That's good enough for me."

"You sound pleased that he's dead," George said.

"Doesn't matter to me one way or the other. If that lily-livered, weak-kneed son of his hadn't brought you here, the whole thing would be over and we could get on with the business of making wine. But no, Mr. Bruce Ladington has to make a stink about what seems perfectly obvious to me, that the old bastard decided he'd had enough of his family and packed it in, checked out, said adios. As far as I'm concerned, if I had to put up with these people, I'd swallow pills too."

"Doesn't anyone like anybody around here?" George asked.

His question brought a smile to Grosso's lips. "Not much," he said, breaking into what passed for a laugh. "You want to see where Ladington ended up? Come on. I'll show you."

We followed him around to the side of the castle. Grosso stopped, went to the edge of the moat, and peered down into it. "Right there," he said, pointing.

We stood next to him and looked down.

"A secluded area of the property," George said.

"No more so than most," Grosso said.

"You have lights out front," George said, "illuminating the moat. I don't see any lights here."

"You're right," said Grosso. "It gets pretty dark on this side."

"Those are nasty looking rocks," I said.

"Did Mr. Ladington often come out here at night?" George asked.

Grosso shrugged and screwed up his face. "Not so I can recall."

"The assumption is that he took the pills, left the house,

came here, felt the effect of the pills, and fell into the moat," George said.

"That's what they say," said Grosso.

I hesitated before asking, "Did you see him come out of the house that night, Mr. Grosso?"

His broad face turned hard. "Are you asking whether I might have pushed him into the water?"

"No. I just thought—"

"You want to know who killed him—*if* he was killed and didn't do it himself? Just take a look over there." He pointed to the neighboring vineyard, the one owned by Bob Jenkins. "Bad blood between them, Bill and Jenkins. They've been fighting over rights to Halton Mountain ever since Bill bought this place. Damn near shot each other a few times."

"Is the mountain really that important?" George asked.

Grosso guffawed. "You'd better damn well believe it is," he said. "You plant the right vines on that mountain and you'll one day produce the best cabernet in the world. I've been in this business all my life, started as a kid working for my father. He was a pretty good wine maker but didn't have the gumption to go out on his own. Always working for somebody else, like me. I've worked for a lot of people in this valley, some good, most bad. You get people with money who think that's all they need to make good wine. You tell 'em how to do it and what they need, but all their goddamn money clouds their brains. They know it all. So they end up producing second-rate wine, only they think it's great because their taste buds are in their bank accounts. Halton Mountain? Important? It's the best piece of grape-growing land in all of California."

"Was Mr. Ladington one of those people with money who thought he knew more than he did?" I asked.

"Bill? No. That crazy bastard—pardon my French—he loved the idea of making fine wine, and he listened to me.

Well, most of the time. It was like he found religion when he bought this place, put all his crazy past behind and decided to make this winery work. Of course, he never did get over his love of the ladies. Married that piece 'a work, Tennessee, because she made him feel like a kid again. Women can do that to you—if you let 'em. There were lots of things I didn't like about Mr. Bill Ladington, but I respected him when it came to this vineyard and what he wanted it to be. You can respect a man and hate his guts at the same time."

"Is it possible that Mr. Jenkins was here the night Mr. Ladington died?" George asked.

"Sure it is. Jenkins was always sneakin' over here to see what we were doing with our vines and the wine. Wouldn't be surprised if he was in cahoots with our French friend, Saison."

"I thought she and Bill Ladington were partners," I said.

"Doesn't mean anything with that lady. Stab you in the back as soon as look at you. We've had lots of Frenchmen come through the valley, their noses up in the air, thinkin' they're the only ones who know how to make wine. Truth is, they come here to learn from us. Saison's no different, except she's a woman. Bill had his blinders on when he met her, fell for her so-called French female charms. Wouldn't have happened if she'd been a man. Excuse me, I've got things to attend to."

George and I watched him lumber off, shoulders back, a swagger to his gait because he'd set us straight.

"Surly chap," George said, lighting his pipe.

"A proud man, like his boss. As he said, he had respect for Bill Ladington."

"And hated his guts, as he also said."

I looked down into the moat where Bill Ladington's body had been found and felt a chill, and wrapped my arms about myself. "Feel like a walk?" I asked.

"Sure you don't want to go inside? You're cold."

"More psychological than temperature," I said.

We strolled along the moat to the rear of the castle and stepped up onto the expansive patio overlooking the vineyards beyond the moat. The footbridge was down, but no security guard was on duty.

"It's beautiful, isn't it?" I said. "Not only the land, the idea that those millions of vines all over the valley will, if handled with care, become fine wine."

"It takes a certain type of person, I'm sure, to coddle grapes through the wine-making process. A very patient person."

"Or an incurable romantic like William Ladington."

I looked over to the neighboring vineyard owned by Robert Jenkins, then to Halton Mountain. "If that mountain is as valuable as everybody says it is, I imagine people would kill for it."

"Wouldn't be very neighborly."

"Neighbors have killed neighbors for lesser reasons—a barking dog, a fence that's too tall."

George drew on his pipe, squinted, and said, "Isn't that Bruce's wife?"

"Yes, it is."

Laura Ladington stood alone at the far end of the vineyard. She appeared to be slightly bent over; a hand held one of the stakes.

"Shall we say hello?" I suggested.

We crossed the footbridge and slowly made our way between the long rows of stakes until we were within fifty feet of her. She sensed our presence and turned quickly, like a feral animal startled by a predator.

"Hello, Laura," I said pleasantly, advancing toward her.

She straightened, then seemed to fold within herself as though she lost air. Her frightened eyes were open wide. She started to say something but turned away.

"It's so peaceful out here," I said.

"Yes," she said in a voice carried away on a breeze that ruffled her hair. She wore a shapeless knee-length dress as gray as her mood, and sandals.

"Is Bruce back at the house?" I asked, trying to make conversation but concerned that the wrong topic would send her scurrying away.

"Yes."

"We took a ride today," I said. "Just to get away for a few hours."

"That's nice," she said.

"You should do the same," George said.

"I don't drive."

"I don't either," I said, laughing. "But I can fly a plane."

"You can?"

"Yes. I learned last year in my hometown. Cabot Cove. It's in Maine. Have you ever been to Maine?"

"No."

Her pain surrounded her like a visible aura.

"Would you like to come with us when we take another ride?" I asked. "We're planning to go to some of the other vineyards. They have an aerial tram at Sterling Vineyards, and I'm dying to take a hot air balloon ride."

"I don't think so, but thank you for asking. I'd better get back. Bruce will be looking for me."

"The offer still holds," I said. "We'd love to have you join us."

She walked away.

"Pathetic creature, isn't she?" George said as we watched her navigate the trellises on her way to the castle.

"Breaks my heart," I said. "Do you get the feeling that if she could open up, she'd have a lot to tell us about Ladington's death?"

"It's been my experience that it's the quiet, withdrawn

members of a family who know the most. She must be carrying a very heavy burden."

"As well as carrying a child," I said.

He looked at me. "She's in the wey?"

"I said I think she's pregnant."

"So did I. 'In the wey'—Scottish for being with child."

"Oh. She wears those baggy dresses and dusters, but that slight bulge tells me she's in the early stages of a pregnancy."

"A blessed event for Mr. Bruce Ladington."

"I'd like another, longer conversation with her."

"And I'm sure you'll arrange it. Ready to go back and face the other inmates at the asylum?"

I chuckled. "I hadn't thought of it that way, but the description does seem to fit. Yes, I'm ready to go back. Let's not forget we have our meeting with the sheriff in the morning."

"I'm looking forward to it," he said. "I find myself looking forward to anything except these people Mr. Ladington left behind."

"Don't make me feel guilty for bringing you into this. We can always leave."

"Oh, no, Jessica. Now that I'm in, I'm in all the way and for the duration. I just hope we resolve this before we must leave to get back to our regular lives."

He took my hand, squeezed it, and grinned. "I should consider moving closer to you," he said. "Spending time with Jessica Fletcher is infinitely more interesting than chasing British serial killers and mad-dog rapists."

"I'm not sure that's a compliment," I said, laughing as I led him across the drawbridge.

"Oh, it is, Jessica. It certainly is."

Chapter Twenty-one

Edith Saison and a man we hadn't seen before greeted us as we entered the castle.

"Mrs. Fletcher," she said, "I'd like you to meet Yves LeGrand."

"Did you have a pleasant flight?" George asked after we'd exchanged greetings.

"As pleasant as airline travel can be these days," he replied.

"You should try Virgin Atlantic," George said. "Very much the way air travel used to be."

LeGrand pointedly ignored George's pitch for the British airline by rolling his eyes and wrinkling his nose. He was a distinguished-looking gentleman whose French accent matched Edith's. He was tall and reed-thin, his double-breasted blue blazer cut to mold his upper body; his gray slacks had a razor crease. I assumed he'd changed upon arriving; you couldn't get off a long flight looking that good. He wore a white silk shirt open at the collar, and a red-and-blue ascot. His deep tan looked permanent.

"Yves and I are partners in our vineyard in France," Edith said. "As you know, we became partners with Bill."

"So he told me," I replied. "You were bringing some special vines to graft onto his native rootstock."

"Shoots," Yves corrected. "They're called shoots."

"I'm afraid I'm not especially well versed in grape growing and wine making," I said.

"But well versed in many other things, I'm sure," said Yves, charmingly.

"Bill obviously told you a great deal about our partnership before he died," Edith said.

"You asked me that once before," I said. "No, he had very little to say, just that he was excited about the potential of the wine you were planning to develop together."

"Exactly," Edith said. "It was his enthusiasm that promised to make the partnership work. That, and the superior cuttings we've brought with us. I'm sure he indicated to you that he wanted his work to go forward even after he died."

It sounded to me as though she was trying to line me up as a witness on her behalf. If so, she was due for a disappointment.

"Have you started grafting your shoots to the Ladington rootstock?" George asked.

"Oh, no," Edith said, becoming animated. "That won't happen until the question of ownership is resolved."

"Ownership of Ladington Creek?" I asked.

She became conspiratorial as she whispered, "Of course. Our agreement was finalized in Curaçao. We both own houses there."

"So I understand."

"If that dreadful woman, Tennessee, insists upon claiming rights to this vineyard, there will never be a superior cabernet from it."

"She *is* the widow," George said.

"Under fraudulent circumstances!"

"It was a pleasure meeting you, Mr. LeGrand," I said. "I'm sure we'll be seeing more of each other."

"The pleasure was mine, Mrs. Fletcher."

"A grotty couple if I ever saw one," George muttered after they'd walked away.

"Grotty?"

"British slang for shabby."

We'd reached the door to Bill Ladington's study when the door opened and Bruce and Laura stepped into the hallway.

"Hi," Bruce said. "Have a nice day?"

"Yes, quite," George said. "You?"

"So-so," Bruce replied.

"I meant to ask you when we were outside, Laura, about your migraine," I said. "Are you feeling better?"

"Yes, much better," she said, wandering down the hall.

"That's good to hear," I called after her.

"See you at dinner?" Bruce asked.

"Yes." I put a hand on Bruce's sleeve to detain him. "While I'm thinking of it, was there a glass found on your father's desk the night he died?"

"Glass? No. At least I don't think there was. Why?"

"We were wondering how—if he committed suicide—he washed down the pills," George said. "I understand he was a big man. Must have needed to take a lot of them to kill a man his size."

"A glass? No. There wasn't a glass. But I see what you're getting at," Bruce said, animatedly. "If there was no glass, then there was no suicide."

"Perhaps he took the pills in the small bathroom off his study," George offered. "You know, drank water in there, then brought the empty bottle back to his desk."

"But he didn't commit suicide," Bruce said. "That's the whole point."

George grunted.

"You're right," Bruce said, "about the glass. I'm really glad you two are here. I never would have thought of it. See you at dinner." He followed his wife down the hall.

I looked through the open door into the study, motioned for George to follow, and we entered the room, closing the door behind us. I went to the small bath off the study and looked inside. It was as neat as the proverbial pin. There was a stall shower, sink, and toilet. On the sink's countertop were two glasses. One held a toothbrush and small tube of toothpaste. The other contained a comb and nail file. I looked for a paper cup holder or glass for drinking. There wasn't any.

When I returned to the study, George had removed a book from the shelves and was perusing it. I came to his side and saw that it was a guide to pharmaceuticals.

"Looking for what pills Ladington was supposed to have taken?" I asked.

"As a matter of fact, yes. I thought there might be a page turned down, or something highlighted."

"And?"

"Nothing."

He continued leafing through the book while I went behind the desk and sat in the leather chair. "Ladington was a neat man," I said absently.

He agreed.

"I somehow think of men his size as not being fastidious," I said.

"An erroneous assumption."

"Yes."

"Inconceivable to me that a man of Ladington's business success and wealth wouldn't have an updated will."

"At least not one that anyone knows about."

I ran my hand over the surface of the desk. It was highly polished; I could see my reflection as I leaned over it.

"Hardly the sort of man to be content with having his body found in a moat," George said.

Bruce Ladington interrupted our musings. "I'm glad you're still here," he said, lowering his voice and coming close to us. "I thought you might be interested in knowing that Tennessee threatened Dad on more than one occasion."

"Physical threats?" George asked.

"Yes. I saw her point a gun at him once."

"Obviously she didn't pull the trigger," George said.

"No, but she wanted to."

"How long ago did that happen?" I asked.

"It happened more than once," Bruce said. "The last time was about a month ago. She's got a mean streak in her, Mrs. Fletcher, a real mean streak. She wanted Dad dead so she could have this place all for herself."

"What about the French couple?" George asked. "They seem to think they'll be getting the winery by virtue of their business relationship with your father."

"And they'd gladly kill to get it," he said. "I don't trust them any more than I trust Tennessee."

"Mr. LeGrand wasn't here when your father died," I said. "He couldn't have killed him."

"But Edith could have. Dad and Edith were fighting over the partnership the night she arrived. I heard her tell him that if he didn't give in, she'd see to it that he didn't live to enjoy the superior cabernet she intended to produce here on Halton Mountain."

"What were they fighting about?" I asked.

Bruce shrugged. "I don't know. Like I told you before, Dad didn't ring me in on his business dealings."

"But you did hear her threaten him."

"Yes. She got loud at that point."

"Such threats seldom progress to murder," George said. "Do you know why your father had this book, Bruce? It was on the shelf here in the midst of books on making wine. Out of order, it would seem." He showed the pharmaceutical guide to him.

"No," Bruce said. "I never saw that book before. Are

you—I mean, are you thinking that because he had such a book he probably did take his own life?"

"I'm thinking nothing of the sort," George said. "Just curious."

"Well, if you are thinking along those lines, you can just forget it. I just thought you'd want to know about the threats to Dad's life. Somebody in this house killed him. That's why I asked you here, to prove that."

"I thought you asked us here to ascertain the truth," I said.

"Well, sure," he said. "Of course. But the truth is that my father was murdered."

He abruptly left the room.

"I have a suggestion, Jessica."

"Yes?"

"I don't think we're going to learn anything useful until we meet with the sheriff in the morning and get some indication of what the autopsy reveals. In the meantime, why don't we put aside any thoughts of how Mr. William Ladington died and simply enjoy ourselves for the rest of the evening?"

I couldn't stifle a laugh. "Do you think that's possible?" I said. "Enjoy ourselves here?"

"Of course it is," he said with bravado. "All we have to do is—"

My sudden and involuntary gasp cut him off.

"What is it?" he asked. "What's wrong?"

"There was someone at the window looking in at us. I think it was—no, I'm sure it was Raoul, the driver."

George went to the window and peered out. "Well, he's gone now," he said, closing the gap in the drapes.

I shivered. "Raoul makes me nervous."

"Oh? He seems like a harmless enough chap to me."

"There's something in his eyes. Lots of anger bottled up. I have a sudden need for a nap."

"Splendid idea. Make us feel as though we're on vacation."

But as I lay awake in my bed, I didn't feel at all like someone on a holiday.

I was gripped with a sudden anger and resolve. Until that moment, I'd been ambivalent about being involved in William Ladington's death. Bruce had been persuasive in his zeal to learn the truth about how his father had died, and I wanted to help him reach some sort of closure. But now, I was the one who wanted to get to the truth, for my own sake. Someone at the winery was a murderer, and whoever that person was couldn't possibly be happy having us snooping around trying to prove it.

Chapter Twenty-two

"Did you enjoy your day?" Roger Stockdale asked George and me after we'd been seated for dinner.

"Yes," I said. "An interesting day. Wasn't it, George?"

"Yes, quite interesting."

"What did you do?" Tennessee asked.

"Oh, we drove around, had a pleasant lunch," I said. "We ate at Ladington's Steak House."

"Really?" said Tennessee. "What caused you to go there?"

"We just happened on it," George said. "The chicken salad was very good."

"I can't bear to go near it after that waiter was killed," Tennessee said.

If she had, in fact, engaged in an affair with Louis Hubler, her demeanor and words didn't reflect it.

"I can certainly understand that," I said. "Did you know him?"

"I knew who he was. Bill managed affairs there."

Interesting choice of words, I thought.

"I seldom went there," she added. "Why he had to have a restaurant is beyond me. Ego, I suppose. Something else with his name on it."

"I was glad when he opened it," Bruce said from across the table. "We really like going there, don't we, Laura?"

"What did you, a vegetarian, ever find to eat?" Wade Grosso asked Laura. "Hardly your sort of menu."

"I did fine," she replied.

"Nothing but a bottom-line loser," Stockdale said. "Bill didn't know anything about running a restaurant. It lost money from the day it opened."

I observed Tennessee throughout the conversation because I wanted to gauge her reaction to our having gone there for lunch. Her expression didn't change, no sign of anger or concern. The lady was cool.

"What else did you do?" she asked.

"I had a mud bath," I said, laughing. "In Calistoga. Have you ever had one?"

She ignored my question by asking her own: "Which spa did you go to?"

"The Hampton."

I didn't know whether Tennessee knew the waitress, Mary Jane Proll. If she did, was she aware of the romantic link between Mary Jane and Hubler? I decided to find out.

"My attendant at the spa used to work as a waitress at Ladington's Steak House," I said. "Mary Jane Proll."

Tennessee didn't have a visible reaction to my mention of the name. But Roger Stockdale did.

"I know her," he said. "She waited on me when I went to the place. You say she's working at a Calistoga spa?"

"Yes."

"Was it a coincidence you ended up having her as your attendant?" he asked.

I wasn't sure whether to be truthful or not. I decided to be. "Actually," I said, "we sought her out."

For the first time, Tennessee's deportment changed. Her lips became thin and her eyes bored holes in me. "Why, might I ask, did you seek her out?"

"We were told by someone else at the restaurant that your husband and the dead waiter might have had problems between them. I wanted to see what that was about."

Stockdale picked up on Tennessee's mood shift. "Don't

you think you're out of bounds, Mrs. Fletcher?" he said, trying unsuccessfully to maintain a well-modulated voice. "You're invited guests, no matter what your reason for having come here. A man—a *great* man, I might add—is dead. There is a vineyard to run, and a lot of legal issues to resolve. Having you chasing after waitresses who used to work for Bill is an intrusion into what are distinctly private matters." To further make his point, he stood and walked with conviction from the room.

Wade Grosso ignored Stockdale's sudden departure and asked Tennessee, "Anything new on the autopsy and funeral plans?"

"No," she responded. "I'm meeting with the lawyers in the morning."

Edith Saison and Yves LeGrand looked at each other as though trying to determine who should speak. Edith got the nod.

"Speaking of lawyers, Mrs. Ladington," she said in a measured voice, "Yves and I have retained our own counsel here in California. You'll be hearing from him."

"Is that so?"

"Yes. It's become obvious to us that you don't intend to honor our partnership agreement with Bill."

"You bet I don't," Tennessee said.

"Why don't you talk about this another time?" Bruce suggested, weakness in his voice indicating he wasn't sure he should be saying it.

"I'll discuss what I want, when I want to," Tennessee snapped at him.

Consuela and Fidel's timing was good as they entered the room carrying our dinner on trays—grilled salmon, steamed vegetables, and a simple salad with oil-and-vinegar dressing. Obviously, Bill Ladington's passing had resulted in a different approach to menu planning. Light was in, fat was out.

Silence fell over the room as everyone started eating. Stockdale returned and took his seat without saying anything.

"Mrs. Fletcher and George are meeting with Sheriff Davis in the morning," Bruce said.

The lifting of forks to mouths stopped. Tennessee spoke.

"I have been extremely patient," she said, looking directly at George and me. "I've allowed you into my home because Bill had asked you to come here before he took his life, and because his son, my stepson, wanted you here. But I now find the intrusion to be a burden. I do not need either of you speaking with our law enforcement officers about Bill's unfortunate demise. I'm well aware that you are a famous mystery writer, Mrs. Fletcher, and that you work for Scotland Yard, Mr. Sutherland. But you have no official capacity where Bill's death is concerned, and I insist you stop poking your noses into what are family matters."

George spoke. "As Mrs. Fletcher said at a previous dinner, Mrs. Ladington, we will be happy to leave. You're right. We have no official reason for being here." He stood and added, "Frankly, Mrs. Ladington, I find you and your family and friends to be insufferable." He looked down at me. "Come, Jessica. I need some air."

As George led me from the dining room, Bruce followed.

"Please don't leave," he said as we headed down the main hallway to the front door. "The hell with them."

"We didn't come here to be insulted," George said. "Their behavior is deplorable."

"I know, I know," Bruce said as we reached the door and opened it. It was a dull night, with low gray clouds obscuring the moon and stars; mist in the air filtered the light from outside fixtures mounted high on steel stanchions.

"I'm going back and straighten them out," Bruce said.

We ignored him and stepped outside, the mist moistening our faces as though we were sprayed with an atomizer.

"I'm sorry," I said.

"Nothing to be sorry about. I know one thing."

"What's that?"

"If one of them is a murderer, I'd like to be the one to hang him."

"Him?"

"Or her."

We walked slowly along the edge of the moat, heading toward where Ladington's body had been found. George lit his pipe; the smoke thickened the mist and swirled around our heads. The grass was wet and glistened in the artificial light, until we turned the corner of the castle and were in darkness. We reached the place we'd examined earlier. The grass in that area was matted and scuffed from the activity of pulling Ladington from the moat, and any police investigation that had taken place. The steady drone of the hundreds of windmills across the valley was like a one-note Gregorian chant.

"He stood right here," George muttered.

"It doesn't matter," I said. "Let's go back inside, get our things and—"

It happened so suddenly my reaction was delayed. One moment I was standing next to George, the next moment he was gone. The earth at the moat's edge had given way beneath his weight. He'd slid straight down into the moat, his pipe flying into the air, a garbled, involuntary groan trailing behind him.

"George!" I yelled. I took a step closer to the edge, realized that I, too, might slip, stepped back but leaned forward. Although there was virtually no light, I saw him looking up at me from ten feet below. He appeared to be standing.

"George, are you all right?"

His response was another groan, longer and sustained this time.

My concern was the water in the moat. At the moment, because he was standing, he didn't seem to be in danger of drowning. From what I could see, the water was up to his thighs. But what if he collapsed, keeled over, went under?

"I'll get help," I said. I ran to the front of the castle, tried the door, opened it, and burst inside. I ran down the hall, and went to the dining room where everyone was standing and yelling at each other.

"I need help," I shouted.

"What's the matter?" Stockdale asked.

"George has fallen into the moat."

"He *what*?" Grosso said.

"He's in the moat. Please, come quick. We have to get him out of there."

They followed me out of the castle to where George had fallen. Grosso had grabbed a flashlight on his way and trained its beam down into the moat. George's face was illuminated. He still stood there, the front of him pressed against the moat's wall.

"Get a rope," someone said. Raoul ran off, returning a minute later with a coil of stout clothesline.

"Are you hurt, George?" I asked.

"My back," he replied. Pain was evident in his voice.

"I'll lower you down," Grosso said to Raoul. "Bring him up."

My heart pounded and my throat went dry as I watched them prepare to bring George up from the water. Grosso tied one end of the rope around Raoul's waist. The winery's driver got to his knees, backed to the edge, and lowered his legs. Grosso held the other end with both hands. "Easy now," Grosso said. "Don't worry. I won't let you fall."

There was silence as Grosso lowered Raoul over the edge and down to where he stood next to George.

"How deep is it?" Bruce asked.

"Up to my hips," the shorter Raoul responded loudly.

"Put the rope around him," Grosso commanded.

Once Raoul had secured the rope about George's waist, Grosso asked, "Can you grab hold of the rope, Inspector?"

"Yes," George said, "but I don't think I can pull myself up."

"You won't have to," Grosso said. "We'll do all the pulling."

The vineyard manager turned to us. "Come on now, grab the rope and pull with me," he said, laughing. "Just like tug-of-war. Remember? Ready? Okay, here we go. One— two—three—*pull!*"

I winced as George's pained cry assaulted my ears, but I kept pulling along with the others. Although it seemed an endless process, he was up over the edge within a minute. He lay on his stomach on the wet grass, his body heaving from exertion and the pain he was experiencing. I knelt beside him. "We'll get you inside, onto a bed. You'll be fine."

My assumption at that moment was that we might need a stretcher of sorts to move him. To my relief, he turned onto his back and, with a hand from Grosso and Raoul, sat up, moaning as he did. I touched his trouser leg. It was wet from the water he'd been standing in.

"Maybe we should call an ambulance," I said.

Instead, again with help, George got to his feet. He was bent over from the spasms in his back, but other than that he didn't seem the worse for wear. I walked at his side as we went back inside the castle and up the stairs to his bedroom.

"You're lucky you didn't hit one of the rocks," I said.

"I know," he managed. "I need to stretch out. And get these wet pants off."

Bruce pulled George's shoes, socks, and trousers off and draped a sheet over him. Bruce, Laura, and I were the only ones in the room with him.

"Feeling better?" I asked.

"Yes, much, thanks. Clumsy fool is what I was. I shouldn't have gotten so close to the edge."

"It's a good thing the moat wasn't filled," Bruce said.

"That's for certain," I agreed. "George, do you think you should go to a hospital, get an X ray, have a doctor look at you?"

"No, no need for that, Jessica. I've had my back go out on me before, too many times as a matter of fact. Usually, a good night's sleep on a hard mattress, like this one, straightens everything out."

"I don't know," I said. "I really think—"

"I can take care of him," Laura said, surprising me. "I was going to be a nurse but—"

"Laura knows a lot about medicine," Bruce offered.

"I'm sure you do, Laura," I said. "But George seems to be all right, and I can tend to any needs he might have. Thank you for offering."

She nodded and left.

"Anything I can do?" Bruce asked.

"No, thank you," George responded.

"I told everybody to lay off you. I told them we're fortunate to have you as guests and to start treating you with respect."

"Thank you," I said, wondering whether anyone cared what Bruce wanted.

"Well, I'm glad you weren't hurt," Bruce said. "Bad, that is. I'll be going. Do you want Mercedes to bring you up some food? You didn't eat much at dinner."

"Thank you, no," I said. "We're just fine."

He backed from the room, wanting to stay but knowing it wasn't what we wanted. When he was gone, I sat on the edge of the bed and placed my hand on George's. "Are you okay?" I asked.

"No, but I will be by morning. Do you know what I was thinking, Jessica?"

"What?"

"While I was down in that damnable moat, I was thinking—no, wondering is more accurate—whether Ladington fell into the moat, or was pushed."

"A possibility," I said, "although the assumption is that whatever poison he ingested took effect and caused him to fall."

"Whatever poison," George said to no one in particular. "That assumption exists, Jessica, because an empty pill bottle and an alleged suicide note were found in his study. There hasn't been an autopsy finding as yet. Maybe he didn't ingest poison. Maybe he was simply pushed into the moat and died from impact with those rocks."

Mention of the huge bolders in the moat sent a chill down my spine. If George had fallen headfirst and . . . it was too grim to contemplate. "Maybe we'll find out more in the morning when we meet with Sheriff Davis," I said.

I went to the window and looked out. The mist had turned to a drizzle, slow but steady.

"Can I get you anything, George?"

"No, thank you, Jessica."

I looked at him. His eyes were closing.

"I'm going to go read," I said. "I think we both can use a good sleep." I came to the side of the bed, leaned over, and kissed his forehead. "See you at breakfast?" I asked.

"Absolutely," he said, grabbing my hand and squeezing it. "Eight o'clock?"

"In the dining room."

"In the dining room."

Chapter Twenty-three

The following morning, I waited until 8:10 before leaving the dining room, going upstairs, and knocking at George's door. His "come in" sounded pained.

He was dressed except for shoes. He was on the bed, his body twisted into a question mark.

"Your back," I said. "It's worse."

"Yes, damn it!" he replied without changing position. "It felt better when I got up. But while I was showering it tightened up again."

"I'm so sorry," I said. "We've got to get you to a doctor."

"Nothing they can do for it. I've been to doctors back home. They prescribe a muscle relaxant. I brought some with me, took two tablets this morning. It doesn't help. Rest. That's the only thing that helps."

"Then you must rest. We'll stay here at the castle today. You'll put your feet up, and I'll read a good book. I've brought several with me."

"No," he said, struggling to straighten out and propping himself up against the headboard. "You've got the meeting with Sheriff Davis this morning."

"That can wait. The important thing is you and your—"

"No, Jessica. I want you to keep that date with the sheriff."

"And leave you here alone? Absolutely not."

"I insist. Go see what the sheriff has to say. We've come

this far. I'd hate to drop the ball now. I'll be fine, waiting here for you to return. The young Mrs. Ladington offered to be of help should I need it, although I doubt if I will."

"All right," I said. "I'll bring you up some breakfast."

"Just something light. Juice, tea, a piece of Danish. Nothing with marmalade. Why the British love marmalade so much is a mystery to me."

I couldn't help but laugh. "No marmalade," I said.

I returned to the dining room where Bruce, his wife, Laura, and Roger Stockdale were having breakfast.

"Where's your friend?" Stockdale asked between forkfuls of scrambled eggs.

"Not feeling well," I said. "His back still hurts."

"I'm sorry to hear that," Bruce said. "Anything we can do?"

"Yes. Keep an eye on him. I'm off to meet with the sheriff. Actually, there are two things you can do for me. I'll need a ride to Sheriff Davis's office."

"I'm heading into town anyway," Stockdale said. "I'll be happy to drop you off."

"Thank you," I said. "And I wondered, Laura, whether you'd be good enough to check in on George now and then. I don't want to impose on your day but—"

"Of course," she said. "Don't worry about him."

"I won't, knowing he's in capable hands. Thanks."

Laura's response heartened me. It was the first spark of life I'd seen in her. Maybe she was one of those people who need to be needed and who rise to such an occasion. Regardless of why, I was comforted knowing someone would be tending to George while I was away.

I brought a tray to George's room, told him I'd be back as quickly as possible, and returned downstairs where Stockdale waited. We went to the front courtyard and got into the black BMW. Wade Grosso, who was digging up a tree that had died, lowered the drawbridge. I gave him a wave of thanks but he didn't return my gesture.

Stockdale was in a talkative, expansive mood as we drove to Napa.

"Sorry about George," he said. "A bad back can really cripple you. I've had a few bouts with a bad back myself."

"Fortunately, I never have," I said. "You seem to spend all your time at the winery. Do you have a family?"

"Had one. It ended in divorce. I was spending too much time on business and not enough time at home."

"That's always a difficult situation. Do you have children?"

"Two. My former wife raised them. I didn't argue. It was better for them."

I'd learned that he, Grosso, Raoul, and the household staff all lived at the castle. Obviously, working for William Ladington was an all-consuming occupation, not unusual when the boss is as powerful a personality and as demanding as Ladington had been. But I also knew that people who willingly put themselves in that position expected large rewards for their dedication. What was Stockdale's payoff? From what I could ascertain, he wasn't in line to inherit any part of the Ladington winery, nor was Raoul, or Grosso, or the serving staff.

Or were they?

According to Tennessee, her dead husband hadn't updated his will since divorcing his fourth wife. I had trouble accepting that. Men who've achieved significant financial success don't go through life without having put in place appropriate legal documents to ensure an orderly disposition of their assets.

Then again, a will doesn't have to be formally drawn. In many states, a handwritten letter suffices. When I was having my will drawn up years ago, I remember my Cabot Cove attorney mentioning that California was one of those states. If that was true, it was possible Ladington had made his wishes known in just such a letter. If he had, where was it, and who did he designate as beneficiaries of his years of work and success?

"You know, Mrs. Fletcher," Stockdale said, "all this talk about Bill being murdered is unnecessary."

"Oh?"

"It just muddies the waters. The fact is, he killed himself because he knew he was dying anyway."

"I wasn't aware of that," I said.

"Yeah. Cancer. He had a year at most."

"Who diagnosed it?"

"His doctor in Los Angeles."

"He didn't have a local physician here in Napa?"

"No. He and his L.A. doctor go back years."

"Is the doctor still in Los Angeles?"

"He sure is. Six feet under. He died."

How convenient, I thought.

"Was Bill Ladington given a written diagnosis concerning his cancer?"

"I don't think so. Bill confided in me soon after returning from Los Angeles. He wanted me to know because he'd promised that I'd receive a financial stake in Ladington Creek if he died."

I fell silent. I didn't want to challenge what he'd said because I didn't have anything upon which to base a challenge. At the same time, I had to wonder whether Ladington had, in fact, made such a verbal promise. Tennessee was claiming ownership of the winery by virtue of being Ladington's wife. Edith Saison and her partner, Yves LeGrand, said the winery belonged to them because of their partnership with Ladington. And there was Bruce.

"What was Bill's doctor's name?" I asked as Stockdale pulled up in front of the Napa sheriff's office.

"I forget," he replied, not at all convincingly.

"I'm sure his wife will know," I said, not wanting to let him off the hook so easily.

"Tennessee?" he said scornfully. "The only thing she knows is when her next hair and facial appointments are. Sorry to be so blunt, Mrs. Fletcher, but that's the truth. Here we are. How will you get back?"

"I'm sure I can arrange something," I said, opening the door.

"How come you don't drive?" he asked. "I thought everybody drove these days."

"Just never got around to it," I said. "Thanks for the ride. I'll see you later in the day."

I watched him drive off, then entered the building and told a uniformed officer at the desk who I was, and that I had an appointment with Sheriff Davis. He made a call. A minute later Davis entered the lobby. He was as casually dressed as when I'd first met him. This day he wore jeans, sneakers, a navy-blue T-shirt, and a tan safari jacket. The bulge of a handgun in a holster was visible through the jacket.

"Good morning," he said, smiling and extending a beefy hand. "Where's your buddy?"

"George hurt his back. He fell into the moat last night at Ladington Creek."

"How did that happen?"

"An accident. He got too close to the edge and the ground gave way beneath him."

"Not too serious I hope."

"No. He just needs a day or two of rest, flat on his back. I know you invited us to be here this morning because George is a Scotland Yard inspector. I hope you're not disappointed in just me showing up, a mystery writer."

"Of course not," he said. "It's a privilege to have someone of your stature, Mrs. Fletcher, as a guest of the department. Come on in my office and have a cup of coffee."

His office reminded me a little of our sheriff's office back in Cabot Cove. Sheriff Metzger, whom I count among my closest friends, didn't dress as casually as Sheriff Davis—he liked wearing an official uniform—but Mort's office reflected a laid-back approach to law enforcement.

Piles of file folders took up most of Davis's desktop; he had to clear some from a chair for me. A dozen photographs, presumably of family, and with a couple of posed shots of Davis with local politicians, hung crookedly on the walls.

"Coffee?" he asked, going to a half-filled pot on a file cabinet.

"Thank you, no," I said, not adding that I'm a bit of a coffee snob, not unlike wine snobs who insist upon certain standards. I'd convinced Mort Metzger to allow me to buy coffee for his office back home, and to teach him how to make a decent cup. He was a good sport about it, and the quality of his jailhouse brew had improved considerably. Before that, it was barely drinkable.

Davis took a seat behind his cluttered desk, propped his feet on its edge, flashed a wide grin, and said, "So, Mrs. Fletcher, you think Bill Ladington was murdered."

I returned his smile. "That's not the case," I said. "I haven't come to any conclusion."

His grin turned to a frown. "That's not what I hear from Bruce Ladington."

"If Bruce told you that, he's mistaken. George Sutherland and I came to Ladington Creek at Bruce's behest. He's convinced his father was murdered and asked us to help him prove it."

"Making any progress?"

"Some, although we're not leaning in any one direction. I'm counting on you to help me decide in which direction to lean. Has the autopsy been completed?"

"You like to get right to the point, huh?"

"I might as well. George and I aren't planning to stay until there's a resolution, but I'd like to have *some* answers before we leave."

"I can understand that. The autopsy. Yes, it's been completed, including a preliminary toxicology report."

I waited, eyebrows raised, for him to continue.

"Bill Ladington did ingest a poisonous substance."

"A prescription medicine?"

"Evidently not. It's some sort of bacterial poison that's found in certain species of fish."

"So unusual a substance that your local medical examiner can't identify it?"

"He's still doing research to be sure. In the meantime, tissue and blood samples have been sent to the state police lab in Sacramento."

"How long will it take that lab to confirm what it is?"

"I don't really know, Mrs. Fletcher. That's beyond my area of expertise."

I thought for a moment before asking, "Why are you sharing this with me? I mean, I appreciate it, Sheriff, but I'm wondering if you have a purpose behind it."

He grinned and lowered his feet to the floor. "I'm getting some pressure to resolve Ladington's death."

"Political pressure, I assume."

"That's right. Ladington was a pretty powerful force around here. He donated big sums to plenty of candidates, including me."

"It's my understanding that he wasn't especially well liked."

"True. He could be pretty gruff, wasn't big on subtlety."

"If Mr. Ladington *did* ingest a poisonous substance, that would give credence to the suicide theory, wouldn't it?" I asked. "Unless, of course, someone else poisoned him."

"Uh huh. If the ME had identified some pills, you know, sleeping pills, antidepressants, ordinary prescription drugs,

I'd say that it would be hard to disprove suicide. But this exotic substance complicates it. Wouldn't you agree?"

"I follow you. Someone might have *fed* such a substance to him. There was a suicide note, wasn't there?"

"An ambiguous one, Mrs. Fletcher. Typewritten."

"Signed by Ladington?"

"No."

"Did it mention that he'd been diagnosed with cancer, and had a year to live?"

Davis's laugh was involuntary, a short burst. "Ladington had cancer?"

"That's what his business manager, Roger Stockdale, told me a few minutes ago. He drove me here from the winery."

"That's news to me. No, the note didn't mention that."

"Any chance of my seeing the note?"

"No, but I'll let you read a photocopy. The original is secured in our evidence section."

He pulled a sheet of paper from a pile on his desk and handed it to me.

To Whom It May Concern:
Life has become unbearable and I no longer wish to live.

"That's it?" I said.

"That's it."

I handed the paper back to him.

"I can't imagine William Ladington bothering to type such a short note," I said. "Can you?"

"Seems unlikely. It was written on the Canon portable typewriter we took from his study. No doubt about that."

"Anyone could have used it," I said. "What about the empty pill bottle? Was that checked for residue?"

"Yes, it was. Clean."

"Nothing to match up with what the ME found in his body."

"Right."

"Prints on the empty bottle or note?"

"Ladington's prints on the bottle. Partials on the note, not enough to come up with an ID."

"Sheriff, there's some debate about whether there was a glass on the desk along with the empty pill bottle and note."

He shrugged. "Who says there was?"

"No one," I replied. "George and I simply assumed that there would be if Ladington had swallowed a sizable number of pills."

"No, no glass. At least I didn't see one."

"Bruce Ladington also says there wasn't a glass. From his perspective, that means it had to have been a murder. Of course, he's wrong to assume that."

"I'd say he is. Look, Mrs. Fletcher, can I be perfectly straight with you?"

"I hope you would be."

"I wasn't thrilled that you and your Scotland Yard friend arrived in the midst of an ongoing investigation. It's been my experience that the fewer people snooping around the better."

"I understand."

"Personally, what I'd like to see is this end up a simple case of suicide. It would make my job a lot easier."

"But?"

"But it's looking more and more like Bruce Ladington is right, that his father was murdered."

"He's been steadfast in that belief."

"Yeah, I know he has. You and your buddy are staying in the castle. What's going on there?"

"You're not the only person who's been asking me that."

"Really? Who else?"

"A friend of mine, Neil Schwartz. He's a writer who—"

"I know all about Mr. Neil Schwartz. He's been bugging me day and night looking for information about the waiter from Ladington's restaurant who was stabbed to death."

"Is there a connection?" I asked.

"None that I can see. You could do me a big favor and tell your writer friend to back off."

"I doubt he'd listen to me. What *is* new in that case?"

"You too?"

"Seems fair to ask. You're suggesting that I help you by passing on what I learn by virtue of being a houseguest at the winery. Information flows two ways."

"Fair enough. There's a drug connection with the waiter's murder."

"Bill Ladington mentioned that when I first met him. It's definite?"

"Looks that way."

"Was the young man selling drugs?"

He nodded. "Nothing big time. Started out supplying friends, that sort of thing. But it appears he started going beyond that. I suppose the money was too tempting. It usually is. The big question is who *his* supplier was. The state police undercover cops are investigating that end of it. The drugs are coming in from San Francisco, no surprise."

A uniformed officer interrupted us. "This fax just came in," she said, handing it to Davis.

He scowled as he read it.

"I suppose I should be going," I said.

His response was to hand me the fax. It was from the California forensic lab in Sacramento.

The substance found in the recently deceased William Ladington has been confirmed to be tetrodotoxin, a powerful poison, a nerve toxin, commonly found in fugu, or puffer fish. It is produced in the fish by a bacterium, and is almost always fatal when attacking the central nervous system. Puffer fish is a popular sushi ingredient in Japan. Certain portions of the fish are edible, provided the sushi chefs are skilled and knowledgeable in preparing it. Because of the potential danger it poses, fugu chefs in that country are licensed by the government.

Recommendation: Investigate the recent diet of the deceased to determine whether it included sushi that might have contained puffer fish.

It was signed by the chief of the forensic lab.

"Was Ladington a sushi lover?" the sheriff asked.

"Judging from meals I saw him eat, I doubt it," I said.

"Never touch it myself," he said.

"May I have a copy of this?" I asked.

"Keep it to yourself?"

"Myself, and George."

"All right."

He had a photocopy made.

"You said you had a ride here this morning," Davis said as he walked me to the lobby.

"Yes. I'll need a taxi."

"I'll have someone call you one. It'll be here in a minute or two."

He went to the desk officer, told him to get me a cab, and joined me outside on the front steps.

"Tell your friend I hope his back is better."

"I will. In your investigation, have you come up with any information about relationships the murdered waiter might have been involved with?"

"Sexual relationships? Romantic? No. Why?"

"I just wondered whether anyone has told you that Bill Ladington's wife, Tennessee, might have been having such a relationship with Louis Hubler."

Davis stared at me.

"Just wondered."

"Were did you hear that?"

"From a former girlfriend of the waiter. She worked as a waitress at Ladington's Steak House until the night of his murder. She left immediately afterward."

"You believe her?"

I shrugged. The taxi pulled up. Davis waved the driver away.

"I'll be happy to drive you wherever you want to go, Mrs. Fletcher, just as long as you keep talking."

Chapter Twenty-four

"Where to?" Sheriff Davis asked after we'd gotten into his unmarked car.

"I was planning on going back to the Ladington castle to look in on George."

"Mind if we take a detour?"

"Depends on where to," I said.

"I thought you might like to meet our ME."

"I'd like that very much."

"Great. Maybe you'll tell me more on our way about this alleged affair between Tennessee Ladington and Louis Hubler."

"I'm afraid I've told you all I know."

"I doubt that, Mrs. Fletcher. What about this former waitress who told you the story?"

I recounted what I knew about Mary Jane Proll and her accusation that Tennessee had been sexually involved with Mary Jane's boyfriend, Louis Hubler.

"Did she say anything about her boyfriend using and selling drugs?" he asked as he pulled up in front of the local hospital two minutes later.

"No. Bill Ladington was the one who brought it up to me. What's your medical examiner's name?"

"Bill Ayala. Came here from Chicago ten years ago. He's good."

"I'm sure he is."

Davis led me through the admitting area to the rear of the hospital utilized by Dr. Ayala and his staff. The ME was reading a newspaper in his office when Davis poked his head through the open door. "Catching up on the news, or reading your horoscope?" he asked with a chuckle.

"Both," Ayala said, dropping the paper to his desk and standing. He was a light-skinned black man with a youthful face and engaging smile, and wore a white lab coat over a blue button-down shirt and gold tie.

"I'd like you to meet Jessica Fletcher," Davis said.

"This is a real pleasure," Ayala said. "I read you were vacationing in Napa Valley."

"It's turned out to be not much of a vacation," I said.

"Oh?" He invited us to take seats across the desk from him.

"Mrs. Fletcher has been looking into Bill Ladington's death," said Davis. "She and a friend from Scotland Yard are houseguests out at the Ladington castle."

"Is that so?" Ayala said. "Scotland Yard? What's their interest in it?"

"Strictly unofficial," I said. "Mr. Ladington's son, Bruce, is convinced his father was murdered."

"So the sheriff has told me. You're functioning on behalf of Bruce Ladington?"

"I wouldn't say that," I responded. "I'd met his father the day he died. I, ah—"

"Mrs. Fletcher writes murder mysteries," Davis said.

"I'm well aware of that," Ayala said. "I saw you on the Larry King Show."

"My goodness. That was a couple of years ago."

"But I remember it well. I've read some of your books. I'm impressed with your grasp of medical forensics."

"Thank you. I have a good consultant back home in Maine, a doctor friend."

"Aha. I'd be happy to consult with you."

"And I may take you up on it one of these days. The sheriff told me this morning that a substance was found in Ladington's body, some exotic poison from puffer fish."

Ayala looked quizzically at Davis.

"Mrs. Fletcher seems to have a penchant for coming up with information, Bill, and is willing to share it with me. Only fair to share with her what I know. I gave her a copy of the fax that came through this morning from Sacramento."

"Interesting, wasn't it?" Ayala asked.

"I'd never heard of such a poison," I said.

"I'm aware of it, but don't know much about it. That's why I sent it to Sacramento."

"Did your autopsy of Bill Ladington indicate he had cancer?" I asked.

Ayala frowned. "No. No sign of any disease, aside from the results of high blood pressure, and an ulcer the size of a quarter in his stomach. Cancer? Why do you ask?"

"One of his employees told me that Ladington had a doctor in Los Angeles, an older man now deceased, who'd informed Ladington of the cancer a year ago."

"What sort of cancer?" Ayala asked.

"He didn't specify."

"I'm sure this doctor was wrong," Ayala said. "There was no sign of cancer in Bill Ladington. There was the head injury."

"Head injury?" I said, surprised.

"I didn't mention that to you," Davis said to me.

"What sort of head injury?" I asked.

"Blunt force injury," the sheriff said. "To the left side."

"Perhaps it happened when he fell into the moat," I offered. "Those rocks in there look menacing."

"You're probably right."

"Unless someone hit him on the head," Sheriff Davis offered.

"Which would rule out suicide," I said.

"A reasonable assumption," said the sheriff.

"Judging from an external examination of the wound, I'd say it was a rock that caused the injury," Ayala said. "The discoloration on his left temple and cheek was widespread, consistent with having struck his head on a rock."

A buzzer sounded on Ayala's phone.

"Yes?" he said. He frowned. "Tell him I'm busy," he said and hung up the receiver. He shook his head. "That writer from San Fran, Neil Schwartz, calling again," he said to Davis.

"Your buddy," Davis said to me.

I smiled.

"He is tenacious," Ayala said. "You and he are friends, Mrs. Fletcher?"

"Yes. We go back a long way."

"He's for real?" Ayala asked pleasantly.

"Oh, yes. He was a police officer in New York City. A good one, I'm told. He turned to writing when he retired, mostly poetry. He has a contract from *Vanity Fair*."

"About the murder of the waiter from Ladington's Steak House."

"I believe that started it for him. But I'm sure Bill Ladington's death, especially if it was murder, has taken center stage."

"You'd never know that by talking to him," Sheriff Davis said.

"What do you mean?"

"All his questions have to do with the waiter," Ayala replied.

"All his questions to me have been about Ladington," I said.

"Well," Davis said with a sigh, "you never can tell about writers." He quickly added, "Present company excluded."

"No need to exclude me," I said. "Tell me more about the blow to Ladington's head."

"As I said, a broad injury to his head," Ayala said. He consulted his autopsy report and read from it: "Gross discoloration of left side of face, including temple, cheekbone, and jaw line. Significant swelling and bruising. Some bone fragments invaded soft tissue. Internal bleeding between the dura and inner surface of the skull. I'd say he died somewhere between nine-thirty and eleven."

"Was the blow to the head the cause of death?" I asked. "As opposed to the poison?"

"Hard to say," the ME responded. "Tetrodotoxin is a pretty potent poison, although the level found in Ladington was small. The blow to his head caused intracranial damage. It's my professional opinion that it was the chief cause of death, although the poison might have done it, too, if he'd lived a little longer." The ME got up from behind the desk. "You'll have to excuse me. I have a meeting to get to. It was a real pleasure meeting you, Mrs. Fletcher."

"For me, too," I said, shaking his hand. "Does the family know of your conclusions about how Bill Ladington died?"

"I intend to call them later today," Davis said.

"Is there a phone I can use to make a local call?" I asked Dr. Ayala.

"Use this one," Ayala said, pointing to the one on his desk on his way out.

"I want to see how George is doing," I said, fishing the Ladington Creek Winery's number from my purse.

Mercedes, the housekeeper, answered.

"This is Jessica Fletcher," I said. "I'm calling to see how Inspector Sutherland is feeling."

She said nothing in response. Bruce came on the line a few seconds later.

"He's doing fine," he told me. "Laura's been looking in

on him. She brought him some tea. She says his back is a little better."

"That's certainly good to hear," I said. "I shouldn't be much longer."

"Do you need someone to pick you up?"

"No, thank you. Sheriff Davis is driving me."

"He is?"

"Yes. Please tell George hello from me and that I'll be back as soon as possible."

"I will."

"How's your friend?" Davis asked as we left the hospital and went to his car.

"Feeling better."

"Glad to hear it."

"I should go back."

"Sure, only I was wondering whether you were up for another detour."

"Someone else for me to meet?"

"No. Someone *I'd* like to meet."

"Who might that be?"

"The waitress who told you about the affair between the waiter and Tennessee Ladington. Mary Jane is her name?"

"Yes, but—"

"I could go up to Calistoga alone," he said, starting the car, "but since you've already met her, she might be more willing to talk to me if you make the introduction."

"I doubt that," I said.

"Why?"

"We didn't part on the best of terms. She tried to boil me alive."

"Whoa."

"In the mud bath. She's an unpleasant young woman. At least she was with me. She's frightened of Ladington's people."

"Did she tell you why?"

"No. She just turned up the heat. She didn't appreciate the questions I was asking."

I looked at my watch. Ten-thirty.

"All right," I said, "I'll go with you, but I would like to be back in time to have lunch with George."

"Shouldn't be a problem," he said. "I just want you to know how much I appreciate this, Mrs. Fletcher."

"No, I'm the one who's appreciative. I met with you to see what I could learn about William Ladington's death."

"Yeah, but I'm the one who's ended up learning things. Tell me again about this Mary Jane—"

"Proll. Mary Jane Proll."

"Right."

I recounted for him the trip George and I had made to Calistoga after having had lunch at Ladington's restaurant where we learned about Ms. Proll. He listened quietly, nodding now and then, focusing on his driving. When we reached Calistoga and were a few hundred yards from Hampton Spa, he pulled to the side of the road.

"She's likely to be not very happy having you bring me to her," he said. "I'd appreciate it if you could smooth the way, grease the skids."

"I'll do what I can. She claims to be afraid of Ladington, or at least of some of the people who surrounded him. She specifically mentioned his driver, Raoul. I don't think she'll be happy to see me, either."

We pulled up in front of the spa, parked, and I led us inside. The same woman who'd greeted me the last time sat behind the desk.

"Hello," I said.

"Hi." She cocked her head and narrowed her eyes. "You were here just a few days ago."

"Yes, I was. I had a mud bath. Mary Jane Proll took care of me."

Her expression soured.

"I was wondering if she was working today."

"No."

"Day off?"

"She quit."

"Permanently?" I asked.

"Permanently and last minute. She really left me in the lurch. We had reservations booked for her, but she just didn't show up this morning. I called her apartment. She said she was leaving town."

"Today?"

"I suppose so."

"Could you tell us where she lives?" I asked.

The woman looked at Davis.

"This is Sheriff Davis," I said.

"I thought so. I've seen your picture in the papers. I don't think I should be giving out employees' home addresses."

"This is an official police matter," Davis said.

"Has she done something wrong?" the woman asked.

"Just tell us where she lives," he said in a gentle, yet firm voice.

She consulted a notebook from a drawer and wrote on a slip of paper, and handed it to me.

"Thanks," I said.

"You just can't depend on help anymore," she said. "They have no sense of loyalty or responsibility."

"I know what you mean," Davis said. "Much obliged."

"Do you know where this is?" I asked as we got back into his car.

"Yes, I do. An apartment complex east of town."

The complex was a five-minute drive from Hampton Spa. The two-story buildings, with small porches in front of each unit, were stacked up one behind the other on a low terraced hill, with a narrow road separating them. Mary Jane's apartment was in the third building from the base of the hill.

We got out of the car and went up onto the porch. The front door was slightly ajar. Sheriff Davis went to it and knocked, causing it to open a little more. "Hello," he said through the gap. "Anyone home?"

There was no response.

He called her name, pushed the door fully open, and stepped inside. I followed.

We were in a large central room. A dining table was to the left, in front of a low counter separating the room from a small kitchen. Two open doors led to bedrooms.

"Looks like Ms. Proll made a hasty getaway," Davis said, referring to the condition of the room. Clothes had been tossed everywhere. An open suitcase lay on the counter separating the kitchen from the main room.

He went into one of the bedrooms. It was even more chaotic than the living room. Dresser drawers hung open. The door to the closet was ajar, revealing clothing on hangers dangling precariously from a metal rod.

I went to a desk wedged in a corner of the room. Drawers were open and papers and books were strewn across it. A pile of magazines a foot high was on the floor next to a rickety chair. I sat and glanced at some of the materials in front of me. Many of the papers were bills, and offers for credit cards. I looked into the open top drawer to my right and absently pulled things from it. One item was a small green leather address book that was buried at the bottom. I flipped through it, perusing the handwritten names and numbers, and in a few case addresses, noted next to the names. As I was doing it, Davis entered the bedroom carrying a framed photograph.

"This is Louis Hubler," he said, handing me the picture.

"A nice-looking young man," I said. Hubler stared at me with pale blue eyes beneath a mop of blond hair. The picture had obviously been taken in summer. Hubler wore tan shorts and a yellow T-shirt, and a lake could be seen in the background. He had an engaging, wide, crooked smile exposing large, white teeth.

"What a shame," I said, handing the photo back to Davis.

"A young man with his future all in front of him," Davis said, shaking his head. "Damn drugs destroy too many young lives."

"You sound convinced that drugs were involved," I said, continuing to flip through the address book.

"I don't think there's much doubt, Mrs. Fletcher."

"Did he have drugs in his system?"

"Marijuana. A high level, according to Dr. Ayala."

"But that doesn't mean he was murdered *because* of drugs," I said.

"No, it doesn't, at least on the surface. The undercover narcs will hopefully come up with something on that. Any idea where she might have gone?"

"No. I know nothing about her. I've been looking through papers here hoping I'd come up with something, some indication of where she has family, or had lived previously."

"I checked the other bedroom," he said. "Neat as a pin."

The sound of the front door being closed caused both of us to turn.

"Who are you?" a young woman asked as she appeared in the doorway. She was short and chunky, and had close-cropped brown hair. She wore very tight jeans and a sweatshirt with U. of Cal–Berkeley imprinted on it.

"I'm Sheriff Davis," he said. "This is Mrs. Fletcher."

"What are you doing here?"

"Looking for Ms. Proll," I said. "Do you live here with her?"

"I did." She didn't sound happy.

"It looks like she's gone," Davis said.

"She sure is. She, like, threw some things in a bag this morning and took off."

"Do you know where she went?" I asked.

"No idea, but I wish I did. She owes half the rent for this month, and owes me money too."

"She'll probably be back in touch with you," I offered, not really meaning it. "Do you know why she left in such a hurry?"

The woman shook her head and said, "I don't care. She babbled about some bad guys being after her. She was, like, paranoid, you know."

Davis showed her the photo of Louis Hubler. "This was her boyfriend, wasn't it?" he asked.

"Until he started messing around with that old woman and got himself killed."

"Old woman?" I said. "You mean Mrs. Ladington?"

"Yeah."

"Mary Jane told you about it?"

"Yeah. She was, like, really bummed out."

"Did she talk to you about who might have killed Hubler?" Davis asked.

"She figured it was either old man Ladington or his wife."

I continued looking through the green address book while the conversation was taking place.

"Does Ms. Proll use drugs?" Davis asked.

His question visibly unnerved Mary Jane's roommate. She turned and went to the living room. Davis followed. "I ask only because it might help identify who killed Hubler," I heard Davis say.

"What do you think I am, like, dumb or something?" the woman said. "Talk to a sheriff about drugs? Give me a break."

I turned the pages in the address book until I'd reached the end. The final page contained a list of phone numbers. Unlike the rest of the book, in which names were entered in alphabetical order, these numbers were jumbled together with no regard for the alphabet. I stared at the list as I heard Davis ask, "Do you know whether Louis Hubler dealt drugs?"

"I heard something like that,'" she replied.

"Does your roommate, Ms. Proll, deal drugs?"

"Do you have a warrant or something?"

"No," said Davis. "We're just trying to get to the bottom of things."

"Who's she in there?"

"Mrs. Fletcher? She's a famous writer of murder mysteries. She's helping in the investigation."

"Well, I'm not talking to you anymore unless I get, like, a lawyer or something."

"You won't need a lawyer," Davis said. "Thanks for your cooperation."

I slipped the address book into the pocket of my jacket as Davis reappeared.

"We might as well leave," he said.

"Yes. There's nothing more to do here," I said, standing.

We said good-bye to Mary Jane's roommate on the way out, got in the sheriff's car, and he drove me back to Ladington Creek.

"Thanks for your help," he said, stopping at the raised drawbridge. Wade Grosso stood at the other end.

"And thank you. It's been an interesting day."

"Look, Mrs. Fletcher, I think having you inside the castle could be helpful. Obviously, you and your Scottish buddy, Sutherland, seem to have a knack for finding out things. I'd appreciate your keeping in touch."

"Of course. You've been very generous with what you know."

"Give me a call in the morning. And tell him to lower the bridge."

"I will," I said, "but I'll walk over. Thanks again."

I got out of the car and motioned for Grosso to lower the

bridge. He went to the wooden box by the front door, activated the switch, and the bridge creaked down until it spanned the moat. I walked to the midway point, turned, waved to Sheriff Davis, and continued across until reaching the drive in front of the castle. I watched the sheriff drive away.

"Have a nice day, Mrs. Fletcher?" Grosso asked.

"Yes, very. You?"

He didn't respond. Instead, he returned to the box and drew the bridge back to its upright position. I entered the castle, paused in the huge foyer, reached in my pocket, withdrew the green address book, closed my eyes against the thoughts I was having, decided to put them off for now, and went upstairs in search of George.

Chapter Twenty-five

The door to George's room was open when I arrived. He wasn't there. I dropped off my purse in my room and went downstairs where I bumped into Raoul, who'd just come in from outside.

"Hello," I said. "Have you seen Inspector Sutherland?"

"No, ma'am," he said, and walked past me.

I went to the office. Roger Stockdale was sitting behind Bill Ladington's desk. "Have you seen George?" I asked.

"He was outside a half hour ago," he said, glancing up from what he'd been doing and returning his attention to it.

My next trip was to the French doors leading to the patio. I stepped through them. It was a splendid afternoon, sunny and seasonally cool, a "fat day" as Seth Hazlitt would say. I looked out over the vineyards and saw Wade Grosso at the edge of the Ladington Creek vineyard. He was talking to a man I'd seen before at a distance, the neighboring vintner, Robert Jenkins. I looked in the other direction and saw George sitting on a wooden bench with Bruce; that he'd felt well enough to leave his room heartened me.

He saw me and waved.

"Good afternoon," I said to the security guard who sat in the director's chair by the manually operated drawbridge across the moat. He nodded and mumbled something. I crossed the narrow wooden bridge and headed for George and Bruce. As I got closer, Bruce got up and walked in my direction. I could see that he was upset; his face was fixed in a sad expression, and as he came abreast of me, I thought I saw traces of tears on his chubby cheeks.

"Hello, Bruce," I said, smiling.

"Hello, Mrs. Fletcher," he said.

"I see you and Laura have been taking good care of George."

"He's feeling better," he said, lowering his head and walking past me.

George stood to greet me.

"Feeling better, I see," I said.

"Yes, thank goodness. I'm being prudent in my movements, however. Easy for my back to go out again."

"I imagine. What were you talking with Bruce about?"

"A number of things, Jessica. He's a very sad young man."

"Poor man. He looks miserable. Did he have anything new to say about his father's death?"

"No. He just keeps repeating that someone killed him. He told me quite a bit about his relationship with his father and stepmother. No love lost between him and Tennessee. I found myself vacillating between sympathy for him and a certain degree of scorn. I'm not especially proud of the latter feeling, but he's typical of people I've known who offer themselves as doormats, then whine about being stepped on."

"I understand what you're saying. A practiced victim."

"Exactly. I don't know why he chose me to be his sounding board, but he did. I suppose because I'm not part of his usual world and—"

"And what?"

"And because we have something in common."

"Which is?"

"We're both men."

I paused, then asked, "Why is that important?"

"He shared some personal information with me about his marriage to Laura."

"Oh?"

"Yes. As we've observed, it isn't a marriage made in heaven."

When he didn't continue, I said, "And?"

"The young Mr. Ladington is sterile."

"I see." My immediate thought was of having made the observation that Laura might be pregnant.

George was thinking the same thing. "If his wife is pregnant as you claim," he said, "it's doubtful the father of the child is her husband."

"He told you this, George?"

"Yes. According to him, they've discussed various medical approaches to the problem of not being able to have children. I'm not terribly up on such things. Of course, this is just one of many problems with their marriage. His father's dislike of Laura hasn't helped, nor has his father's disdain for his son." He looked me in the eye. "Are you certain, Jessica, that she's pregnant?"

"No. She looks to me as though she is, but I could be mistaken."

"I'd like to know with certainty."

"I suppose I can ask her, although I'd feel a little awkward probing an area that personal."

"Play it by the proverbial ear, Jessica. Tell me about your meeting with Sheriff Davis."

"Interesting," I said, sitting on the bench with him. "A poisonous substance was found in Bill Ladington, some sort of a rare poison found in puffer fish."

"I've read about puffer fish. They serve them as sushi in Japan, I believe."

"That's right, but they're only served by chefs licensed by the government. The medical examiner here, a very nice chap named Bill Ayala, sent the samples to the forensic lab in Sacramento. He gave Sheriff Davis a copy of the preliminary report."

I handed him the photocopy Sheriff Davis had given me. George chewed his cheek as he read.

He handed the paper back to me and asked, "Did the medical examiner indicate how quickly the poison acts?"

"No. I meant to ask but forgot."

"That would be useful information. I have a close friend in Edinburgh, an expert in toxic substances. His book on the subject is required reading in every criminal justice class. Our MEs consider it a bible. I can call him."

"Please do. Sheriff Davis also showed me Ladington's supposed suicide note."

"Supposed? You don't buy it?"

"Not at all. It was typewritten and not signed. It was addressed to whom it may concern. All it said was something like 'Life has become unbearable and I don't want to live any longer.' That was it."

"You've had a busy day."

"More than you know. Sheriff Davis and I went to Calistoga to talk with Mary Jane Proll, the young woman from the spa."

"And?"

"She didn't show for work, We went to her apartment. Her roommate said Ms. Proll tossed some clothing in a bag and took off this morning. The roommate confirmed in a roundabout way that the murdered waiter, Louis Hubler, used drugs and might have sold them. Oh, and I learned from the ME that there was a heavy level of marijuana in Hubler's body at the time of death."

"Let's go in," he suggested. "I'll call my friend in Edinburgh."

As we stood, I again looked to where Wade Grosso had been talking with Ladington's neighbor and competitor, Robert Jenkins. They were gone.

"I'd like to speak with the neighbor," I said as we headed back to the castle.

"I agree," George said. He walked stiffly, bent slightly forward.

"It still hurts," I observed.

"Yes, but nothing like this morning. Clumsy of me, falling into that moat."

"At least you didn't hit your head on those rocks. Dr. Ayala told me the autopsy on Ladington showed an injury to the left side of his head that caused internal bleeding. There were bone splinters, he said."

George's laugh caused him to grimace. "I wish you worked for me at the Yard," he said. "You collect more information in less time than any of my senior investigators."

"Thanks for the compliment, but I didn't have to work very hard for it. It's Dr. Ayala's opinion that the blow to Ladington's head was the proximate cause of death. The amount of poison in his body was small, although the doctor also says that if Ladington had lived longer—hadn't hit his head—the poison might have eventually done its job. Between Louis Hubler's murder, and Bill Ladington's death, murder, or suicide, the sheriff seems desperate for any help he can get. I told him about the rumor that Tennessee and Hubler had been having an affair. Mary Jane Proll's roommate was aware of it because Mary Jane told her about it."

We entered the castle and went to the small office from which I'd made calls before. I handed George my AT&T credit card. He called his friend's number, and said, "Rufus, George Sutherland." After some preliminary chat, George started asking questions, jotting the answers on a pad. Fifteen minutes later he said, "Much obliged, Rufus. My best to your wife." He hung up.

"Well?" I asked.

"The man is a walking encyclopedia on poisons," George said. "Let me see." He consulted his notes. "Puffer fish are found in warm waters, Central America, Australia, South Africa. There are numerous species—Rufus says as many as ninety—the poison is found in the fish's ovaries. The problem, according to Rufus, is that cooking doesn't destroy the poison. It has to be removed before cooking and serving. It effects the central nervous system, first manifests itself as difficulty in speaking, then moves on to cause respiratory arrest. It can produce a reaction in as little as ten minutes, or as long as three hours. If a person survives for as long as twenty-four hours, it usually means he'll make it. More than fifteen hundred people in Japan died from puffer fish poison in the fifties, sixties, and seventies. An interesting aside from my learned friend—Haitians, at least those devoted to voodoo and the zombie ritual, sometimes use poison from the puffer fish."

"Remind me never to take part in a Haitian voodoo ritual," I said.

"Should we ever end up together in Haiti, I'll do that. By the way, Rufus also said there's been a recent problem with the poison from puffer fish infecting other marine life. Sea urchins have been dying off in droves in the Caribbean, especially off the coast of Curaçao. There are people who enjoy the roe from sea urchin, and are dying from the poison."

"Curaçao," I said. "Ladington, and Edith Saison and Yves Legrand, have homes there. I think that most everyone at the castle has spent some time there recently."

"Something else to consider," he said. He handed me his notes. "We should destroy these."

I put them in my jacket pocket.

"Let's go upstairs," he said.

He opened the door. Standing close to it was Tennessee Ladington.

"I was just passing," she said.

George and I glanced at each other. She'd been standing there listening through the door.

"Excuse me," she said, and walked away.

Chapter Twenty-six

We sat in George's room sipping sparkling water that Laura had brought him earlier in the day.

"An interesting scenario," George said. "Ladington ingests this poison found in puffer fish, then goes to the edge of the moat and falls in, either because the poison had began to take effect, or because he was a clumsy fool like yours truly."

"The assumption has been all along that he took whatever killed him in his study. But that empty pill bottle doesn't make any sense, does it? He didn't take some prescription medicine, an overdose of an anti-anxiety drug or similar medication. I can't imagine that the puffer fish poison—or poison from sea urchins infected with it—would be in an amber pill bottle. The lab tests on the bottle revealed nothing, no trace of any substance."

"Someone put that bottle there to make it appear at first glance to have been a suicide. The same with the so-called suicide note."

"All right, let's go on that assumption. If someone did place those things on the desk in an attempt to make it appear that Ladington took his own life, he or she wasn't thinking very clearly. That person should have known that the autopsy would reveal the type of poison that was used. Whoever killed Bill Ladington was a bit of a bumbler."

"A real *fouter.*"

"Pardon?"

"Scottish for bumbler."

"Oh. It's also unlikely that someone planning to kill himself would choose such a poison."

"Why?"

"Too exotic, too unsure. Ladington wasn't an expert on poisons. He had a pharmaceutical guide in his study. No, he would have chosen a more mundane drug or combination of drugs. Someone fed it to him, most likely through food."

I went to the window, looked out, and said without turning, "Your friend in Edinburgh said the poison could take effect in as soon as ten minutes, or might take as long as three hours."

"Correct. Did the medical examiner give an approximate time of death?"

"Between nine-thirty and eleven. They discovered his body at ten-thirty."

"What time was dinner served that night?"

"Cocktails at seven, dinner at eight, I assume. It seems never to vary."

"Within the time frame for a reaction to the poison, according to your friend."

"Exactly."

"George, who found Ladington in the moat?"

"Bruce."

"How did that come about?"

"He told me he went looking for his father because he wanted to discuss a business issue with him."

"I thought Ladington kept Bruce *out* of the business."

"I remember him saying that, but it doesn't mean it applied to everything. Bruce told us he sometimes works in the wine-tasting room. He might have wanted to talk to his father about that. What's next, Jessica?"

I turned from the window. "It's a pretty day, George.

How about paying a neighborly visit to Mr. Jenkins next door? Is your back up to it?"

"I'll manage."

We went to the front of the castle where George's rental car was parked. Although Jenkins's vineyard abutted Ladington Creek, it was a long way around to reach its entrance. Considering George's back problems, it wouldn't have been prudent to walk.

I was halfway in the car when I said, "I just thought of something. Wait here a minute."

I entered the castle through the front door and went down the hall to the small office from which George had called his friend in Edinburgh. The pad of paper that had been on the desk was gone. I'd hoped to head that off, but I was obviously too late. My concern was that the pressure of George's pen might have left an indentation of what he'd written on the blank sheets. Since Tennessee seemed to be the only one who knew we were using that office, it was fair to assume that she'd taken the pad. Too late to worry about it now. I fingered the notes I'd put in my jacket pocket and made a mental note to discard them somewhere away from Ladington Creek.

"What did you forget?" George asked when I rejoined him.

I told him.

"I should have thought of that myself," he said. "But I suppose my scribbling won't mean much to Mrs. Ladington."

"Just the fact that we were asking about poison will mean something to her," I said. "Are you able to drive?"

"Of course. Just point the way."

The entranceway to Shelton Reserve Vineyards was considerably shorter than Ladington Creek's, and was paved with red brick. A sign in front heralded free wine tasting; I wondered whether the owner had decided not to charge as a competitive move against Ladington's fee-for-tasting. The main building was not nearly as large or lavish as the Ladington castle, but it was not unimpressive. It sprawled long and low, with lots of glass and stone.

We parked in a space near the entrance, got out, and entered through the visitor's door. There were quite a few tourists gathered in a gift shop, and we could see into the tasting room where two young women served tiny glasses of wine to tasters lined up along a lengthy counter.

"Over there," I said, pointing to a sign indicating where the offices were located.

We entered a reception area; a middle-aged woman sat behind a desk talking on a phone. She glanced up, indicated with a finger that she'd only be a minute, and finished her conversation.

"Can I help you?" she asked.

"We'd like to speak with Mr. Jenkins," I said.

"Do you have an appointment?"

"No, we don't," I said. "We're staying next door at Ladington Creek. My name is Jessica Fletcher. This is George Sutherland."

"Jessica Fletcher. Oh, yes, I should have recognized you. I have many of your books."

"That's always good to hear."

She turned to George. "And you must be the Scotland Yard detective I've been hearing about."

"You've been hearing about me?"

"Absolutely. Everyone's talking about Scotland Yard being involved in the investigation of Bill Ladington's murder."

"I'm afraid these people are wrong," George said. "I'm simply here as a tourist and friend of Mrs. Fletcher."

The woman's expression said she wasn't buying it.

"Would it be possible to meet with Mr. Jenkins?" I asked.

"Let me see if I can find him," she said, holding down a button on the elaborate phone on her desk: "Bob Jenkins, please contact the office."

A moment later a man's voice came through the phone's tiny speaker. "What's up?"

"Two people to see you, Bob. Jessica Fletcher and the Scotland Yard inspector, Mr. Sutherland."

"What do *they* want?"

"They're right here with me, Bob—*listening*."

Jenkins's sigh could be heard over the speaker. "All right," he said. "I'll be there in a few minutes."

We chatted with the woman behind the desk until Robert Jenkins arrived. He was of medium height, with floppy brown hair tinged with silver combed back along his temples; the top of his head was bald. His face was long and angular, Lincolnesque, with green eyes set deep beneath prominent salt-and-pepper eyebrows. He wore chinos, a plaid shirt, leather jacket, and brown-and-black running shoes. I judged him to be in his early fifties. He exuded energy and impatience.

I introduced George and myself.

"What can I do for you?"

"We're staying next door at Ladington Creek. We—"

"I know all about you," Jenkins said in a surprisingly high voice. "You're trying to prove Ladington didn't commit suicide."

"That's hardly true," I said. "What we *are* doing is looking for the truth."

His thin mouth twisted into a crooked, cynical smile. "The truth?" he said. "The truth is that Mr. William Ladington got what he deserved. There wasn't anybody in the valley who liked him or his gang over there at the castle. He threatened half the population here, including me. You know what, Mrs. Fletcher? It doesn't matter why Ladington died. It doesn't matter whether he poisoned himself, or whether somebody else did the deed. Everybody's better off with him gone."

"Why did you say 'poisoned himself'?" George asked.

"That's what they're saying."

"That's what *who's* saying?" George pressed.

"Everybody in the valley."

So much for the autopsy results remaining secret, I thought. Either the sheriff s department, the ME's office, or both were sieves.

"Do they say what sort of poison?" I asked.

"Not that I've heard."

"You and Mr. Ladington certainly weren't friendly neighbors," I offered.

His guffaw said it all.

"And I understand that Halton Mountain might be at the root of it," I added.

Jenkins screwed up his face in thought before saying, "Come with me."

We followed him from the office, past the tasting room and gift shop, and out through a back door that led to the vineyards. Jenkins said nothing as he led us along the narrow paths between hundreds of stakes supporting the vines. We kept walking until we reached the end, at the foot of Halton Mountain. Jenkins stopped, looked up at the barren hillside, turned to us, and said, "If it wasn't for Bill Ladington, my vineyard would stretch up to the top of Halton. Shelton Reserve's cabernet would be the best in the world."

"Who owns that mountain?" George asked.

"It's mine," Jenkins responded. "It was grandfathered into my deed for this property. The Jenkins family has owned this land for generations. Nobody contested my right to Halton Mountain until Ladington arrived, set his sights on it, and started challenging my claim. He and his goddamn lawyers—he's used dozens of them—have tied up the ownership of Halton for years. When things didn't go his way in some hearing, he'd storm over here and threaten me."

"Physical threats?" I asked.

"You bet. He's pointed guns at my head, told me he'd bury me up there on Halton under his vineyard. Not friendly neighbors? I hated the man! When I heard he was dead, the first thing I did was pour myself a big, stiff drink and toast the news."

A small groan came from George, and he twisted his torso against discomfort in his back.

"We should go," I said. "My friend's back is acting up."

"From falling into Ladington's stupid moat?" Jenkins said.

"Word does get around, doesn't it?" I said.

"First thing I'd do if I had that property is fill in that damn moat."

"Is there a possibility you might one day end up with Ladington Creek?" I asked.

"Depends on what his estate decides to do with it."

I paused before suggesting, "If you owned Ladington Creek's vineyards, you'd also own Halton Mountain."

"That's right. But if you think that would be a reason for me to kill Ladington, you're making up stories like in your books. I've got to get to work. Thanks for stopping by."

He turned and headed back toward the main building, with us falling in line behind. It was obvious that George's back was going into spasms again, and I wanted to get him to his room as quickly as possible.

Jenkins said good-bye to us at the main entrance. As he turned to go inside, George asked, "Have you been to Curaçao lately?"

Jenkins frowned. "No. Why would you want to know that?" he asked.

"Just curious," George said. "A pleasure meeting you, Mr. Jenkins."

Tennessee was in the foyer when we entered the castle.

"I saw you over at Jenkins's vineyard," she said. "Have a pleasant chat with the charming Mr. Jenkins?"

"Very pleasant," I said. "Excuse us. George isn't feeling well." He was now bent into a pretzel.

We went up the stairs to his room where George removed his shoes and sport jacket, loosened his tie, and got on top of the bed. He let out a sigh of relief.

"Feel better?" I asked.

"Yes. Too long on my feet. Jessica, I'm sorry for being such a hindrance."

"You're nothing of the sort. Now relax, close your eyes, take a nap."

"What will you do with the rest of the day?"

"I think I'll kick off my shoes, too, put my feet up and make some notes. I can usually think more clearly when I put things on paper."

I went to the side of the bed, touched his hand, kissed him on the forehead, and left.

Chapter Twenty-seven

I didn't realize how tired I was until I'd removed my shoes, sat in an easy chair, and rested my head against the chair's back. I had to fight to keep my eyes from closing. A quick trip to the bathroom and some cold water splashed on my face made a difference. I pulled a yellow legal pad from my overnight bag, returned to the chair, and started noting my thoughts.

Cause of death—Poison (tetrodotoxin), and/or blow to left side of head (rocks in moat?)

Time of death—Approx: 9:30 p.m.

Body found in moat by son, Bruce Ladington

Empty pill bottle (no trace elements in it) and "suicide note" found in Ladington's study. Note typewritten, not signed. Ignore. Obviously no suicide. Someone wanted it to look like suicide.

SUSPECTS:

Wife, Tennessee—Obvious dislike of husband. Was present night he died.

Son, Bruce—Dominated by his father, browbeaten. Loved him, needed his approval. Determined to prove father was murdered.

Daughter-in-Law, Laura—Withdrawn, almost, antisocial. Obviously not a fan of Bill Ladington. Pregnant? If so, who's the father? Bruce tells George he's sterile.

Vineyard manager, Wade Grosso—Hard to read. Sounds like he hated Ladington, yet speaks with certain respect of him. Big enough to deliver a fateful blow if injury to head was deliberate. ME doesn't think so.

Business manager, Roger Stockdale—Unhappy fellow, made negative comments about Ladington on first meeting. Claims Ladington verbally promised him some sort of partnership down the road. Believe him? Lied about Ladington having cancer? Autopsy says he didn't have cancer. Ladington lied to *him*?

Neighbor, Robert Jenkins—Seething hatred for Ladington. Possible motive of money, Halton Mountain, etc.

Edith Saison and Yves LeGrand—Partners with Ladington in vineyard, claim partnership entitles them to Ladington Creek. Much to gain.

Housekeeper, Mercedes—Cynical type. Hard to conceive of someone like her killing somebody. But . . .

Staff, Fidel and Consuela—Ladington inherited them. Know little about them. Ladington's overbearing manner as boss sufficient motive to kill him?

I stopped writing, sat back, and tried to think of other possible suspects. Of course.

Chef, Nick—Poison given to Ladington in food? Likely. So, who is Nick? Find out more about him.

<u>*MOTIVES:*</u>

Halton Mountain ownership—Bob Jenkins most interested.

Money—Tennessee, Edith, Yves, Stockdale (if to be believed about being promised something by Ladington), Bruce, by extension Laura.

Personal hatred—Ladington alienated lots of people, including family and employees. If personal motive, suspects number in the hundreds.

<u>*NOTE:*</u>

Curaçao connection. Ladington had home in Curaçao and everyone spent time there recently. Met Yves and Edith there (they own home there too). Tetrodotoxin found in Curaçao, killing sea urchin.

Hubler, murdered waiter—Connection with Ladington's death? Tennessee having affair with Hubler. Ladington know of it? Drugs involved? Neil Schwartz more interested in Hubler death than Ladington. Why?

I took another break and paced the room. I couldn't identify what was nagging me at that moment, couldn't put a finger on the vague, shadowy shape that floated in my head, almost discernible but not quite.

I read over my notes, then decided to go downstairs and see who might be around. I wandered into the kitchen where the housekeeper, Mercedes, and the husband-wife team of Fidel and Consuela were sitting at the table drinking coffee and tea.

"Can I help you?" Mercedes asked in her usual antagonistic tone, not looking up.

"Just restless," I said. "A cup of tea sounds appealing."

"Help yourself," she said, pointing to a kettle on the

stove that was still steaming; a small bowl of teabags was next to it. I considered leaving the kitchen; her manner was off-putting. Instead, I made myself a cup of tea and joined them. Fidel and Consuela finished what was left of their black coffee and left. I expected Mercedes to do the same. Instead, she displayed a rare smile, which softened her round face. She sat back, crossed her large arms across her sizable bosom, and said, "Well, now, Mrs. Fletcher, have you solved the murder?"

Her question took me by surprise and I had to pause before answering with my own question: "Are you sure Mr. Ladington was murdered?"

"I just know what I hear, Mrs. Fletcher. Seems to me Bruce is hell-bent on proving the old man was done in by somebody."

"He is convinced that's what happened," I said, sipping my tea. "But what do *you* think? You've worked here in the castle for a long time. You obviously know the people who live and work here as well as or better than anyone."

"I've seen a few things in my years here."

She closed her eyes and pursed her lips as though tasting an unpleasant thought. I waited. She opened her eyes and spoke plaintively, capturing a bittersweet reflection.

"It was good here," she said, more to the room than to me. Mr. Ladington bought this place and made it into something he could be proud of. I worked for him in Hollywood and he brought me here." Her smile was small. "Those Hollywood days were wild, Mrs. Fletcher. The man seemed hell-bent on destroying himself. Nothing but parties and drinking and women, so many women."

"His wives," I said.

"And others," she said, shaking her head. "He didn't seem to care about whether the movies he made were good or bad, just as long as they made enough money to keep him and his crazy lifestyle going. But then something happened."

I waited.

"He changed, he did. He packed up his production company and house and left without as much as saying goodbye to his friends. He came up here, bought this place, and called me."

"How long after he left did he call you?"

"Not long, a month or so. I was so surprised. I'd decided to leave Los Angeles and go live with my son and daughter-in-law in Oregon. But Mr. Ladington was persuasive, I'll say that. He said he couldn't survive without me running his house. I suppose I was flattered. I came here and made sure everything ran right, that he had good meals and didn't go back to his old ways, carousing and drinking and all the rest. But then—"

"Then what?"

"Then that woman came."

"Tennnesse?"

"That's the one. A real gold digger is what she is, Mrs. Fletcher, a scheming, conniving manipulator. Wrapped him, the old fool, around her finger. And that son of his. Well, I suppose he's blood and that counts for something, but everybody around Bill Ladington sucked the life out of him. You might say they all killed him."

"How so?" I asked.

"They're all takers, Mrs. Fletcher, not a giver among them. That Mr. Stockdale is a thief if I ever saw one."

I couldn't help but laugh at her bluntness.

"He's got his eye on the missus, too. I see things like that. I may not have a fancy education, but I know people."

"I don't doubt that for a minute," I said, meaning it. "It may be true that the people he surrounded himself with, as you put it, 'sucked the life out of him,' but someone *really* killed him—physically. You still haven't told me who you think might have done it."

She started to say something, stopped, stood, wiped her large, red hands on her apron, and went over to where her purse lay on a cupboard. She took something from it, returned, and handed me a photograph. It was of a young man and woman. The woman held an infant.

"A nice-looking family," I said.

"My son, daughter-in-law, and grandson in Oregon."

I wasn't sure how to respond. The whole conversation was out of character for her, including sharing something about her family with me.

"Do you see them often?" I asked.

"I'll be seeing a lot more of them," she said, taking the picture from me. "I'm leaving here—for good!"

"Oh? When?"

"Day after tomorrow. My son's coming down to pick me up. I'll be staying with them. His wife wants to go back to work, so I'll watch the little one."

"That sounds wonderful."

"I can't stay here, not with this gang of vultures. Good riddance to them, I say."

"I understand," I said.

She slipped back into her uncommunicative mood.

"Thanks for the tea," I said, standing and moving toward the door. "I wish you well in your new life."

I was in the hallway and on my way to the stairs when the thing that had eluded me earlier in my room suddenly snapped into sharp focus. It was the photograph of Mercedes's son and family that did it. A photograph! There was a photo I'd seen that had meaning. What was it? Where was it?

I was trying to come up with the answer when Roger Stockdale appeared. "You have a phone call, Mrs. Fletcher."

I went into the office area where a receiver lay next to a phone. Stockdale pointed to it.

"Hello?" I said.

"Jess, it's Neil."

"Hello, Neil, I—"

"I know. I'm not supposed to call you there. But I need to talk to you."

"I'm listening."

"Not on the phone. Can we get together? Say in a half hour? I can pick you up."

"Oh, Neil, I don't think so. I—"

I looked at Stockdale's desk. On it was a framed picture of him and people I assumed were his former wife and their children. They looked blissfully happy; the picture had been taken on a ski slope.

I heard Neil ask, "Jess? Are you there? Jess? Are you—?"

"I'm sorry, Neil. My mind was elsewhere."

"Look, I can pick you up. We can maybe get a cup of coffee or a drink and—"

"I need to swing by Cedar Gables Inn," I said.

"Yeah? Okay. I can drive you there."

"Good. I'll be waiting out front. I'll make sure the draw-bridge is down."

He laughed. "Drawbridge!" he said. "What a joke! I'll be there in fifteen minutes."

I went upstairs to check on George, who was sitting up in bed reading a book.

"I'm running back to Cedar Gables," I said. "I seem to remember having seen something there that might have a bearing on Bill Ladington's death. I'll try not to be long. Neil Schwartz is driving me."

"He's here?"

"On his way. How's your back?"

"Better now, but getting up and about is always the test."

"I suggest you not put it to the test until I return, sometime before dinner."

Fidel, who was out front watering plants, lowered the drawbridge just as Neil arrived in his champagne-colored Lexus. He jumped out of the car and came around to open the door for me. He wore a blue blazer that appeared to be new, a red-and-black checkered button-down shirt, tan slacks with a sharp crease, and brown tasseled loafers.

"Want to go right to Cedar Gables?" Neil asked once we were on our way.

"If you don't mind."

"I don't mind at all. Checking in on your friends?"

"Something like that. You said you wanted to talk to me."

"It can wait."

"Maybe it can't," I said. "I mustn't be away long. George's back went out and I promised him I'd return in time for dinner."

"Okay. I've been doing some serious digging, Jess. When you told me that Ladington's wife was getting it on with the waiter, Hubler, that sent me in a new direction. I've been talking to dozens of townspeople who knew Ladington and his wife. Evidently the affair between Hubler and Tennessee wasn't such a big secret. A number of people were aware of it. I spoke with one guy who knew Ladington pretty well. He told me that Ladington also knew about the affair and said he was going to kill Hubler."

"This source of yours is certain that Bill Ladington knew his wife, Tennessee, was involved with Hubler?"

"Absolutely certain. Ladington told him he wanted to cut Hubler's heart out. That's a direct quote."

"Hubler *was* stabbed," I said. "In the heart."

"Exactly. Know what I think?"

"What?"

"I think Ladington killed Hubler, and his wife, Tennessee, killed him."

"Because her husband killed her lover?"

"Sure. Makes sense, doesn't it?"

I didn't answer. Instead, I asked, "What about drugs being involved, Neil? Everyone seems to believe drugs were a factor."

"They're wrong," he said as we pulled onto Coombs Street and stopped in front of Cedar Gables. "It's such a knee-jerk reaction, Jess. Cops immediately assume drugs are involved in every crime. Not in this case. It was lust and jealousy, pure and simple."

"You sound absolutely convinced."

"I sound that way because I am."

"I'd like to speak with this person who claims Ladington threatened to murder Hubler."

"No can do. I promised him anonymity. I can't break that promise."

"Coming in with me?"

"Sure. I'd like to meet your friends."

Craig was away, but Margaret greeted us as we came through the door.

"Hello, stranger," she said.

"Hi, Margaret. This is my friend Neil Schwartz."

"The writer," Margaret said, shaking his hand. "People around town have been telling me about you."

"I'm not sure whether that's good or bad," Neil said with a laugh.

"You're investigating William Ladington's death for a magazine article."

"That's right."

Margaret turned to me. "How's your stay going out at Ladington Creek?"

"All right, although George fell and hurt his back."

"Oh, I'm sorry to hear it. What brings you here?"

"I should have called first, Margaret, but I was in a rush."

Her eyebrows went up. "Something to do with Ladington's murder?"

"Possibly. Is your guest upstairs in the Churchill Chamber?"

"No. They all went out. Why?"

"I was wondering whether I could go up and take a look at the guest diary."

"Guest diary?" Neil said.

"Yes." To Margaret I added, "You know, the one where happy guests wrote their thoughts, and even included pictures."

"I'll go get it for you," Margaret said. "You and Neil settle in the den."

"Wow," Neil said when he saw Craig's shiny motorcycles. "Interesting way to decorate a B-and-B."

"It puts the male guests at ease, I'm told."

Margaret returned a minute later carrying the diary and handed it to me. I started at the beginning, flipping quickly through the thick book, stopping only to examine photographs as they appeared. Neil sat and viewed the book with me.

"What are you looking for?" he asked.

"I'll know it when I see it," I replied. Margaret had excused herself to help in the kitchen.

Although it wasn't my intention to read any of the guests' diary entries, it was difficult not to, so charming were many of them. Neil, too, had me stop a few times when an entry caught his eye.

I was three-quarters of the way through when the picture I was seeking appeared. It was a small Polaroid snapshot of a couple posed in front of one of the many hot air balloons for which Napa Valley is known, which take thousands of tourists each year into the air above the valley. Neil sensed I'd found what I was looking for.

"Who are they?" Neil asked.

"I'll fill you in once I've sorted out why this photo is here," I said.

Margaret poked her head back into the room. "Find what you're looking for?" she asked.

"Yes. Mind if I take this picture? I'll bring it back."

"Sure."

I placed the Polaroid in my purse and stood. "Can you give me a lift back to the castle?" I asked Neil.

"Of course, but I'd really like to know what that picture's all about."

"Please, Neil, not now."

Neil, obviously angry at my reticence, preceded me through the door.

"Be out in a minute," I yelled to him.

I showed the photo to Margaret. "Do you remember these guests?" I asked.

She took the snapshot and brought it closer to her eyes, then smiled. "Of course I do. They were here about a year ago. Craig and I got a kick out of them."

"Why?"

"They stayed with us for two nights. They were sort of— well, sort of secretive, like a couple of international spies."

I laughed. "What did they do?"

"In and out at odd hours, always whispering to each other, stopping their conversations abruptly whenever Craig or I approached. 'Typical French,' Craig said when they were gone."

Neil returned to the open door. "Come on, Jess, I haven't got all day."

"Sorry," I said, kissing Margaret on the cheek and going to the car with him.

He was obviously still annoyed. I considered telling him

what the photo meant to me, but still felt uncomfortable sharing it with him. To be honest, I wasn't sure myself what it meant, if anything, and I didn't want to give him fuel for speculation until I had something tangible to back it up.

Neil's face was grim, his lips set in a hard, thin line. He gripped the steering wheel as though trying to squeeze something from it, and pulled away faster than necessary.

"Please slow down," I said in response to squealing tires as he sped around a corner.

He did, but his expression was still one of irritation.

"Neil," I said, "I know you're upset but—"

"I thought we were friends."

"We are."

"Sure doesn't sound like it. All I've been asking is that we keep each other informed about what's going on with the murder. You're inside the house. I'm not. I'm working the street."

"And you seem to be successful at it."

"That's not the point. Sure, I'm good at getting people to talk openly to me. That's why I called and said I wanted to talk to you this afternoon. I want to wrap up the story on Hubler for the magazine. Now that we know that Ladington killed the kid because he was having an affair with his wife, I'd like you to—"

"Hold on, Neil. I know this unnamed source of yours claims Ladington knew of his wife's affair, and that he made some threat about carving Hubler's heart out, but that doesn't mean Ladington killed Hubler. People make dumb threats all the time."

"I'm convinced Ladington did it. Look, I know you've gotten close to the sheriff. I'm sure he respects you and listens to you. He won't give me the time of day."

"And?"

"And—I think he should have this information I've come up with."

"I told him about the affair between Hubler and Tennessee Ladington," I said.

"I want you to do more than that. I want you to *convince* him that Ladington killed Hubler."

"I can't do that, Neil. One, I'm not in a position to convince the sheriff of anything. Two, he's not about to come to a conclusion based upon a claim by an anonymous person."

"Why not? Ladington's dead. Frankly, I don't care who killed *him*. The Hubler case is the one I'm interested in."

I hesitated before asking, "Why is that, Neil? Sheriff Davis was wondering the same thing."

"He was?"

"Yes. I suppose it seems natural to him that the death—if it was murder—of William Ladington would be a much bigger story."

"Well, it isn't. You won't go to bat for me with the sheriff?"

"Go to bat for you? You sound as though you have some personal reason for wanting me to do it, Neil."

He said nothing and accelerated. I reached into the pocket of the teal blazer I was wearing and pulled out the green leather address book I'd found in Mary Jane Proll's apartment. Neil glanced over and saw it.

"What's that?" he asked.

"An address book I took from Ms. Proll's apartment when Sheriff Davis and I were there."

"What did you want that for?"

"There's a page at the back of the book, Neil, on which she'd written some phone numbers. They weren't in the alphabetical sections of the book, which leads me to believe they were grouped together on that page because they shared something in common."

"Like what?"

"I thought maybe you could tell me."

"Me?" He guffawed. "How would I know?"

"Your number in Sausalito is on that page."

"That's—my number?—that's ridiculous. Why would my number be there? I didn't even know her."

"I can't answer that," I said. "But here it is." I held it up so he could see it without taking his eyes from the road for more than a second.

"No idea, Jess," he said.

"I have to turn this over to Sheriff Davis, Neil. I didn't want to do that until I had a chance to ask you about it."

He swerved up onto the shoulder of the road, came to a jarring stop, and turned to face me. "What are you suggesting, Jess?" he asked, pleading for an answer, not belligerent. "Do you think that my number being in her address book has some sinister implication? What the hell are you doing?"

"Neil," I said, "I'm not suggesting anything, and I'm certainly not assigning something sinister to it. But you claimed you didn't know Mary Jane Proll. I accept that— except, why would she have your phone number included in a list of numbers at the back of her book? I think that's a fair question to ask. The sheriff will certainly ask it, too."

"And I can't give you an answer."

"Fair enough. Would you take me back to Ladington Creek now?"

For a moment, I wondered whether he might strike me, or insist I get out of the car. This was so unlike the Neil Schwartz I knew, the tough ex-cop with a poetic bent, a loving husband, father, and grandfather, a good friend.

He smiled and shook his head. "I'm sorry," he said. "It's just that my editor is putting pressure on me to get the article to her. I have no idea why my phone number is in that book, and frankly I don't care. Sure, give it to Sheriff Davis. It means nothing."

"I'm glad to hear that, Neil."

He checked his side-view mirror and pulled out onto the road. Fifteen minutes later we were crossing the drawbridge.

"Thanks for the lift, Neil. And I'm sorry if I sounded accusatory. I feel under some pressure too, to get to the bottom of things. George and I only have a few more days before we head home. Let's not let this detract from our friendship. We go back a long way together."

"We sure do. Let's keep in touch, huh?"

"Of course. You're staying in Napa a little longer?"

"No. I think I'll head home. I have enough to put together the article."

"That's good to hear. Thanks again."

He kissed my cheek and reached across to open my door. As I exited the car, the door to the castle opened and Tennessee Ladington came through it, followed by the driver, Raoul. I looked at Neil; was he about to get out of the Lexus and approach Tennessee? I considered for a moment introducing them because I was experiencing some guilt over not having been cooperative with him. But I shelved that instinct, and was relieved when he put the Lexus in reverse and drove away.

"Hello," I said, approaching Tennessee and Raoul.

"Friend of yours?" Tennessee asked. Raoul glowered at me, his usual expression.

"Yes," I said. "An old friend. I see I'm in time for cocktails and dinner."

"I'd like a word with you," she said.

"Of course. Let me see how George is doing and—"

"He's fine. Please."

"All right."

I followed her to a wing of the castle where the bedrooms were located, segregated by heavy wooden double doors leading to a long corridor. The master bedroom was at the end; we passed four other bedroom doors on our way, all shut.

The master bedroom was very large. A white, frilly, lightweight comforter covering a king-sized bed was in perfect concert with the rest of the room's decidedly feminine decor, which was somewhat incongruous with the masculine image Bill Ladington had presented. Tennessee noted my interest in the room.

"*Everything* wasn't Stetson hats and stuffed animal heads on the wall with Bill, Mrs. Fletcher," she said. "He had his soft side, too."

"I'm sure he did."

"He was pleased to let me decorate this room. When we married, this space looked like an army barracks. He gave me carte blanche with our bedroom and loved what I did with it. We spent many wonderful intimate moments here."

She invited me to sit in a small upholstered chair in front of an elaborate makeup table.

"I'm afraid I owe you an apology," she said.

"For what?"

"For the way you and the inspector have been treated here."

"We both understand the strain you've been under."

"I appreciate that," she said, sitting on the bed's edge. She crossed her long legs and sighed. "I never smoke in this room. I promised Bill I wouldn't."

"It certainly makes for a sweeter-smelling bedroom," I said.

"It was always sweet in here, Mrs. Fletcher. Bill was getting old, but he remained a very virile man right up until he died."

I was beginning to feel uncomfortable. I felt like George having a man-to-man talk with Bruce about Bruce's sterility problems. Was I about to be engaged in a woman-to-woman talk about her deceased husband's virility? I hoped not.

"I'm sure you're finding us a different breed of people than you're probably used to, Mrs. Fletcher."

"Would you call me Jessica? Or Jess?"

"Yes, I'd like that."

"A different breed?" I said. "I'm not sure that's true, although there are things that have—well, that have surprised me."

"Beginning with me?"

"No. I find it interesting that you allow Ms. Saison and Mr. LeGrand to stay here considering their designs on the winery."

It was more of a snort than a laugh. "Excuse me," she said. She left the room and returned smoking a cigarette. "With Bill gone, it doesn't make much difference whether I smoke in here or not."

I didn't say I would have preferred that she honor the deal they'd had.

"You were talking about Edith and Yves," she said, balancing an ashtray on her knee as she sat on the bed.

"That's right. She says they're entitled to ownership of Ladington Creek by virtue of their partnership with your husband."

"Well, they're wrong," she said, blowing a thick, blue cloud of smoke into the air and snuffing out her cigarette. "As far as having them here, it gives me a chance to keep an eye on them. Bill taught me that. Stay close to your enemies."

"I suppose there's wisdom in that," I said, "although I'm sure it's not easy for you."

We didn't say anything for a few moments. Finally, she said, "You haven't asked me whether I murdered Bill."

"Did you?"

"No. No one did. He committed suicide."

"With poison?"

"Yes. But then he fell into the moat and hit his head. Sheriff Davis called and told me what the autopsy revealed."

"I see," I said.

"I'm sure you do. If you research your murder mysteries as thoroughly as you've looked into Bill's death, they must be very good books."

"I like to think so. Tennessee, neither George nor I believe that your husband intended to kill himself. We're convinced that someone gave him the poison. Whether that was the proximate cause of his death or not is irrelevant."

"Irrelevant? He died of an accidental head injury."

"Not if the poison caused him to fall into the moat. Even if it didn't—even if he simply lost his balance—someone *attempted* to poison him. That's attempted murder."

"Are you looking at me, Jessica?"

"Should I be?"

"I didn't try to poison Bill."

"Fair enough," I said. "How does the murder of Louis Hubler fit in with all of this?"

"I haven't the slightest idea. Do you have ideas about it?"

Be direct? Bring up her alleged affair with Hubler?

"Were you having an affair with Hubler?"

She reacted by smiling and slowly shaking her head. "What powerful things rumors are," she said softly, lighting another cigarette.

"Were you?" I repeated.

"If I were," she said, "that would make you suspect me in that death, too, wouldn't it?"

"Those powerful rumors you mentioned involve you in an affair with Hubler, your husband knowing about it, him killing Hubler, and you killing your husband because he'd murdered your lover."

"My goodness," she said with exaggerated surprise. "Shakespeare couldn't have done better."

I laughed. "Now that I've told you what I've been hearing, Tennessee, I'd better look in on George. I'll see you at dinner?"

"Yes, of course."

I stood and was halfway to the door when it opened. Roger Stockdale glanced at me in surprise and confusion.

"Jessica and I were just having a heart-to-heart," Tennessee said.

"You were?" Stockdale said.

What struck me was that he evidently was comfortable simply walking into her bedroom. No knock on the door, no asking whether she was "decent."

"I must be going," I said.

I went directly upstairs. George's door was open. He was standing in front of a mirror straightening his tie.

"I see you're feeling better," I said.

He turned and nodded. "Much better, thank you. Did you find what you were looking for at your friends' B-and-B?"

"Yes."

I showed him the photograph I'd taken from Cedar Gables.

"Familiar faces," he said.

"Aren't they?"

"And?"

"They told me this was the first time they'd been to Napa Valley. Obviously, it isn't."

"I wonder why they bothered to stretch the truth."

"I intend to ask them."

"I'll be interested in their answer."

"So will I. I need to freshen up. Cocktails at the usual time?"

"So I'm told by Laura. She's been quite solicitous, playing nurse to me. I like her."

"Did you discuss her pregnancy?"

"Of course not. It wouldn't have been gentlemanly of me to probe such a delicate subject."

"I've come to the conclusion, George, that the only delicate subject around here is the relative quality of the wine. Give me ten minutes."

Chapter Twenty-eight

Everyone was in the drawing room when George and I arrived. Raoul stood at his usual place behind the bar; others clustered in various parts of the room. Bruce noted our entrance and came immediately to us.

"Hi," he said. "Is your back feeling better, Inspector?"

"Much, thank you. I took it easy today."

"I guess that's the best way," Bruce said. He appeared to be even more nervous than usual. There was perspiration on his forehead and upper lip, although the room was somewhat chilly. I saw that Laura stood at the opposite end of the room talking with Roger Stockdale.

"How is your wife feeling?" I asked.

"No more headaches, thank goodness. Sheriff Davis called this afternoon. He said you'd been with him."

"That's right."

"He said Dad probably died from hitting his head on the rocks."

"So he told me."

"But there was poison in his system, too. Somebody did murder him. He probably fell into the moat after the poison started to work."

"That's one possibility," George said.

"You said you and Laura enjoyed going to your father's steak house," I said.

"That's right, until that waiter was murdered."

"And your stepmother said she never went there."

"She's a liar. I know she used to stop in there at night for a drink. Plenty of times."

I considered asking him whether he was aware that his stepmother had been having an affair with Louis Hubler, but thought better of it. His hatred of her had been so apparent from the beginning that it would be difficult to give any credence to anything he might say about her.

Yves LeGrand and Edith Saison joined us.

"You look lovely," I told her.

"Thank you, Mrs. Fletcher. I understand you're the one to ask about progress in the investigation of Bill's death."

"That's hardly accurate," I said.

George tossed a conspiratorial glance at me and said to Bruce, "Let me get you a drink."

"Get me a—?"

He took Bruce's arm and led him to the bar, leaving me alone with Edith and Yves.

"I stopped in at Cedar Gables Inn this afternoon," I said. "It's a B-and-B owned by friends of mine. Do you know it?"

Frowns creased their brows.

"It's a lovely place. They have a diary of sorts, a scrapbook, in one of the rooms, the Churchill Chamber. People who spend time there, many of them honeymooners, write in the book. Some even include pictures of their stay in Napa Valley."

"Interesting," Yves said in his alluring accent. To Edith he added, "We must stay in this charming place Mrs. Fletcher speaks of the next time we visit."

"Excuse us," Edith said, turning and walking away. Yves nodded, and went after her.

"Well?" George asked me when he returned to my side.

"I wasn't direct," I said, "but I'm sure they knew what I was saying, and why I was saying it."

"They continue to deny they were here in Napa Valley before?"

"By inference, yes."

We didn't have a chance to discuss it further because Roger Stockdale joined us. "Good evening," he said. "Was your visit with the sheriff this morning fruitful?"

"To some extent," I replied. "I also spent time with the medical examiner."

"Oh?"

"The autopsy on Bill Ladington didn't show any sign of cancer."

"Interesting."

"I thought so. Was your only source of information Bill himself?"

He thought before answering. "Yes. He was the one who told me, but that's no surprise. No one else knew."

"He shared it with you but not with his wife or son?"

"Bill trusted me implicitly, Mrs. Fletcher. I'm the only person in his inner circle who can claim that."

George spoke. "I understand you were promised some sort of partnership by Mr. Ladington."

"I wouldn't call it a partnership, Inspector, but he did assure me that I would become a participant in the vineyard's profits once the new varietals bore fruit and produced the quality of cabernet they promised."

"But only if he died," I said. "I think that's what you told me."

"You're wrong. I was to share in the profits whether he was dead or alive. His concern was that if he were to die, I was not to be cut out by the vultures around him."

George laughed. "I always enjoy vultures with names," he said.

Stockdale looked around the room. "Take your pick," he said. "There wasn't one of them who cared whether Bill lived or died, and he knew it. He didn't trust anybody. Is that paranoia? Sure it is, but there's that old saying that just because you're paranoid doesn't mean someone isn't following you. He built the moat, had guns around, hid money in different places to keep it out of their hands." He swept the room with his own hand to indicate that he was referring to them all. "He was a very unhappy man."

"He seemed happy to me," I said.

"He put on that façade, Mrs. Fletcher. Underneath, he was miserable."

"Dinner is served," Tennessee announced from the doorway.

We went to the dining room and took our seats at the large table. Everything seemed the same—until the kitchen door opened and salads were brought to us, carried not by the soon-to-depart Mercedes, or by Fidel and Consuela, but by Nick, the chef whose routine had been to cook lunch at the house, then go to the restaurant bearing Ladington's name to handle dinner there. He wore kitchen whites and a tall white chef's hat. He was a handsome man, no older than thirty-five, with a dark complexion and a heavy twelve-o'clock shadow.

When he'd left the room, I asked, "To what do we owe the presence of the chef this evening?"

"For what he's being paid, we might as well have him cook decent dinners for *us*," Tennessee said from the head of the table. "The sous chef is handling dinner at the restaurant. I'm selling the joint as soon as the estate is settled and I can find a buyer."

"I understand Mercedes is leaving," I said nonchalantly, taking a bite of salad.

"You seem to know everything," Tennessee said. She had changed into a sequined red halter top and tight white slacks for dinner, and had pulled her long blonde hair back into a taut ponytail. She wore less makeup than I was accustomed to seeing on her.

"Unfortunately, I don't," I said. "Know everything. I wish I did."

"Meaning?"

"Meaning, I'm sure I share what all of you desire, to know what really happened to your husband."

"We already know that, Mrs. Fletcher," she said, her lip curling. "Frankly, I find you and your charming British friend to be more amusing than efficient. Sheriff Davis told me what happened when he called today. Bill took poison, but before that could work he fell and struck his head."

"Or someone in this room fed him that poison," George said.

Wade Grosso cleared his throat, causing everyone to look at him. He said to me, "Do *you* think one of us killed Bill?"

I chose not to reply.

Bruce said animatedly, "Dad *was* murdered. And what conclusion can anyone come to except that somebody close to him is the murderer?"

They all stared at him without saying anything.

Nick delivered the soup course, and we ate in silence until I announced, "We'll be leaving here tomorrow." I glanced at George, who masked any surprise my pronouncement might have caused him.

"You can't," Bruce said from his seat across from me.

"I'm afraid we must, Bruce," I said. "We both have to get back to our respective homes and lives. It's evident to me that our presence here has been an extremely unwelcome one, and I'm old enough to know when a welcome has been outworn."

Bruce said to George, "How can you just leave when you know someone has been murdered? Don't you have some sort of ethics at Scotland Yard?"

George smiled and said calmly, "Oh, yes, we have many codes of ethics at the Yard. But Jessica and I also have our personal lives to consider. We came to this lovely valley to relax and enjoy each other's company. I think it's time we did that."

"You'll be leaving in the morning?" Tennessee asked as Fidel and Consuela cleared the soup bowls and Nick delivered the main course, lovely-looking breasts of chicken and braised root vegetables.

"Some time tomorrow," I responded. "This looks delicious."

My announcement of our planned departure created two distinctly different reactions. Bruce and his wife became sullen, although it was hard to determine Laura's true feelings because she was sullen so much of the time. On the other hand, spirits seemed to pick up with Tennessee, Roger, and Wade.

In between those diverse reactions were Edith and Yves. I couldn't read what either of them was thinking. When I confronted them about Cedar Gables Inn, I had expected them to agree with me that it was, indeed, a lovely place and that they'd spent a pleasant time there. At least that would have been the way I would have handled it. If asked why I'd said earlier that I'd never been to Napa Valley, a simple laugh and reference to having forgotten would have sufficed.

After dinner, as George and I were leaving the dining room, Tennessee encouraged us sweetly to ask for help if we needed it when leaving in the morning. I thanked her, and George and I went outside for some air. It was a pristine night, with millions of brilliant white stars against a black sky. And it was chilly; the sound of hundreds of windmills keeping the vines warm provided a low drone over the valley. George lit his pipe and drew contentedly on it.

"How's your back?" I asked.

"It was all right for a while, not perfect but better. Beginning to trouble me as we sat at dinner. What made you decide to announce we were leaving?"

"To create a sense of urgency."

"With *them*?"

"With me. Truth is, we have a couple of days before we have to leave. I thought I would call Margaret and Craig and see if our rooms at the inn have become available. Spend our last days there."

"Without a resolution to Ladington's murder?"

"Don't think that doesn't bother me. But resolving who killed him really isn't our responsibility. It never was."

"You won't hear an argument from me, Jessica."

He groaned; his hand went to his back.

"You're in pain."

"This chilly air isn't helping."

"Come," I said, taking his hand. "Let's get inside."

This particular spasm had come on quickly. By the time we'd reached the door and stepped into the hallway, he was almost doubled over. I helped him up the stairs and to his room, where he stretched out on the bed with a long, deep sigh of relief.

"What can I get you?" I asked. "Do you want me to call a doctor?"

"Oh, no, love. This is all I need."

"I feel so guilty," I said.

"Guilty? You don't control the weather."

"I wasn't talking about the weather. There's been such tension here, I'm sure it's contributed to your bad back."

"Nonsense. No more talk about that."

There was a knock at the door. It was Laura Ladington.

"I saw the inspector and you come in, Mrs. Fletcher," she said. "Is he all right?"

"No, he's not," I said. "His back seems worse."

She looked past me at George, who managed a wave.

"Is there anything I can do?" she asked.

"I don't think so." I turned to George: "Can we get you anything?"

"Thank you, no."

I thanked Laura for asking. She looked as though she was about to leave, but her hesitation was obvious. She whispered, "Could I speak with you privately?"

"Of course."

"After you've taken care of the inspector."

"Meet you downstairs?"

"Outside," she said, fear in her voice. "In the vineyard."

"Fifteen minutes?"

"Yes."

She backed away, and I closed the door. George was now sitting up. His raised eyebrows asked the obvious question.

"She wants to speak with me privately."

"Interesting. The quiet Mrs. Ladington is about to become vocal."

"Maybe it's nothing."

"Maybe. But I have a gut feeling—no, a feeling in my back—that she's about to tell you something meaningful."

"We'll see. Sure I can't do anything?"

"Nothing. Go. Have your private conversation with Laura. Then report back as quickly as possible."

"Yes, boss." I tossed him a small salute, got a cardigan from my room, slipped it on, and headed for the vineyard.

Chapter Twenty-nine

The hand-operated wooden drawbridge over the narrow part of the moat, to the rear of the castle, was down when I arrived. One of the security guards sat dozing in the chair. My presence startled him awake.

"Good evening," I said.

"Oh, hello."

"Lovely night. A little chilly."

"Yes, it is."

"Did Laura Ladington come out here a few minutes ago?"

"Yes, ma'am. She's out there in the vineyard."

I looked past him and saw Laura standing where George and I had last encountered her. Were it not for the moonlight, she would have been invisible among the vines.

I crossed the drawbridge and approached slowly. She appeared to be ill. She was bent over, supporting herself by holding one of the stakes.

"Laura?' I said, stopping a few feet from her.

"I—I'm sorry," she said. "I was nauseous. I must have eaten something that—" She began to cry, softly at first, then loud sobs that caused her body to heave. I closed the gap between us and placed my hand on her shoulder.

"What is it?" I asked. "Nothing served at dinner tonight seemed to—"

"It wasn't food. It wasn't anything I ate. It's—"

"It's your pregnancy," I said.

My blunt statement caused her sobbing to cease.

"How did you know?" she asked.

"Women in the early stages of pregnancy often don't realize how soon they begin to show," I said lightly. "You *looked* pregnant to me."

"Oh, God," she said. "How did I get into this mess?"

"I can't answer that," I said. "I assume Bruce is pleased."

"Bruce? He doesn't—"

"Doesn't know? You haven't told him?"

"Yes, he knows."

"He noticed, too."

She shook her head. "He hasn't had a chance to notice, Mrs. Fletcher. We haven't slept together for a long time."

"How many months are you?" I asked.

"Three, I think."

I wasn't sure how far to probe into what was obviously a very personal situation. Yet I felt I had to, knowing through George that Bruce was sterile.

"I know I'm prying, Laura, but since you've opened up to me, I feel somewhat justified."

"It's all right," she said, her crying now under control.

"I've been told, Laura, that your husband isn't capable of fatherhood. Is that true?"

Her voice tightened. "How did you find that out?"

"It doesn't matter. What *does* matter is whether the situation you find yourself in has any bearing on your father-in-law's death."

"No. Of course it doesn't."

"Then why did you decide to confide in me tonight?"

"I don't know why, Mrs. Fletcher. It was foolish of me. I'm sorry."

She turned to leave.

"Laura," I said.

She stopped, turned, and faced me.

"Who's the father of your child?"

The light from the moon illuminated her face, which was now hard, even hateful.

"Who, Laura?"

"That bastard, Ladington."

"Ladington? Not Bruce."

"No."

"Your father-in-law."

"Yes."

She ran from me in the direction of the drawbridge and the house.

Chapter Thirty

"That is a shocking revelation," George said after I'd returned to his room and told him of my conversation with Laura.

"I'm still in shock," I said, sitting on the edge of the bed and trying to process what I'd been told.

"How could a father do such a thing to a son?" George asked, as though seeking wisdom from an unseen force in the room. "The man must have been a monster to rape his own daughter-in-law."

"If it was rape," I said.

"Good God," George said. "If it wasn't rape—if it was consensual—it's even more perverted in a way."

"Do you think he could possibly have deliberately impregnated Laura to punish Bruce?"

"If so, it makes his actions even more despicable. At least if he'd had a sexual relationship with his daughter-in-law out of lust for her, it could be understood. Not condoned, of course, but understood in human terms. But if it was an act of aggression toward his own flesh and blood, it reaches the level of evil."

I simply nodded.

"She didn't indicate why it happened?"

"No. It was enough for her to tell me at all. The moment she did, she was gone, scurrying back to the castle."

"Why do you think she told you, Jessica?"

"I've been trying to figure that out since it happened. Confess? Salve her conscience."

"Deliver a message to you?"

"About the murder? That's the most logical reason. I asked her about that. I didn't get an answer."

George stood stiffly and went to the window. "Who else knows?" he asked.

"I don't know."

"Was Ladington killed because of it?"

"A good possibility."

"If Tennessee knew, it could have angered her to the point of killing her unfaithful husband," he said.

"The same could be said for Bruce. Laura told me that Bruce knows about the pregnancy, but she didn't say whether he knows his father was responsible."

"What do you suggest we do with this information, Jessica?"

"That's one of many questions swimming around my brain. I can't help but wonder who else in this household has been having affairs. There's Tennessee having had her fling with Louis Hubler. She might have entered into that relationship to get back at her husband—*if* she knew he'd fathered Laura's baby."

"If so, it would be a more benign form of revenge than killing him. What about the others?"

"Hard to say," I replied, "not knowing their own personal secrets. Stockdale burst into Tennessee's bedroom while I was there with her. I have the feeling it isn't the first time."

"An affair between them?"

"Possible," I said.

"Our charming French friends," George said. "Any idea why they'd been here in Napa Valley before, but found it necessary to lie about it?"

"No. Where does this leave us? It appears that Ladington

was murdered for one of two reasons: lust and/or jealousy, or money."

"Two of the more common motives."

"Let's say it was lust or jealousy, George. What I can't sort out is the ingestion of poison and his fall into the moat. Did someone push him? If so, that could have been the result of a jealous rage. But he was poisoned, too. That's a much more premeditated approach and would take careful planning."

He returned to sit beside me on the bed and laughed. "Maybe two people tried to kill our philandering vintner, one with poison, the other by pushing him to his death. Hardly likely that the same person tried both methods."

"Not necessarily," I said. "The murderer might have tried poison, saw it wasn't working—or working too slowly—and finished him off in a more forceful way. Belt and suspenders."

I observed him as he sat next to me. He was deep in thought.

"What are you thinking?" I asked.

"That we're overlooking Miss Laura. We're sitting here speculating about how her pregnancy might have prompted someone to kill. But we're not taking into account that she had as much, or more, motive for killing her father-in-law. Let's say it was rape. She wouldn't be the first woman who'd sought revenge on her rapist."

"Well," I said, standing and stretching against a pain that had developed in *my* back, "I don't think this changes our plans to leave tomorrow."

"I'm in the mood for a drink," he said.

"I'll join you. It's been that sort of an evening."

We went down to the drawing room where George pulled down a bottle of single-malt Scotch from behind the bar. "You?" he asked.

"I'll have some of that Ladington Creek cabernet," I said.

We held up our glasses in a toast. As we did, Nick entered the room.

"Sorry," he said. "I didn't think anyone would be here."

"No problem," George said. "Please join us."

"That's what I came in for," Nick said, going directly to the bar. He went behind it and poured bourbon into a water glass, "Aah," he said, taking a healthy swig. "This may be wine country, but there's nothing like a good bourbon." He wore jeans, a white V-neck sweater that exposed a bush of black chest hair, a well-worn leather jacket, and loafers sans socks.

"I agree," said George, "especially one of your single-barrel varieties."

"We've never been formally introduced," I said. "I'm Jessica Fletcher, and this is George Sutherland."

He shook our hands.

"I know who you both are," he said, drinking again; his glass was almost empty. "Famous mystery writer and Scotland Yard detective." He finished off his drink and refilled his glass. "So, who done it?"

"Murdered William Ladington?" I said.

"Yeah. Somebody did, that's for sure."

"I thought *you* might have some answers," I said, "working here and at the restaurant."

He crossed the room, fell into an easy chair, and raised his glass. "To the end of the Ladington era."

We took chairs near him.

"You sound almost pleased that the 'Ladington era' has ended," I said.

"Pleased? No. Indifferent. The man was crazy, impossible to work for. And that wife of his. The current one, I mean." He affected a southern accent. "Madame Tennessee." He snickered and drank. "She got what she wanted. She married the old fool for his money. Looks like her plan paid off."

"We had lunch one day at your restaurant," George said.

"Not my restaurant. I'm out of there. I'm heading home to San Francisco, to my old job at Fleur de Lys. You know it?"

"A very nice French restaurant," I said. "I've eaten there. Why did you leave to work for Bill Ladington?"

"We all have our moments of insanity, Mrs. Fletcher. That was mine. It doesn't matter. I've had enough of this valley and the people who make wine. They're all a little nuts. Don't you agree?"

"I can't say that I've met enough of them to come to that conclusion."

George sat forward in his chair, his glass cradled in his hands. "Since you're leaving," he said, "Mr.—what is your last name?"

"Potmos."

"Mr. Potmos. Since you're leaving, I feel comfortable being direct in asking you questions."

"Questions?" His eyebrows went up. "Am I being interrogated by Scotland Yard?"

"Of course not," George responded. "But Mrs. Fletcher and I are leaving in the morning and our natural curiosity is getting the better of us."

"Yeah, yeah, I know, the kid brought you here to prove his old man was murdered. No luck, huh?"

"Solving crimes often involves luck, Mr. Potmos, more than most police officers like to admit. But maybe we'll get lucky with you."

"Shoot. I've already been questioned a couple of times by Sheriff Davis and his people about the Hubler thing. Nothing to hide. What do you want to know? Who do I think killed Bill Ladington?"

"A good place to start," I offered.

"When Mrs. Fletcher and I—" George started to say.

"Please, it's Jessica," I said.

"And I'm Nick. You were saying?"

"I was saying," George continued, "that when Jessica and I had lunch in Ladington's Steak House, we noticed you had a sushi bar. Unusual fare for a steak house, we thought."

"*Mea culpa*," Nick said, holding up his hands in mock defense. "I convinced Ladington the place needed something different instead of just greasy steaks and french fries. He didn't like the idea, but he let me put in the sushi bar."

"Did the fish offered at it include puffer fish?" I asked.

Potmos shrugged. "I don't know what Ye used. Not my thing."

"Ye? Was he Japanese?"

"Yeah. Nice little guy, but he split a few days after Hubler was killed. I didn't bother finding a replacement for him. I closed the sushi bar down, as I'm sure you noticed. Ye ordered fish from different places, San Fran, L.A., lots of places."

"Including Curaçao?" I asked.

"As a matter of fact, he did, but not through the usual suppliers. Ladington hooked up with some source in Curaçao. He has— had—a home there. Insisted we order from them."

"Bill Ladington arranged it?"

Potmos thought for a moment. "No. Tennessee did."

George and I glanced at each other.

"Why?" Potmos said.

"Nothing specific," I said. "To your knowledge, was Mrs. Ladington having an affair with your waiter, Louis Hubler?"

Potmos laughed loudly, got up, and went to the bar. "This deserves another drink, a double." He returned to his chair with his glass filled again, sat back, crossed his legs, and grinned. "You were asking about Tennessee and Louis. My, how word does fly. Yeah, they had something going between them. She made a pass at me, too, only she's not my type. A little long in the tooth for me."

I didn't say what I was thinking.

George said, "You spent your evenings at the restaurant, Mr. Potmos, preparing dinners for customers. You obviously interacted a great deal with staff, including Louis Hubler and a waitress named Mary Jane Proll. Ms. Proll told us that she and Louis had been dating. Is that true?"

"Dating? That's an old-fashioned term. Did they get it on now and then, out in the car, in a storeroom? Yeah, they did."

"Were they drug users?" I asked.

"Oh, boy, now we're getting heavy," Potmos said with a laugh.

"Not nearly as heavy as murder," George offered. "Were they drug users?"

"Some weed now and then, maybe an upper. Ecstasy when they were partying, nothing more than that."

His cavalier attitude about drug use was unsettling, even distasteful. I seemed to be reading almost every day about young men and women suffering serious illness, even death, through the use of so-called recreational drugs. How sad.

"Where did they get the drugs?" George asked.

Potmos shrugged and drank. "Where does anybody get drugs? Dealers. They run it up from San Francisco."

"Did either of them *sell* drugs?"

"Hubler did some selling. Minor stuff at first, just enough to support his own use. But then he got more ambitious. I guess the money was better than minimum wage and tips."

"There's been speculation that Bill Ladington might have murdered Hubler out of jealousy about his wife."

"It's crossed my mind."

"Or Mrs. Ladington. Ms. Proll told us Hubler had ended the affair."

"Another possibility. How about Mary Jane? She was jealous as hell, seething with rage at being dumped for a senior citizen."

George looked at me and smiled.

"We've thought of that," I said. "Of the three, which one do you think killed Louis Hubler?"

"Hey, why all this interest in Hubler? I thought you were here to nail the old man's killer."

"There might be a link between the two murders," George said.

"Well, good luck," Potmos said, draining his glass of its amber liquid, and standing. He crossed the room in the direction of the door, stopped, turned, and said, "You didn't ask whether I killed old man Ladington."

"Did you?" I asked.

He shook his head. "Hubler, either. Have a good night."

When he was gone, I asked George what he thought.

"Interesting, arrogant chap. Do I think he might have provided the poison that Ladington ingested? No, I don't. Someone else either got hold of the puffer fish ingredient from the sushi bar, or brought it back with them from Curaçao. Either way, I know one thing."

"What's that?"

"The Hubler and Ladington murders are, most likely, not connected."

"Why?"

"Instinct, based upon what I've gleaned from people we've talked with. And you? What do your instincts say?"

"My instincts are talking louder lately. Tell you what. I want to call Sheriff Davis and see if we can get him here tomorrow morning. He gave me his home phone number."

"And?"

"I think we might provide for an interesting breakfast before we leave Ladington Creek. I'd like the sheriff on hand."

"You'll fill me in, I'm sure, before this so-called 'interesting breakfast.' "

"Of course I will, but not here. Is your back up to a ride?"

"Even if it were broken, I wouldn't miss this conversation for anything."

Chapter Thirty-one

We drove first to a pay phone from which I called Sheriff Davis at home. His wife, a pleasant woman, answered and brought her husband to the phone.

"Mrs. Fletcher," he said.

"Hope I'm not disturbing a favorite TV show."

"Not at all. I was in my workshop putting finishing touches on a piece of furniture I'm building. It's my hobby, woodworking."

"I'm always impressed with people who can do that," I said. "I won't keep you from it for more than a minute. I was wondering whether you were free in the morning to join George and me for breakfast at Ladington Creek."

Davis laughed gently. "What's the occasion?" he asked.

"George and I will be leaving in the morning. In a sense, it will be our farewell breakfast with all the occupants of the castle. One of them murdered Bill Ladington, and I think we know who it is."

There was a moment of silence on the line before Davis said, "Have I got this right, Mrs. Fletcher? You and your Scottish friend intend to accuse someone at breakfast?"

"Exactly," I said.

"Well, Mrs. Fletcher, I don't see how I can say no to an invitation like that. What time?"

"They usually gather between seven and seven-thirty."

"I'll be there."

"You might want to station some of your deputies in a car outside, on the other side of the moat. Just in case our plan works."

"All right."

"Thanks, Sheriff. I'll see you in the morning."

We next drove to a nearby bakery and coffee shop that was ready to close, but whose owner graciously invited us to sit and order cappuccinos, and the last piece of coconut custard pie in the display case. We had the place to ourselves, which was ideal for the topic of discussion, the murder of William Ladington. I laid out for George the conclusions to which I'd come, and what I thought we should do with them.

"I don't know," he said when I finished, fishing his pipe from his jacket, remembering he couldn't smoke inside, and returning it to his pocket. "You're suggesting we accuse someone of murder without having the proverbial smoking gun."

"Which we'll never have," I said. "I'm counting on the vulnerability of the murderer, George. I've seen it happen more than once before. As you well know, plenty of murderers have been put away on purely circumstantial evidence, even without a body. I've also seen pretty tough characters fess up when confronted with compelling circumstantial evidence. I think it's worth a try."

"I'm not arguing with you, Jessica. I've heard my share of such confessions, too. I suppose we can apply the old adage, nothing ventured, nothing gained. I'm with you."

"Good."

He shook his head. "You're determined not to leave here without some sort of resolution."

"Does that surprise you?"

"It might with someone else. With you? No. You agreed to help Bruce Ladington prove that his father had been murdered, and you don't want to let him down. I quite understand that."

"I'm glad you do. But the big question is, do you agree with my thesis?"

"Yes." He held up his hand. "However, I hope you aren't disappointed if your theory fails to elicit an admission of guilt."

"I'm prepared for that."

There was one sliver of pie left on the plate.

"Go ahead," I said.

"No, no, no, it's for you."

"I insist."

"I wouldn't think of taking the last piece."

"I wouldn't either."

George said, "Let's go. We have a busy morning ahead of us."

"Yes."

We stood and looked down at the table.

"Please," he said.

"Absolutely not."

He scooped up the slice with his fork, paid the bill, and we returned to Ladington Creek where we sat in my room for another hour going over what we intended to do at breakfast, speaking in hushed tones, even passing each other notes to avoid any possibility of being overheard. Finally, he wrote his final note: *I'm going to bed.*

Why are you writing me that? I wrote. "Go to bed," I said loudly.

He laughed. "I will," he said. "Good night, Jessica."

"Good night," I said, laughing, too. "Sleep tight. See you at breakfast."

I expected to have trouble sleeping, but it turned out not to be the case. I awoke rested and content, very much at peace with myself and with what George and I were about to do.

It was early, a few minutes past six. I took a leisurely shower, packed my bag, dressed in my traveling clothes, and sat on the window seat. It promised to be a fair day, although as George had pointed out, the weather in Napa Valley could be changeable.

At seven, I went to George's room and knocked.

"Come in," he said.

He was dressed and packed, too.

"Ready?" I asked.

"Yes."

"How's the back?"

"Just fine. Nothing like a good night's sleep to straighten out the kinks."

"Glad to hear it."

"Is the prosecution ready?" he asked lightly.

"I think so. My concern is that they all won't be there."

"We'll just have to hope that they are. Actually, we only need one—the *right* one."

Wade Grosso and Roger Stockdale were seated at the table when we entered the dining room. They'd been served juice and coffee.

"Good morning," I said pleasantly, slipping into the chair George held out for me.

They returned the greeting.

"Are you on your way?" Grosso asked as Consuela entered carrying a tray with their breakfasts.

"Yes, we are," George said, laying his napkin on his lap. "Where are the others?"

As he asked it, Tennessee arrived, followed closely by Edith Saison and Yves LeGrand. Tennessee took her usual spot at the head of the table; Edith and Yves sat across from me.

"All packed?" Edith asked.

"Yes," I said. "Who's doing the cooking this morning?"

They all looked at Tennessee.

"Nick. He'll be doing three meals a day here until he leaves for San Francisco. I've closed the restaurant. Nick has another week before he leaves."

"That's good to hear," I said. "It must be a real luxury to have a professional chef on hand."

"We'll manage when he's gone," said Tennessee.

Bruce and Laura walked in as Tennessee was telling Consuela what she wanted for breakfast. Consuela evidently knew Edith's and Yves's preferences because she didn't bother asking them.

Tennessee called after Consuela: "Take Mrs. Fletcher's and Inspector Sutherland's order." To us she added, "I'm sure you want to be on your way as early as possible."

Before I could respond, Raoul came through the door. "The sheriff is here," he said.

"The sheriff?" Stockdale said in some surprise.

"I should have mentioned," I said. "I invited him to have breakfast with us. I was sure you wouldn't mind."

There were puzzled looks around the table before Tennessee said, "Happy to have him. Maybe he has something new to report on the investigation, although his call yesterday seems to have wrapped things up."

"We'd like breakfast, too," Bruce said, obviously annoyed that he and his wife had been ignored.

"Go tell Nick what you want," Tennessee said flatly. "It's not a resort."

As Bruce went to the kitchen, I observed Laura. She avoided my eyes, which was understandable considering the revelation she'd made to me the previous day.

"Good morning," Sheriff Davis said.

"Good morning, Sheriff," Stockdale said, standing. "A pleasure having you here. Please, sit down and join us."

He sat next to me.

"Catch the murderer yet?" Grosso asked through a mouthful of scrambled eggs.

"No," Davis replied. He glanced at me. "But I think we're getting close."

"That's good news," Edith said.

"Only if it's not you," Tennessee said. "Who heads the list?"

Davis started to respond but I said, "I'm sure the sheriff has a busy day and would like breakfast."

"Go get Nick," Tennessee told Stockdale, who dutifully got up and went to the kitchen. He returned with the chef, who took Davis's order for pancakes, bacon, orange juice, and coffee.

"Much obliged," Davis said after placing his order.

Bruce cleared his throat, coughed, and asked Davis, "Has it been determined, *really* determined, what killed Dad? You said it was his head hitting rocks in the moat. Is that a proven fact?"

"Yes," Davis said. "Dr. Ayala, the ME, now confirms it was the blow to the head that killed your father, Bruce."

"What about the pills?" Stockdale asked.

"They weren't any pills," Davis answered. "He was also poisoned by puffer fish."

"What the hell are they?" Grosso asked.

"A rare fish that's often used in sushi, at least in Japan. Very deadly if it isn't handled right. Your father had some in his system, but because he was such a big man, and the amount of poison was small, it wasn't sufficient to kill him. No, he died from a brain hemorrhage, either because he slipped into the moat and hit his head, or—"

"Or what?" Stockdale asked.

"Or was pushed into the moat by someone. If that's the way it happened, whoever did it is a murderer."

"Sushi," Grosso grumbled. "Raw fish. How anybody can eat that stuff is beyond me."

Yves stood and came around behind Edith's chair. "You'll excuse us," he said. "Obviously, none of this involves us."

"I think you ought to sit down and stay a while," Davis said with an edge to his tone.

I touched his arm and said, "It's all right if they leave, Sheriff." I then said to Yves and Edith, "But before you go, there's one question I'd like answered."

Yves's eyebrows arched.

"Why did you lie about never having been to Napa Valley before this trip?"

"You're calling us liars?" Yves said, forcing indignation into his voice.

"I'm saying you were here a previous time." I pulled the photo I'd taken from Cedar Gables from my purse and held it up for them to see. "There's no crime in saying you weren't here before. But why bother denying it?"

Grosso snarled, "This is nonsense. Whether they were here before or not doesn't mean a damn thing."

George and I had discussed why Edith and Yves might have lied, and had come to a conclusion that George now expressed to Grosso, then extended it with his eyes to everyone else at the table. "We know Ms. Saison and Mr. LeGrand had been in Napa Valley before. Do any of you remember seeing them here at the vineyard?"

Silence indicated their denials until Grosso spoke. "I knew they were here," he said.

"Did you?" George said. "Did they stay here at the castle?"

"You know they didn't," Grosso said. "They were at that inn."

"Cedar Gables," I said.

"Whatever," Grosso said with a shrug.

"What were you doing here the last time?" I asked the French couple.

"Come," Yves said to Edith, pulling out her chair.

"You know damn well why you were here," Grosso growled.

"Why don't *you* tell us, Mr. Grosso," George suggested gently.

"Halton Mountain," Grosso said. "They were trying to cut a deal with that bastard, Jenkins, to get control of the mountain."

Stockdale slapped his hand on the table. "You knew that?" he demanded of Grosso.

"Yeah, I knew it."

"Did Bill know?"

Grosso looked at the empty plate in front of him and said nothing.

"Of course you knew it," Edith said, venom in her voice. "You couldn't wait for the deal to go through so you could get your cut."

"Cut? What cut?" Tennessee demanded.

"For helping us gain control of Halton Mountain," Edith replied.

"With Jenkins?" Tennessee said. "Is that true, Wade?" she asked.

He maintained his silence.

"I can't believe this," Stockdale shouted at Grosso, getting to his feet. "You sold us out to these—to these—these foreigners?"

Bruce Ladington suddenly came to life. "Is that why you killed my father?" he shouted, first at Edith and Yves, then at Grosso.

"I didn't kill anybody," Grosso said.

Yves and Edith headed for the door.

"*Au revoir,*" George said.

"You're letting them just walk out?" Bruce said to the sheriff. "They're murderers."

"No, they're not, Bruce," I said.

"Then he is," he said, pointing to Grosso.

"No," George said.

The room fell into a profound silence.

"Who, then?" Bruce asked.

"You, I'm afraid," I said.

"Me?" He shook his head and forced a laugh. "That's crazy. I'm the one who brought you here because I was the only one who believed my father was murdered. I'm the only one who fought to keep the investigation going."

"Exactly," George said.

"I can't believe this," Bruce said, standing. He glared at me. "Why do you think I killed my father?"

I sighed; this sort of confrontation has always been dismaying to me. "First, Bruce, you certainly had motive."

"Motive? I loved my father."

"But he didn't return that love, did he?"

"That isn't true. He—"

"Bruce," I said, also standing and facing him, "you know full well what your father did to you. I'm talking about the final blow, the ultimate display of his lack of love and respect for you."

"What are you talking about?"

"Laura told me," I said.

He looked down at his wife, who sat with her elbows on the table, her head buried in her hands.

"Did you?" he asked her.

"Yes." Her response was barely audible.

"What are you talking about?" Tennessee demanded.

"Bruce can tell you if he wishes," I said. "The important thing is that your husband angered him to the point of murder."

"Doesn't make sense," Stockdale said. "He's the one's been preaching murder all along."

"Which is why we decided he could be the murderer," I said. "I've always had a theory that those who make the most noise about a murder are often the guilty parties. Not always, of course, but enough times to convince me it was true in this case."

George added, "Mrs. Fletcher expressed her theory to me, and I immediately concurred. My experience investigating hundreds of homicides has led me to the same conclusion. These people do it for one of two reasons, either to deflect suspicion from themselves—which, I might add, worked quite well for Bruce in the early stages—or out of a neurotic need to assuage their guilt by calling for justice."

"I didn't poison him," Bruce offered weakly. "I didn't even know he'd been poisoned when I—"

"When you pushed him?" I asked.

"I—I just went out to tell him I was tired of being treated like dirt. I was his son, for God's sake. He barely acknowledged me and never did. And then when Laura told me what had happened, I—"

"What are you talking about?" Tennessee fairly snarled. "What did Bill do to make you so mad that you killed him?"

For a moment, I thought Bruce was going to tell her. He started to shake. His hands were tight fists at his side, and his face became beet red, as though pressure was being exerted from within that threatened to explode his head. Then he began to cry and slumped back down into his chair. He managed to say through his tears, "I never meant to kill him. I just wanted to hurt him the way he's hurt me. He was standing at the edge of the moat. He seemed drunk, unsteady on his feet. His voice was slurred. I was so disgusted with him and—no, disgusted with myself for taking it all these years—I pushed him. That's all. I didn't hit him or anything. I just pushed him and he went down. I heard him hit the water and the sound of his head hitting something solid. A rock."

All eyes were on him.

"Why did you put the empty pill bottle on his desk and write that supposed suicide note?" George asked.

"I guess I panicked. I didn't want anyone to know what I'd done so I decided to make it look like a suicide."

"You didn't even know whether he was dead," I said.

"I just figured he was. I came inside, went to his study, and emptied some sort of pills down the toilet. Dad had that little Canon typewriter next to his desk. He always wrote notes to himself on it. I typed the note and put it on the desk with the empty bottle."

"But didn't you realize that an autopsy would show that he didn't have any medication in his system?" I asked, unable to keep from sounding astonished at his naiveté.

"It turned out he did have a foreign, toxic substance in his system," George offered.

"I didn't poison him," Bruce repeated. "I never wanted to kill him."

I looked around the table and received in return a succession of blank stares.

The sheriff called for his men on his cell phone. A few minutes later, two uniformed officers entered the room.

"Arrest Mr. Ladington for the murder of his father," Davis instructed.

As they pulled Bruce's arms behind his back and secured his wrists with handcuffs, he said, "You don't know how terrible he was to me. So terrible. He hated me. Hated me. All I wanted was for him to love me, respect me as a man. I'm so sorry."

I ached for him as the officers led him away. His final words trailed off, "I loved him . . ."

Everyone in the dining room was stunned into stillness.

"His own son," Tennessee muttered. "How dreadful."

"I suppose I'd best be going now," Sheriff Davis said.

"You haven't eaten yet," I said.

"Not hungry," he said. "Thanks, Mrs. Fletcher, Inspector Sutherland."

He took a few steps toward the door, stopped, turned, and said, "If you don't think Bruce tried to poison his father, who did?"

"Mrs. Ladington certainly had motive," I said. "And she has established a connection with a fish purveyor in Curaçao. Is that where you got the tetrodotoxin, Mrs. Ladington?"

"This is outrageous," she said. "Get out of here! At once!"

Roger Stockdale spoke up: "The poison is irrelevant," he said. "Bruce killed his father when he pushed him into the moat. Poison didn't kill him."

"Absolutely correct," I said. "But there is such a thing as *attempted* murder." I said to Davis, "I'm afraid I don't have any proof that Mrs. Ladington attempted to kill her husband, but maybe if we had a few more days here we could come up with the answer."

"I don't doubt that you would," Davis said. "All of you here are suspects in the attempted murder of Bill Ladington. You're not to leave until I've had a chance to question each of you at length. Understood?"

"Coming, George?" I asked.

He stood.

"I can't say this has been a pleasant week," I said to those left at the table, "but it certainly has been an interesting one. I wish you well, and hope this year's vintage is especially good."

We retrieved our bags from our rooms and stepped outside where the squad car containing Bruce Ladington and the two officers was pulling away. Sheriff Davis stood alone looking up into the sky.

"Beautiful day," he said when we joined him.

"Yes, and we intend to take full advantage of it," I said.

"Do you really think Tennessee Ladington was the one who tried to poison her husband?" he asked us.

"I don't know," I said, "but I think it's a pretty good bet. My suggestion is to follow the puffer fish trail from Curaçao to Ladington's Steak House, and to the castle. Nick might be helpful. The same with the Japanese chef who manned the sushi bar. His name is Ye. I'm sure Nick can put you in touch with him. Fortunately, Bruce cracked easily. Tennessee will be a lot tougher."

"I'll get to the bottom of it," he promised.

"I'd appreciate knowing how it comes out." I handed him my business card with my Cabot Cove address and phone number on it.

"Count on it," he said.

I pulled the small green leather address book from my blazer pocket and handed it to him.

"What's this?" he asked.

"I took it when we were going through Ms. Proll's apartment. I shouldn't have, I know, but my friend's phone number was included with others on a back page. I wanted to ask him about it before turning it over to you."

"Concealing evidence," George said playfully. "She ought to be arrested."

Davis ignored the quip and looked at the back page. His face creased into a multitude of lines. "Your friend the writer, Schwartz?"

"Yes. Neil Schwartz."

"What did he tell you?"

"He said he had no idea why his number was there. I believe him."

I suddenly had the disconcerting feeling that the sheriff was withholding information. "Is there a problem?" I asked.

"No, no problem. Thanks for returning this to me."

"Of course. I shouldn't have taken it in the first place."

"No harm done. What are your plans for the rest of the day?"

"Go back to the Cedar Gables Inn. The rooms we had when we first arrived are vacant again. Our good fortune. Relax a little. Have a quiet dinner—alone. Then, if we can do it, arrange for a hot air balloon ride tomorrow."

"I can set that up for you," he said. "I'll call Ken Custis at Napa Valley Balloons. They run the best operation in the valley. Want to go up with a group, or just the two of you?"

"Just the two of us," we said in unison.

Chapter Thirty-two

We didn't go directly to Cedar Gables. Instead, we drove leisurely on side roads, enjoying the scenery and expressing our respective reactions to what had happened back at Ladington Creek.

When we did walk through the inn's front door, Margaret was there with a large greeting. "How great to see you," she said, hugging me with enthusiasm, showing a little more reticence with George. The rich baritone tones of Bob Dalpe singing *I'm Beginning to See the Light* came from the room's speakers.

Margaret noted my smile at hearing it and said, "I love it. We play it all the time. The guests love it, too. I called the record company and ordered a dozen to sell here at the inn."

"Very smooth style," George said.

"How are you, Inspector?" Margaret asked.

"Quite well, thank you, Mrs. Snasdell."

"So, what's happening out at Ladington Castle?"

George and I looked at each other before I replied, "William Ladington was killed by his son, Bruce."

Margaret gasped.

"He didn't intend to kill his father," I said. "He pushed him into the moat in a fit of anger. Bill Ladington hit his head on some rocks. The son is a pathetic story, Margaret. It's too lurid to replay, I'm afraid."

"How did you?—were you?—did *you* solve it, Jess?" Margaret asked.

"George and I played a small role. But that's all behind us. What we need are our wonderful rooms back, dinner at a nice, quiet spot, and—Oh, by the way, Sheriff Davis is going to set us up for a hot air balloon ride in the morning."

"I know," Margaret said. "He called a minute before you arrived. You're all set with Napa Valley Balloons. They'll pick you up at six."

"A.M.?" I said.

"They can only go up in the very early morning because of winds," Margaret said. "You have to call them at four-thirty to confirm that the weather's okay for a launch."

"Four-thirty?" I said. "In the morning?"

Margaret laughed. "Believe me," she said, "it's well worth it."

The ringing phone drew Margaret to the office.

"Let's unpack," I suggested.

Margaret reappeared. "It's for you, Jess. Neil Schwartz."

"I'll take these up to our rooms," George said, grabbing our suitcases.

"Watch your back," I said.

He went up the stairs without any apparent discomfort, and I took the call.

"Hello, Neil."

"Jess, I have to see you."

"I'd love to see you, too, but I don't think I'll have time before I head home. Where are you?"

"Home. Sausalito. I can drive up right now."

"Neil, I'm sorry, but I've had an exhausting week. George and I intend to relax and—"

"I wouldn't think of interrupting your plans if it wasn't necessary. Please. Just a half hour."

I sighed and thought about the next forty-eight hours. "We'll be driving down to San Francisco the day after tomorrow to catch our flights," I said. "Maybe we can find a few minutes at the airport."

He said dejectedly, "I guess that'll be okay. When's your flight?"

"Three-oh-five. United. George is flying Virgin Atlantic. His flight leaves at four-thirty. You know me. I love to be early. We plan to get to the airport by one."

"I need to see you alone, Jess. It's a very private matter."

"That shouldn't be a problem. We can meet in United's club. I'm a member."

"All right. I'll be there at one."

That night, George and I enjoyed a quiet dinner at Pasta Prego, recommended by Margaret, who called the owner and chef, Marco, to reserve a table for us. We ate lightly— grilled salmon, a salad, and sautéed spinach. Naturally, part of the evening was spent rehashing the week.

"And you have no idea why your friend, Neil, is so desperate to see you," George said.

"None whatsoever. I'm concerned. I wish I hadn't taken that address book from Ms. Proll's apartment and pointed out to the sheriff why I did. I have a feeling Neil is in some trouble because of it."

"You'll find out soon enough. Are you sure I can't convince you to change your plans and fly to London with me? Virgin Atlantic is a unique flying experience, the way flying used to be. They even give you a neck and head massage in first class before landing."

"Sounds lovely, but I have to get home. Maybe in a month or so I can break away and spend a long weekend with you."

"We keep making these tentative plans and never seem to follow through on them."

"We will," I said, hoping it wasn't an empty promise.

Four-thirty the next morning came quickly. George placed the call to confirm the balloon ride and was told the weather was perfect. At six, a young man named David, who said he was a student balloon pilot, picked us up and drove us to a restaurant where others scheduled for flights had gathered. After coffee and donuts, and a briefing about the flights, a professional photographer took orders and we opted for one. We then got back in the vans and drove to the launch area. There were a dozen or so balloons of varying sizes being readied for flight, the gas burners sending hot air up to inflate them. The passengers were expected to pitch in to right the large wicker baskets, and we helped with our rig. We'd been told to wear hats or caps, especially George who, because he's tall, would find his head and hair painfully close to the blasts of hot air that would be activated during the flight.

"All set?" our pilot asked.

"I'm ready," George said, "although I have to admit I *hae nae brou o* this."

"What?"

"Scottish. I said I'm not sure I have a liking for this."

"Why didn't you say something before?" I asked.

"Because you seemed keen on the notion. I didn't want to be a spoilsport."

A few minutes later we were airborne, slowly drifting up into the early-morning sky over Napa Valley, the loud whoosh of hot air being fired into the balloon the only sound to break the stillness. When we'd reached the right altitude, the super-charged flame was turned off and we were in total silence. Dozens of other brightly colored balloons, some larger and carrying six or eight passengers, some smaller like ours with only two or three people in them, were all around us.

"This is so peaceful," I said.

"Great morning to fly," the pilot said.

We chatted about many things, interrupted only when a loud blast of flame and hot air was needed to maintain our altitude of two thousand feet. Below was the lush valley; the vineyards looked as though they'd been painted into the landscape, thousands of rows of vines snaking around and over hillsides, stately buildings set in the middle of them or along roads at their front entrances.

George put his arm around me when I felt a chill in the morning air.

"It's so beautiful," I said.

"Look," George said, pointing over the side of the basket. I followed his finger. It was the castle at Ladington Creek Vineyards.

"Nice to be up here and not down there," I said.

The pilot heard me and laughed. "The famous Ladington Castle. He died, you know. Murdered. His son killed him."

"Really?" George said.

"Heard it on the news this morning," the pilot said. "They solved another murder, too."

"What other murder?" I asked.

"Ladington owned a restaurant in Napa. A steak house. Pretty good food. Anyway, a waiter there was murdered a couple a months ago. Stabbed to death."

He sent another deafening blast of hot air up into the balloon.

"You say they solved the waiter's murder?" George said when there was quiet again.

"That was on the news, too. Looks like drugs were involved. No surprise. Those damn drugs are at the root of most crimes these days. Don't you agree?"

"Yes, of course," I said. "Who are they charging with the murder?"

"Some drug dealer from San Francisco."

"Oh?"

"There were always rumors about drugs being sold out of Ladington's place. This waiter—I forget his name—evidently was holding out on this dealer and got killed for it. What a bunch of animals."

"Certain two-legged animals," I said. "Let's not give our four-legged furry friends a bad name."

The pilot laughed, produced another shot of hot air, and said, "You're right."

"Did they give the name of the drug dealer they've arrested?" I asked.

"Yes, but I don't remember what it was."

We eventually set down in a large parking lot connected to a college. A chase team pulled up in a station wagon, and the crew went through the process of packing up the balloon and wicker basket for use tomorrow. We were driven to another restaurant where a champagne brunch was served. The photographer who'd taken our photo leaning out of the basket as we were about to ascend, gave us a receipt and said the picture would be sent to me in Cabot Cove. We were dropped off at Cedar Gables where we freshened up and spent some time with Margaret and her assistant, Barbara. I called Sheriff Davis from there and asked about Louis Hubler's murderer having been apprehended. He confirmed it was a drug dealer from San Francisco named Jason Morris.

George and I spent the rest of the day visiting vineyards, including the spectacularly beautiful Sterling Vineyard where we finally got to enjoy the aerial tram ride, the stunning views of the valley, and, of course, wonderful wines to sample.

Margaret and Craig treated us to dinner that night at Domaine Chandon, a lovely French restaurant. The following morning, after a hearty breakfast of Margaret's signature almond French toast, we packed our bags into George's rental car and headed for San Francisco, turning in the car at the airport a little before one.

We both had ambivalent feelings during the drive. We'd

managed to salvage a little time to relax and enjoy the valley's abundant pleasures. It had been good being with George, even in the chaotic situation that existed at Ladington Creek. But it would soon be over. In a few hours we'd be on planes flying to our respective homes; no telling how long it would be before we saw each other again.

I tried to put my meeting with Neil out of my mind during the trip but was only partially successful. I turned on the radio twice and tuned to an all-news station, but the apprehension of Hubler's murderer wasn't mentioned. My call the previous day to Davis had eased my mind considerably; I couldn't help but feel that the thing Neil wanted to discuss with me was linked to that murder in some way. Perhaps it still was. But at least his being a suspect in Hubler's murder had been ruled out. Anything else paled in comparison.

Neil was waiting in the United frequent flyer club when we walked in. The woman at the desk confirmed that he was my guest, and we went to a secluded corner of the room. Neil looked at George and started to say something, but George preempted him. "I'll leave you two alone," he said, "and find a good book—and, hopefully, a place where I can smoke my pipe."

"Well, Neil," I said when George was gone, "you sounded upset when you called. Sorry I can't spend more time with you but—"

He drew a deep breath before saying, "Jess, I'm in trouble."

I drew a breath, too, before asking, "What sort of trouble?"

His lip trembled.

"Louis Hubler?"

He nodded. "No, not in the way you think. I mean, it doesn't have to do with his murder."

I waited for him to continue.

"Well, maybe it does."

"Neil, you don't have to tell *me* anything. We're friends. Whatever you've done won't change that. Are you in trouble with the law?"

Another nod.

"Then you should be talking with a lawyer, not a friend."

"I intend to. It's just that—"

"Just that *what*?"

"That I need a friend right now."

"I'm here."

"I delivered drugs to Ladington's restaurant, Jess."

I was stunned. It was inconceivable to me that this gentle, dear man, who'd worked the mean streets of New York as a cop yet wrote poetry in his spare time, who had been devoted to his wife and daughter and grandchildren, could become involved in something so shabby.

I broke our silence. "Why?" I asked.

"Money. What else?"

"You needed it that badly?"

"I thought I did. No, I didn't need it to live. But there were things I wanted that I'd never had. Don't misunderstand. I'm not talking about big-time drug sales—no heroin, no coke, just marijuana, and not a lot of that. And I'm not a drug user except for smoking some weed now and then. I've done that all my life."

"I hadn't realized," I said.

"One or two on the weekend when I was alone, especially after Sandy died. Then I came out to Sausalito and tried to play the bohemian writer. I met some people who were selling marijuana and making pretty good money. I guess I rationalized it, Jess. Everybody smokes marijuana now and then."

I didn't correct him.

"I started driving up to Napa with small bags of it because I figured there was less chance of being caught there. I met Hubler and Mary Jane—"

"Mary Jane Proll?"

"Yeah."

I thought for a moment before saying, "You say you're in trouble with the law? With Sheriff Davis in Napa?"

"He called and said he wanted me to come to his office for questioning concerning drug sales. He asked that I come voluntarily."

"Which is the best thing you could do—with a lawyer."

"I know. I intend to do that tomorrow. That list of names in Mary Jane's address book—the one with my name on it—those were other drug suppliers. Damn, to be included on a list like that is terrible. I mean, the other names on that list are probably hard-core drug dealers and users. That's not me."

I didn't say what I was thinking, that selling drugs is selling drugs—period!

Instead, I said, "You don't have a criminal background, Neil. I'm sure they'll be lenient with you when it comes to sentencing."

"Yeah. But that doesn't take away the stigma with my daughter and grandkids. God, how could I have been so stupid?"

He was sitting slumped forward in the chair, elbows resting on his knees, head in his hands. I touched one of his hands. "What do you want me to do?" I asked.

"Talk to Sheriff Davis on my behalf. Talk to anybody else involved. Intervene for me. I don't want to go to jail, Jess. I was a cop, and a good one. I never took a nickel in graft or bribes. But I know what prisons are like. I wouldn't last."

I glanced at my watch. We'd been talking for a half hour. I turned and saw George come through the door carrying a book and magazines.

"I had to go outside to smoke my pipe," he said. "Am I back too early? I can find something else to do."

"No," I said, "we're finished."

Neil shook George's hand, wished him a safe trip home, and followed me to the club's door. I placed my hand on his shoulder. "I'll make the call, Neil. If there's anything else I can do, just let me know."

"Thanks, Jess. I appreciate it." He looked as though he expected that any attempt to hug me would offend me now that I knew the trouble he was in. I wrapped my arms around him and squeezed hard. "It'll be all right," I said. "It'll be all right."

A few minutes later I told George what had transpired. His only comment was, "I suppose we're all capable of being corrupted, Jessica. I'm sure your friend will be okay."

I passed through Security, gave George a final wave, and felt my eyes tear up.

My flight home arrived on time.

Chapter Thirty-three

Neil received a one-year probationary sentence. He returned to Wisconsin to live with his daughter and grandchildren. *Vanity Fair* canceled his article because the editors felt that his involvement with Hubler and drugs rendered him a partial participant, not an impartial journalist. He was allowed to keep the portion of the advance he'd received, a generous act on the magazine's part, I thought. I never learned how much of an advance the magazine had agreed to pay Neil, but judging from his illegal actions in California, it wasn't as much as he'd indicated.

He called me one night to thank me for having put in a good word with the California authorities.

"You kept focusing on the Hubler murder to keep tabs on whether anyone was looking at you as a drug supplier," I suggested.

"I had the magazine assignment," he said.

"I know, but there was that parallel motive, wasn't there?"

"Yeah, you're right. I'm still in denial, I guess. At any rate, Jess, thanks again. I'm a lucky man. I got off easy."

"And you're a good man, Neil. Stay in touch."

Sheriff Davis also called me one evening.

"Mrs. Fletcher, I thought you'd want to know that we've identified who tried to poison William Ladington."

"His wife?"

"Not alone. She was in it with the vineyard's business manager, Roger Stockdale. They were evidently cozy, Mrs. Fletcher, lovers."

"Have they been arrested?"

"We've charged them with attempted murder and conspiracy. Stockdale skipped town right after you and the inspector left, but was picked up in Texas."

"How did you come up with them?"

"I did what you suggested, followed the puffer fish trail. The housekeeper, Mercedes, came forward after she left the castle to live in Oregon. She knew that the wife had brought the poison into the castle from the restaurant, and knew where the wife had hidden it. She noticed it was gone the night Ladington died. I confronted Tennessee and she did what lots of accused do when they're involved with a conspirator. She pointed the finger at Stockdale, and he accused her when we questioned him alone. No honor among thieves, as they say.

"We pieced together that Stockdale was promised some sort of financial participation in the vineyard by Ladington, but only after he died. Tennessee wanted that to happen sooner than later."

"Well, Sheriff, I appreciate the call."

"My pleasure. How's your friend, Neil?"

I filled him in on Neil's life after his plea bargain of guilty, and his probation. The sheriff and I promised to stay in touch.

Bruce Ladington was originally charged with murder, but a plea bargain reduced it to manslaughter; he was sentenced to fourteen years, with the possibility of parole after four years. I can only assume that the prosecutors, as well as the judge, were as sympathetic as I'd been after hearing what had driven Bruce to push his father into the moat.

I have no idea what happened with Laura and the child

she carried. I only hope that she's able to put her life together and give the child a decent upbringing.

Not long after returning to Cabot Cove from Napa Valley, I spent an evening with Seth Hazlitt and other friends.
After dinner, I recounted in exquisite detail what had transpired while I was in California. One of my guests was
John St. Clair, Cabot Cove's resident wine expert. He'd insisted upon bringing the wine for the dinner party, and included two bottles of Ladington Creek cabernet. After his
first taste, he proclaimed, "Heavenly, with a husky, fleshy-
mouthed taste that oozes across the palate."

"Hruumph," Seth muttered.

"I only hope," St. Clair said, "that the death of William
Ladington, and the turmoil it's created at Ladington Creek,
doesn't ruin the crop there. That would be a tragedy of im-
mense proportions."

Later, talk turned to the novel I'd just started.

"What's it called?" asked Richard Koser, who shoots the
photos for my book jackets.

"Blood on the Vine," I replied. "I'm setting it in a winery
in Northern California."

"Based upon the Ladington incident?" someone asked.

"Oh, no," I quickly said. "That's too real. Actual murders
scare me. I prefer the fictitious kind."

"Wouldn't know it from the way you keep getting yourself involved with real murders," Seth said. "You should
take my advice and stick close to home, make up murders
in your mind and stay away from the real thing. By the
way, heard lately from your *friend* in London, the inspector?"

I smiled. George and I had talked the night before about
my flying to London to spend a few days with him, and I'd
hung a note on my kitchen bulletin board to remind me to
make travel arrangements the next morning.

"Well?" Seth said, bushy eyebrows raised waiting for my answer.

"I would love another glass of that Ladington Creek cabernet," I said, handing my glass to St. Clair. "It is absolutely heavenly, with a succulent nose of black currants, violets, and spices, gorgeous ripeness, and chewy fruit."

Seth winced.

I winked at him, raised my glass, and said, "Salute!"

Here's a preview of the next
***Murder, She Wrote* mystery,**
Murder in a Minor Key,
available now from Signet.

I hadn't seen Wayne Copely since Friday, when he'd graciously escorted our colleague, Doris Burns, and me to the New Orleans Jazz & Heritage Festival. Wayne was a nationally syndicated jazz columnist and native of New Orleans, Doris and I were visitors to The Big Easy—one of many nicknames for the city—she from Princeton, New Jersey, where she was the youngest history professor on staff at the university, and I from Cabot Cove, Maine, where I plied my trade as a writer of murder mysteries. We'd all met as members of an authors' panel, promoting our latest works at a Book Club Breakfast hosted by the *Times-Picayune*, the city's only daily newpaper. Wayne had used the occasion to announce his longtime search for wax cylinder recordings by New Orleans musical legend Little Red LeCoeur.

A turn-of-the-century trumpet player, Little Red's place in the pantheon of early jazz greats was well established in New Orleans, but virtually nonexistent outside that city. Old-timers remembered him as a ginger-haired prodigy with a red-hot temper to match, but one whose music reached heights never claimed before, a sweet sound encompassing the panoramic jazz experience in blues, ragtime, and Dixieland, and presaging the music to come decades later.

"Some said Little Red was possessed by a voodoo

spirit," Wayne had told the Book Club audience, "and when he was under its spell, magic notes poured from his horn—melodic, inventive music, which drew the other musicians of his day like ants following a trail of honey. They were hungry for his sound, in awe of his skill, and jealous of his talent."

If Wayne were successful in his quest for the recordings, he would gain international recognition for the memory of this long-neglected musical genius, and elevate Little Red to the same plateau in the history of jazz as Buddy Bolden and Louis Armstrong. But so far, the cylinders had eluded him. In desperation, he made his public plea for help in finding them.

"Has anyone come forward with information for you?" I asked him as we strolled around the jazz festival, where the air fairly hummed with the strains of gospel, zydeco, bebop, Dixieland, and virtually every other variation of jazz, which drifted out of the tents and rose on the breeze in a delightful cacophony.

"I have a few leads," he said, twirling a pencil between his fingers, "and the paper mentioned it in the article covering our panel." He pulled a much thumbed copy of the magazine *Wavelength* from under his arm. "I've also got a classified ad in here that should churn the waters."

Since then, I'd left two messages on his answering machine and was concerned that he hadn't called back. He'd already missed one appointment with me, and we were supposed to be dining with his sister in the Garden District that afternoon.

Wayne's house in the French Quarter was not far from my hotel, and I walked there Sunday morning. The evening before, the street had been mobbed with people celebrating Saturday night with Hurricanes, a favorite libation in local establishments. Carrying their drinks in go-cups, they hopped in and out of the nightclubs and barrooms, dancing on the *banquettes*—what New Orleanians call sidewalks— and gathering around impromptu performances by free-lance jazz ensembles. Now, the Quarter was eerily quiet, the only sound a janitor sweeping up the crushed cups and other debris that littered the street.

I checked my address book for the number of Wayne's apartment house. An old brown Ford was angled into the curb under a NO PARKING sign in front of the building, which had a facade painted in a soft pink. Iron lacework outlined the balconies that ran the length of each floor, and on which I could see a profusion of green plants and a series of tables and chairs demarcating the individual apartments.

Surprisingly, the double doors leading inside were open. I checked the directory for the number of Wayne's apartment, climbed the stairs to the third floor, and pulled on a brass knocker in the shape of an alligator. The door swung open and a man in a brown suit frowned at me.

"Who're you?" he asked gruffly.

"Perhaps I have the wrong apartment," I said, taken aback. "I'm looking for Wayne Copely."

"What's he to you?"

"I'm a friend, and I haven't heard from him. I was concerned. Are you an acquaintance of his?"

I knew the answer before he gave it, and felt my stomach drop. Men like him have a certain look. It's in the eyes, a world-weariness, a cool appraisal, an unbending attitude worn like a carapace on their backs meant to protect them from the brutalities of life.

"I'm a cop."

"What's happened to Wayne?"

"You look a little pale. Come in and sit down, and I'll tell you."

Numb, I entered Wayne's apartment and slumped down on his green damask sofa. The policeman remained standing on the other side of the glass-topped steel box that served as a coffee table. He tugged at his belt, trying to draw the waistline of his trousers over a protuberant stomach.

"Is he dead?" I asked, trying to regain some semblance of control.

"How did you know?"

His question was like a slap, startling me back to conscious thought. I sat up, alert. After all, I'd had experience with death before.

"I didn't know," I said briskly, "but it's obvious that if the police are here and Wayne's not, then something is drastically wrong."

"When did you last see him?"

"Friday. When did he die?"

"Saturday."

"How did it happen?"

"Hey, lady, I'm the cop here. I ask the questions. Why don't we start over? I'm detective Chris Steppe, NOPD." He pulled a pad of paper from his breast pocket, and looked down at me. "And you would be?"

"Jessica Fletcher."

"Why do I know that name?"

I explained to him who I was, how I knew Wayne, and why I'd become concerned enough to come to his apartment. While Detective Steppe scratched away at his pad, I looked around the room. Wayne's apartment was spare with an innate elegance that was difficult to define. It might have been the warmth of the wooden floor, a scarred broad planked relic from an earlier era. Or it might have been the diaphanous curtains that covered the leaded French doors looking out on the balcony I'd seen from the street. The furnishings were simple—a sofa, a coffee table, a small Oriental rug in front of what I was sure was a decorative fireplace, a line of low bookcases on one wall, and a delicate round table of highly polished dark wood with two matching chairs. No bric-a-brac, no clutter was in sight. There was a calmness to the apartment that I could sense, despite my agitation, a calmness that must have been restful for a high-strung personality like Wayne's.

A door from the living room opened into another part of the apartment, and I could hear someone shuffling around in there, opening doors and drawers.

"Where did you find Wayne's body?" I asked Detective Steppe.

"At the cemetery."

"The cemetery?"

"Yeah. Ironic, isn't it? He was found sitting up against a tomb in St. Louis Cemetery Number One."

"What was the cause of death?"

"Are you sure you want to hear this?"

"Detective, I make my living writing murder mysteries. I read case histories, interview coroners, pore over police photos. I think I have a pretty strong constitution by now."

"No doubt," Steppe said, pushing his pad back down in his jacket pocket. He hesitated a bit, considering what to tell me. He decided not to. "Well, we're not really sure anyway. We won't know officially till the autopsy report comes in."

"But you have an idea, right?"

"I might."

"Did he die in the cemetery?" I asked.

Steppe's eyebrows flew up. "You ask a lot of questions, don't you?" He retrieved his pad. "Where did you say you were yesterday?"

"I didn't," I replied stiffly. "You didn't ask me. But I was at Jazz Fest most of the day, and I can supply you with the names of my companions. In the evening, I went with them to Preservation Hall."

Steppe took some more notes and I got up and paced the room, trying to get a glimpse of the layout of the rest of the apartment, and to see whoever was in the other room.

"You didn't answer my question," I prodded.

"Don't really know," he replied. "I'm not the medical examiner. Now tell me, Mrs. Fletcher, why would anyone want Copely dead?"

I whirled around. "He was murdered?"

"I didn't say that, did I?"

"I don't know that anyone would want Wayne dead, unless it had to do with his research."

I gave Steppe a brief rundown on Wayne's interest in the recordings of Little Red LeCoeur. "But he hasn't found any so far," I added, and then remembered that "so far" was as far as Wayne would be able to go.

"What do you know about voodoo, Mrs. Fletcher?"

"Voodoo? Barely anything at all. Why?"

"Copely was found sitting up against the tomb of Marie Laveau, the famous voodoo queen." He paused, waiting for my reaction.

"I know that Wayne knew something about voodoo," I replied, "but that would be true of anyone raised in New Orleans."

"Did he ever wear a gris-gris, Mrs. Fletcher? You know about them, don't you? They're those pouches on a string meant to bring good luck or ward off evil."

"I never saw one on him."

"Well, his corpse wore one, and there's a little more." He was eyeing me closely now.

"Yes?"

"His hand, Mrs. Fletcher. I saw two puncture marks."

"Does this have something to do with how he died?"

"Probably." Steppe was stalling.

"What could have made those marks, Detective?"

"There's only one thing I can think of, Mrs. Fletcher." He stared into my eyes. "Copely died from the bite of a rattlesnake."